# Tennessee Moon

*Also by N...*
*in L...*
*...n Large Print:*

Snow Fire

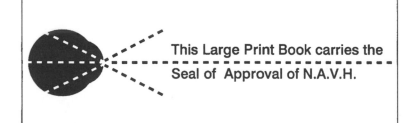

This Large Print Book carries the
Seal of Approval of N.A.V.H.

# Tennessee Moon

# Norah Hess

WHEELER
PUBLISHING

Published in 2003 by arrangement with Leisure Books,
a division of Dorchester Publishing Co., Inc.

Wheeler Large Print Romance.

The text of this Large Print edition is unabridged.
Other aspects of the book may vary from the original edition.

Set in 16 pt. Plantin by Myrna S. Raven.

Printed in the United States on permanent paper.

**Library of Congress Cataloging-in-Publication Data**

Hess, Norah.
    Tennessee moon / Norah Hess.
        p. cm.
    ISBN 1-58724-506-X (lg. print : hc : alk. paper)
    1. Triangles (Interpersonal relations) — Fiction.
2. Cumberland Gap (Tenn.) — Fiction.   3. Stepbrothers —
Fiction.   4. Farm life — Fiction.   5. Large type books.   I. Title.
PS3558.E797856T46 2003
    813'.54—dc22                                           2003057163

*I dedicate this book to my friend John Reed.*

As the Founder/CEO of NAVH, the only national health agency solely devoted to those who, although not totally blind, have an eye disease which could lead to serious visual impairment, I am pleased to recognize Thorndike Press* as one of the leading publishers in the large print field.

Founded in 1954 in San Francisco to prepare large print textbooks for partially seeing children, NAVH became the pioneer and standard setting agency in the preparation of large type.

Today, those publishers who meet our standards carry the prestigious "Seal of Approval" indicating high quality large print. We are delighted that Thorndike Press is one of the publishers whose titles meet these standards. We are also pleased to recognize the significant contribution Thorndike Press is making in this important and growing field.

Lorraine H. Marchi, L.H.D.
Founder/CEO
NAVH

* Thorndike Press encompasses the following imprints: Thorndike, Wheeler, Walker and Large Print Press.

# Chapter One

The belt made a whacking sound as it landed on tender flesh, making the young girl dig her fingers and bare toes into the rough carpet where she had been flung. She bit her tongue so as not to cry out as again and again the leather descended on her bare back where her dress had been ripped to the waist.

Finally a sharp cry of pain escaped her clenched teeth. A cruel hand immediately fastened into the red-gold curls that tumbled around her partially bared shoulders.

Grabbing a fistful of the fine tresses, her tormentor grated out, "What did I tell you about cryin' out and bringin' our neighbors runnin' over here to stick their noses into somethin' that's none of their business? You make another sound and I'll lash you twice as hard."

The belt rose and fell until Kaitlan Barrett fainted. She didn't feel the lifting of the heavy weight that straddled her legs, nor was she aware when heavy feet staggered into an adjoining bedroom. She didn't know how many minutes passed before tender hands carried her and laid her on the narrow cot, facedown.

She came painfully back to awareness as gentle hands carefully washed her bloodied back.

When she whimpered, a voice whispered, "Hush, child. Do you want that brute to come back in here with his belt?"

Kaitlan vigorously shook her head and gritted her teeth as the cleaning of her back continued. She clenched her fists against the pain when a salve was carefully smoothed over her wounds.

It was finally done and she sat up, helping as much as she could when the black woman began to ease the torn dress off her slender body.

"I'm going to make you a special tea now that will help some with your pain and put you to sleep," Hattie Smith said as she divided the heavy red-gold hair into two parts and brought the tresses over Kaitlan's shoulders to keep them off her whipped back.

Kaitlan stared at the lighted lamp whose wick was turned low to conserve the small amount of kerosene that was left in the half-gallon container. She didn't know when there would be any more. The lamp sent out a dim, wavering light, but was strong enough to show the hatred and bitterness in Kaitlan's dark blue eyes: hatred for her brutal stepfather and bitterness for the change that had come into her life soon after he married her widowed mother.

She had been mystified when, two years ago, Yancy Wilson proposed marriage to her ailing mother. Mary Barrett had suffered from lingering tuberculosis for the past five years. She was pale and thin and the beauty she had once possessed was so faded that it seemed the only thing alive in her gaunt face was her warm brown eyes.

But surprisingly, Yancy Wilson — big and attractive in a coarse sort of way — had fallen in love with the delicate Mary.

Mother and daughter had been at the supper table on the eve of the wedding when Kaitlan tried for the last time to dissuade her mother from marrying the man they had known for such a short time.

"I don't trust Yancy Wilson, Mama," she had bluntly stated. "We don't know anything about him . . . where he comes from . . . if he has any relatives. And besides," she went on, resentment in her tone, "I don't know how you could forget Papa so soon and wed again."

"Yancy comes from Maine, and he has a mother and father and a sister. And, honey" — Mary looked sadly at her thirteen-year-old daughter — "I haven't forgotten your father. I never will. No man could ever take his place in my heart. But you know as well as I do, it won't be too long until I join John. I want to make sure there will be someone to look after you when I'm gone."

Kaitlan choked back the tears that gathered in her throat. She knew her mother spoke the truth. Mary had lost all interest in life the day her beloved husband was killed in a mine cave-in. "I don't like for you to talk that way,

9

Mama." She squeezed the frail, white hand, lying on the table. "Besides, Hattie and Peter would always take care of me. Much better than that man."

"I know that, honey, but I don't think the town fathers would allow you to live with a black couple, no matter how much the Smiths love you or how willing they might be to take care of you."

Kaitlan dropped the subject, knowing that her mother wouldn't be swayed.

So the marriage had taken place the next day as planned. Her mother's longtime friends prepared a wedding party for after the ceremony. Yancy had been all smiles, laughing and talking with the men, being very solicitous of his new wife, bringing her a piece of their wedding cake, keeping her cup filled with tea. Kaitlan was beginning to think that maybe they were all mistaken about her new stepfather. Maybe he did care for her mother.

With well-wishes and congratulations to the newlyweds, the guests began to leave. Soon the party was over. As Kaitlan began gathering up cups and glasses and the remnants of the wedding cake, she glanced often at her mother. The celebration had tired Mary. Her features were drawn and there was a weariness in her eyes. Kaitlan looked at Yancy, worry clouding her gaze. Would he be gentle with her mother when they went to bed?

Kaitlan couldn't remember now who looked

the most surprised, she or her mother, when Yancy pulled on his coat and said gruffly, "I'm meetin' up with some friends. I'll see you tomorrow sometime." She could remember, however, that there was relief in both their eyes. At least Mama's tired body would get a rest tonight.

As it turned out, her mother never shared her bed with her new husband. On the third night, when Yancy prepared to leave, Mary shyly hinted that she would not deny his conjugal rights.

He had laughed in her face and said with a sneer, "You skinny bag of bones, you wouldn't last ten minutes the way I ride a woman. I want my bed partner to be as lusty and randy as I am."

Yancy had slammed the door behind him, leaving Kaitlan and Mary shocked, but relieved. They had learned shortly after that he spent his nights with Lulu Collins, the madam of the whorehouse in town, as he had done since he'd first arrived in the area.

No more than a week passed before Yancy began demanding money from Mary, a great deal of money.

"I don't have that kind of money, Yancy," she answered timidly. "What with you not working, there will soon be nothing left of my savings."

"How much do you have, bitch?" he growled at her. "I'll have to make do with it."

"Very little, Yancy. I need it all for food supplies."

"Kaitlan, get in here," he bellowed.

Kaitlan, who had overheard the exchange, stepped into the room, not knowing what to expect as she looked at the belt he had doubled in half and was slapping against his leg. As she waited to be told what he wanted with her, he grabbed her suddenly, spun her around, and brought the belt down across her back. The unexpectedness of it, and the pain, brought a shriek from her lips.

"Stop it!" Mary cried out as he lifted the belt to strike her daughter again. "The money is in my jewelry box in the top dresser drawer."

"That's more like it," Yancy said, a cruel smile twisting his lips as he threaded the belt through the loops of his trousers. "From now on," he warned as he buckled the belt, "anytime you say no to me, your kid is gonna get the belt."

From that day on Mary hadn't crossed her husband once. Still, Kaitlan continued to feel the belt at any imagined infraction of the ridiculous rules he had laid down for her to follow. The house was to be neat and clean at all times even though he tracked in mud and dirt half a dozen times a day, and left his clothes scattered about for her to pick up. She was to have supper on the table every night at six o'clock sharp, even if it was only a pan of corn bread and a jug of buttermilk. Sometimes, if he had been lucky at cards, he would bring home some fatty meat for her to prepare.

Unlike mother and daughter, Yancy didn't lose any weight on the meager diet that barely kept them alive. He was well fed by Lulu.

Then there were the white shirts he liked to wear. He only owned two, and every day Kaitlan had to scrub the alternate one, starch and iron it. One day she slightly scorched the collar of his favorite shirt and received a belting that bloodied her back.

Two weeks into the marriage Yancy had ordered Hattie and Peter to leave *his* house, saying he wasn't going to support their worthless hides. The black couple now lived in a shack in back of the house that had once been a toolshed. Peter had been hired on at the livery, mucking out stalls for a dollar a day. It was thanks to that dear couple that Mary and Kaitlan hadn't starved to death.

Kaitlan sighed. Poor Mama. She had finally given up. Realizing that she could no longer help her daughter, she had lost her will to live. She grew weaker every day and was gradually withdrawing from the world that had treated her so shabbily since her dear John's death.

Kaitlan winced as she tried to lie down on her side. This last beating Yancy had given her was because she had tried to come to her mother's defense.

The only piece of jewelry her mother had that was worth anything was a brooch with a small diamond set in gold filigree. She had kept it hidden from Yancy so that her daughter could have it someday. Then one day, broke as usual, Yancy had been rummaging around in the dresser drawers looking for something that he might be able to sell when he felt the brooch rolled up in a pair of socks.

"So, old woman" — he waved the pin in front of Mary — "you've been holdin' out on me, have you?"

"Please, Yancy," Mary begged, clasping her hands at her waist, "I've kept that for Kaitlan. It's the only inheritance I can leave her."

"Ha," Yancy said with a sneer, "that's a fine inheritance. I probably won't get more than five dollars for it."

With a fire in her eyes that hadn't been there for a long time, Mary held out her hand and demanded, "Hand it over, Yancy."

Kaitlan had silently witnessed the whole scene from the doorway, but when Yancy raised his hand to hit her mother, she sprang at him, scratching his face and yanking at his hair. He let out a howl of fury and flung her to the floor.

And now here she lay, barely able to move from the most brutal beating Yancy had yet given her. Her mother's pleading cries still rang in her ears.

A slight form appeared in the doorway, then came slowly to the bed and sat down on its edge. "My poor, sweet Kaitlan," Mary whispered, smoothing the hair off Kaitlan's forehead. "Your suffering at his hands will soon come to an end. My days are numbered, but I

14

will hang on until you are healed enough to leave this hell my foolishness has caused you to live in."

"Mama, don't talk like that," Kaitlan pleaded as she grasped the pale hand and gently squeezed. "I would willingly suffer more than the lash of his belt just to have you with me."

"I know that, sweet Kaitlan, but I am tired and long to be with John."

Mary dipped her fingers into her dress pocket and brought out four gold coins. Pressing them into Kaitlan's hand, she said, "There's the last of my savings. I had them buried out back. It is enough for you and Hattie and Peter to start a new life somewhere far away."

Kaitlan was too choked with tears to speak. She was gulping them down when her mother rose and quietly left the room. She didn't know then that that was the last time she would ever see her mother.

Mary died quietly in her sleep that night and Kaitlan was unable to get out of bed to attend her funeral, which Yancy arranged to take place the following day.

She cried herself dry that day. Her only consolation was that Hattie said her mother looked so peaceful in death.

A week passed and Kaitlan's back healed sufficiently so that she could get up and around. But though she hadn't seen Yancy since the day of her mother's funeral, she never knew when he might appear. Consequently she spent most of her time with Hattie and Peter in their little shack trying to think where to go and how to get there. So far they had come up with only one conclusion. They were going to leave Pennsylvania.

A week later Kaitlan received a letter that settled their destination. They would move to the Cumberland Mountains in Tennessee where a small farm waited for them. After she read the letter out loud to the stunned Hattie and Peter she pulled a rickety chair over to the shack's one small window to read the letter again, this time more slowly.

The letter was from her grandfather Barrett, a relative she'd never even known:

"Dear Kaitlan Barrett, I am a neighbor of your grandfather, Rufe Barrett. He is poorly, so I write this as he says it.

Dear Granddaughter, me and your father had a falling-out when you was just a baby. I kept track of him for several years, but then he seemed to disappear. It was only three weeks ago that I learned of his death. That gave me a great sadness. I wanted to make peace between us before I died.

Death is not far off for me. It is like a wolf stalking a deer, and like a wolf, death will be the winner.

I am leaving you my small farm, which lies at the bottom of the Cumberland Gap.

Its soil is rich and bears me good crops and there is plenty of tender grass for livestock. I leave you a mule for plowing, a handsome stallion for riding, a couple cows, two hogs, two dozen chickens and a rooster, and my old hound dog named Ringer.

I think, Granddaughter, if you and your mother will give it a chance, you will love the Cumberlands and its people as I have. The power that the mountains have on people is something to see. A person has to be careful not to lose his soul to them.

I hope, Granddaughter, as my only living relative, you will accept my little farm and tend it as I have for so many years. Your grandfather, Rufe Barrett."

There was a postscript. "Your grandfather passed away two days after I wrote this for him. He was a grand old man, loved by everybody. Us neighbors hope that you and your mother will come here to live as he wished you to. We all will take turns tending the livestock until we hear from you.

Maybelle Scott."

Kaitlan let the letter drop into her lap, bitter tears burning her eyes. Why couldn't this letter have arrived three years ago, she asked herself, when Mama was a little stronger? Then she never would have met Yancy Wilson, who had turned their lives into a living nightmare.

17

She knuckled her damp eyes and returned the letter to its envelope. Mama was gone now and she must go on without her. She would make a new life in which her brutal stepfather would have no part.

# Chapter Two

After what seemed like an endless journey by wagon, Kaitlan and her friends finally reached the majestic Cumberland Mountains. It was April and spring was staining winter-brown fields and woods a pale green. Delicate buds of trailing arbutus and trillium were opening up, along with fragile silver bell.

"It sure enough takes your breath away, don't it?" Peter spoke in hushed tones.

"It's a wondrous land," Kaitlan agreed.

The more practical Hattie said, "Yes, it's pretty. Now whip up the horse, Peter, and let's try to find the farm before the sun sets. We may be some distance away from it, and I'm sure tired of sleeping on the ground."

As the wagon rolled along the dirt road, Kaitlan caught glimpses of a river through the foliage of pine and elm. She sniffed the odor of black river-bottom earth and pine woods and hoped that her new home was somewhere in the vicinity. She felt so at peace with the tangled woods to her right and the river on her left. She could heal in these mountains.

"I see somebody walkin' up ahead," Peter said after a while. "You want me to stop the horse when we come to him and ask him if he knows where your grandpaw's place is?" He looked over his shoulder at Kaitlan.

"Of course she wants you to, fool," Hattie snapped. "How do you think we're going to find the farm if we don't ask directions from someone?"

"Don't get all het up, woman," Peter retorted. "I just asked."

Kaitlan hoped that the man ambling along a few yards ahead could give them directions. All three of them were travel-weary.

When the wagon drew near the man, he stepped off the road to let them pass. Peter pulled in the horse and Kaitlan smiled down at the man, who looked as old as the mountains. His toothless face was wrinkled like the skin of a withered winter apple. His homespun trousers had only one strap hanging over his bony shoulder, and his shapeless brown hat looked as if he had sacked potatoes in it.

"Howdy, missy." His bright brown eyes twinkled admiringly at her. "Are you lost? You're a stranger to me. I know everybody in the Gap."

"In a way I guess we are strangers," Kaitlan said, returning his warm smile. "We're looking for the Rufe Barrett farm."

The old man squinted his eyes at her. "Are you Rufe's grandaughter?"

"Yes, I am," Kaitlan answered. Her outstretched hand was grasped by rough, callused fingers in a warm handshake. "My name is Kaitlan."

"That was your grandmaw's name, a real fine

woman. We buried old Rufe next to her a few weeks back."

"I received a letter from Maybelle Scott telling me that my grandfather had passed away. I'm sorry I never knew him."

"He felt bad that he never got to know you too. Are you gonna be livin' among us, or are you gonna sell the place?"

"Oh, we're staying. I already love this glorious country."

Nodding his approval, Kaitlan's new neighbor said, "I'm Lish Jones. My place is over yonder on the branch." He jerked a thumb over his right shoulder. "Today is my turn to look after Rufe's stock. His farm — or your farm, I should call it now — is a couple more miles up the road."

"Climb in, then." Kaitlan scooted over to make room for him to sit beside her. "We'll go there together."

When Lish was settled at her side, Kaitlan said, "Meet Peter Smith and his wife Hattie. They are old friends who will be living with me."

Lish nodded. "Howdy," he said, but he didn't offer his hand to Peter.

"Will I have neighbors, Lish?" Kaitlan asked as Peter touched the horse on the rump with the whip and set the wagon in motion again.

"Why sure, they's plenty of families livin' in the Gap area." Lish went on to describe many of his neighbors and Kaitlan listened with interest, all the while taking in the beauty of the passing countryside.

A quarter of an hour later, Lish broke off his recital to point and say, "Right around the bend comin' up, you can see your new home."

Kaitlan shot to her feet, holding on to the back of Peter and Hattie's seat as the buggy followed the curve of the road. When Peter pulled the horse in, she stared and stared at the picturesque cabin and outbuildings before her. Here was a place where she could live in peace, never again to fear her stepfather's cruel hand.

Rufe Barrett had built his place on a piece of land convenient to the river, with the Cumberland Mountains as a backdrop. Half the land was covered with trees — oak, walnut, and elm. The rest was ready to be tilled when the soil dried a little more.

"The river borders the land for two miles," Lish went on to say, "and a year-round creek runs back of the cabin."

"Do I see a fruit orchard behind the barn?" Kaitlan shaded her eyes against the sun. "I see something all in bud."

"It sure is an orchard. The best in all the Gap. Your grandpaw, when he and his wife came here to settle, brought with him apple, pear, and cherry shoots all wrapped up in wet sacking. And for your grandmaw he brought a yellow rosebush and planted it right outside the kitchen door. It will be full of blooms the last part of June, the sweetest-smellin' things you

22

ever put to your nose."

Hattie squirmed impatiently and Kaitlan said, "Well, let's go take a closer look at my new home. I'd like to look around outside before the sun goes down."

Lish gave her one of his wide smiles. "If your grandpap could see you, he'd be mighty pleased the way you're so eager to see his place. He sure was proud of it."

Hattie gave such a loud sigh of relief when the buggy began to move again, Kaitlan felt like grabbing her shoulders and giving them a hard shake. The mountain people would never like and accept her if she continued to be impatient and unfriendly.

When Peter pulled the buggy up in front of the log cabin, a woman turned from peering through one of its windows. Ignoring Kaitlan and the Smiths, she glared at Lish and complained, "There's dust an inch thick on everything. I don't know why you ain't give me a key to get in there and clean the place up."

As Lish helped Kaitlan out of the buggy, he said from the corner of his mouth, "She don't want to clean; she wants to nose around, poke through the drawers and such."

Kaitlan watched the thin woman come stomping toward them and was ready to smile and hold out her hand in greeting. But the other woman's small eyes barely skimmed over her before looking at the Smiths and then back at Lish. When it was apparent she would make no friendly overture, he spoke.

"Maybelle Scott, meet Kaitlan Barrett, Rufe's granddaughter. She'll be keepin' the place clean from now on."

Pretending not to see Kaitlan's outstretched hand, the agitated woman snorted. "Ha! You mean her slaves will."

"We're not slaves, you bony-assed piece of flesh!" Hattie jumped down from the buggy after jerking the short whip from her husband's hands. "Me and Peter have been freed for seventeen years," she continued, advancing on the mountain woman, her eyes shooting fire. "Now you just take you insulting self away from here or I'll take this whip to you."

"Well I never!" Maybelle took a couple of steps backward.

"Maybe you ain't, but you're gonna feel this whip today if you don't start making tracks out of here right now."

Kaitlan started forward to try to make peace between the two women, but Lish caught her arm and held her. "Maybelle started it, so let your woman finish it," he said in low tones.

The menacing black woman coming toward Maybelle was something she had never encountered before. The women of the Gap always drew back from her sharp-edged tongue in fear that she might start some gossip about them. She wavered a moment, then, with her nose in the air, turned and walked stiffly away.

Lish chuckled. "She'll make the rounds now,

24

telling everyone how the black woman threatened her."

"Oh, dear." Kaitlan sighed. "We're getting off to a bad start. Our neighbors are going to decide they don't like us before we even meet them."

"Don't be too sure about that." Lish handed her the key he fished out of his pocket. "The women are gonna be too glad somebody finally stood up to that troublemakin' old maid."

"I hope you're right." Kaitlan sounded unconvinced and looked at her longtime friend. "I do think you could curb that temper of yours a little, Hattie." Hattie's reply was a loud sniff and Kaitlan shrugged her shoulders in defeat. Hattie's temper would always rule her. Kaitlan turned to Lish.

"Will you show me around outside now? We can go inside later after it gets dark."

Kaitlan didn't know anything about farms, but she felt this must be a fine one. The two cows were sleek and well fed and the two pigs in their pen were fat. She thought that the chickens picking at bugs in the grass looked quite happy. When she said this to Lish, he threw back his head and gave a loud cackling laugh.

"I never thought one way or the other whether a chicken was happy. But you sure know when this feller is happy." He motioned to a pen adjacent to the barn. "That's Snowy, Rufe's stallion, galloping toward us. You can

25

see he's happy by the way he's runnin' with his tail up."

"What a handsome fellow!" Kaitlan exclaimed, climbing to the top of the rail fence. She laughed joyously when the sleek white animal pushed his head against her shoulder.

"He likes you." Lish grinned. "He wants you to scratch his ears."

As Kaitlan ran her nails around the horse's velvety ears, Hattie came hurrying up, trailed by Peter, who wore an uncertain look. "Lish," she asked the old man, "what is that small building back of the cabin?"

"You're talkin' 'bout the one at the edge of the woodlot. Rufe had that put up to house the men what come to cut his tobacco."

"It looks well built," Hattie said, a gleam in her eyes that made Kaitlan wonder what was going on in her mind.

"It is well put together. Anything Rufe did was done right."

"I see it's all set up for housekeeping."

"Sure is. Ever'thin' a body needs is in there."

"Me and Peter want to live in it." Hattie looked challengingly at Kaitlan.

"You want to live in it?" Kaitlan looked puzzled. "Why? Don't you want to live with me?"

"Kaitlan, honey, that has nothing to do with it," Hattie said earnestly. "Me and Peter have never had a home of our own and I've longed for it for a long time." She laid a hand on Kaitlan's knee. "Nothing will change. It will be like it has always been. The only thing different will be that come evening, after supper, me and Peter can sit on our own little porch and listen to the night sounds, then later go to sleep in our own little cabin."

Kaitlan looked down at the two faces gazing hopefully back at her. All her life they had been a part of her family, taking care of her and Mama. It had never entered her mind that these two dear people would want what was only natural: a home of their own.

She climbed off the fence and put her arms around Hattie. "My dear friends," she said with damp eyes, "of course you may have the cabin. I'll deed it over to you tomorrow."

"Hallelujah!" Hattie cried, hugging Kaitlan so hard her breath came out in a loud whoosh. She stood back then and after wiping her tears said, "Let's go look at your place now."

The main cabin was larger than it looked from outside. Most of the back of the building was hidden by spreading pines. Inside it was divided in half, the front part consisting of a combination kitchen and sitting room, the back divided into two bedrooms. The sitting room had a large fieldstone fireplace that took up half an outside wall, with a wide raised hearth and a wooden mantel made from a peeled, split oak log.

In the kitchen area was a smaller fireplace with a brick oven built into one side of it. The furniture was plain but built well by a local cabinetmaker.

As Maybelle had claimed, dust was thick on everything. However, it was too late in the day to do much about it. Dusk was setting in, and as Hattie lit a couple of candle lamps she told Peter to build a fire in the kitchen fireplace. "I'll make us some supper and we'll clean everything tomorrow."

"Will you have supper with us, Lish?" Kaitlan invited. "Hattie is a fine cook."

He glanced at Hattie, and then shook his head. "Not tonight, thank you. I've got a pot of collard greens and sowbelly waitin' for me at home. All I have to do is bake a pan of corn pone." He nodded to the Smiths, and Kaitlan followed him out onto the porch.

"Thank you for tending to the stock, Lish, and for showing me around the place. I hope you come often to visit."

"I'll look in on you every day or so to see how you're makin' out." He grinned. "I think you'll be all right with that Hattie around. I'm half afraid of her."

Kaitlan laughed. "So are Peter and I. But inside she's a fine Christian woman and will help anybody in need."

"If you say so. She and her husband will be the first colored folks to live in the Gap. I guess people will want to take their measure at first." Lish stepped off the porch, ready to leave. He paused when he heard the yowling and baying of dogs. He looked up at Kaitlan and said, "That's mine and Rufe's hounds. Ringer is in the lead. They've took up the scent of a skunk or maybe a panther."

"Panther! Do we have panthers around here?"

"Yeah, we do. The Cumberlands are full of them. Don't ever go out after dark without Ringer at your heels."

Kaitlan shivered. "Once the sun goes down I'll not stick my head outdoors."

Lish looked at her in amusement. "You will in time. You'll get used to livin' with all the varmints. But before I go, let me whistle Ringer in so you two can meet. Not knowin' you, he might take a bite out of you when he comes home." His eyes twinkled. "Especially that sharp-tongued Hattie."

Lish gave a long, shrill whistle and the yowling stopped immediately. In another few minutes two long-eared hounds burst through the forest, then came to a skidding halt when they saw Kaitlan. Lish took her arm and spoke to the dogs in the same way he might speak to a child.

"Fellers, this is Kaitlan. You belong to her now, Ringer, since ol' Rufe is gone." He snapped his fingers at Ringer. "Come here, boy, and meet her."

Ringer stood a moment, and then, wagging his tail, came slowly toward her. Kaitlan held her hand down for him to sniff. He took his time doing it, but when he pushed his nose into her palm, she smiled.

"He's accepted you, Kaitlan," Lish said softly. Kaitlan rubbed the smooth head and stroked the dog's long back. When Lish left, Ringer followed her into the cabin.

Hattie cried out in alarm, but Kaitlan shushed her and repeated the same motions Lish had used with her, quietly introducing Ringer to the nervous Smiths. Surprised smiles wreathed their faces when the hound pushed his nose into first Hattie's and then Peter's palm.

To hide her pleasure at Ringer's accepting her, Hattie said gruffly, "Kaitlan, take that hound outside. I don't want him underfoot while I'm making supper." She turned to Peter then and handed him a wooden pail. "Don't you hear that cow bawling, fool? Her udder is full and hurting her. Go milk her."

Peter and Kaitlan said, "Yes, ma'am," in unison and stepped outside, Kaitlan dragging Ringer with her. She sat down on the top step of the porch, the hound beside her, and listened to a new sound: the click and drone of beetles in the grass and the drone of bees among the early blossoms. She was reluctant to leave the serene late afternoon but knew she should be inside helping Hattie with supper.

When she entered the cabin Hattie had three slabs of thick ham frying over the fire Peter had built. "Where did you get the ham?" she asked in surprise. Certainly they hadn't brought it with them.

"There's a larder over there." Hattie pointed to a narrow door at the end of the kitchen area. "It's chock full of hams and bacon and salt pork, potatoes, big heads of cabbage, bags of apples and pears. It's got a spring running right through the middle of it . . . keeps everything cool."

When the slices of ham were cooked through Hattie placed them on a platter and broke six eggs into the same frying pan. "You can set the table now, Kaitlan," she said. "Then take the pan of pone out of the oven." She handed her a dish towel. "For the time being, just dust off the table. We'll see what we can find tomorrow to pretty it up with a tablecloth."

Peter came through the door just as Hattie was putting supper on the table. She glanced into the pail he had put on the workbench next to the fireplace. "That don't look like much milk from two cows." She frowned at him. "Are you sure you got all the milk out of them?"

"I got all there was from one cow. The other one ain't freshened yet." He grinned. "She's gonna drop a calf any day now. I'll have to keep an eye on her in case she needs any help when the time comes to birth it."

Trying not to be too noticeable about it, Hattie hurried Kaitlan and Peter through the meal. They winked at each other, understanding that Hattie couldn't wait to get to her new home, to search out every corner of the rooms, to gloat over them. Neither blamed her.

Her dream had been a long time coming.

After Hattie served them one cup of coffee each, Kaitlan said, "Why don't you and Peter go home now?" She stressed the word *home*. "I'll do up the dishes."

"Well, if you don't mind, honey, I think we will. Don't forget to strain the milk and put it in the larder before you go to bed."

"I'll take care of it. Peter, light the lantern on the porch and take it with you."

"There's no need for that," Hattie said. "I saw a fresh candle on the kitchen table and a jar of tightly capped matches. Anyway, it's only a few yards away."

"I wasn't thinking about when you get inside. Lish was telling me that there are panthers in the mountains and sometimes they come down into the Gap."

"Oh, my goodness." Hattie's face paled. "By all means, Peter, light the lantern."

"I think it's too early for one to be prowling around yet," Kaitlan said, almost sorry she had mentioned the animal. "I'll stand on the porch until you've entered the cabin."

"And have your rifle ready," Hattie ordered as she bustled Peter through the door.

When the Smiths entered their cabin and Peter waved from the door that everything was all right, Kaitlan went back inside and poured herself another cup of coffee. She took it back outside and sat down on one of the chairs lined up on the porch. She also wanted to gloat a little. She wanted to thank God for the good turn her life had taken.

She sat in the muted glow of the sickle moon that was steadily rising through the gathering mist, thinking of her mother, wishing with all her heart that she were here with her. Not only for her gentle company, but to guide her through the running of a farm, to direct her in this new life she was about to start living.

Kaitlan was jolted out of her thoughts at the sound of horse hooves on the rocky trail leading to the cabin. Her nerves tightened. Was it one of her neighbors coming to call, or was it an Indian? She peered through the semidarkness, wishing that she had brought her rifle with her.

Two horses appeared at the edge of the yard, and she could see two men sitting tall in the saddles. She relaxed a bit. They were white men, but that was no real assurance that they were to be trusted.

# Chapter Three

The only sound in the heavy fog was the muted noise of creaking leather and jingling reins as the two men rode toward the Gap. The milky mist was growing dangerously thick and the man leading on the narrow trail said nervously, "I can't see a foot ahead of me. Do you think we ought to rein in and wait for it to lift?"

"And let a hunting panther come along and tear out our throats while we wait?" Matt Ingram said to his stepbrother Nate Streeter. "I smell wood smoke. Old Rufe's place isn't too far away. We can stop there until this fog lifts."

"How could smoke be coming from his place? Nobody lives there now."

"I was talking to Lish a couple weeks ago and he said that Rufe wrote to his granddaughter about taking over the farm. Maybe she's here now."

"I wonder how old she is and what she looks like," Nate said as his horse carefully picked its way around rocks and small boulders. "If she looks like Rufe, I feel sorry for her."

"Her looks won't keep you from trying to get in her bed, though, will they?" There was underlying contempt in Matt's voice.

"Hell, no. All cats look alike in the dark."

"Someday one of those cats is going to

scratch you good. You're gonna get something you're not looking for, and I'm not talking about another baby."

"There's no proof them two women got big bellies from me."

"You know as well as everybody else in the Gap that you fathered those two children."

"I know no such thing. Those women could have been sleeping with half a dozen other men at the same time. They just named me because of our tobacco farm. They were looking for a husband with money."

"They should have named me, then. I'm the one who owns the farm."

"And you never let me forget it, do you?" Nate's voice was harsh with resentment.

"I only mention it when you seem to forget."

"I don't know why I hang around these damn mountains anyway." Self-pity was in Nate's tone.

"You stay here for the large sum of money you receive every fall when the tobacco is sold, the fine horseflesh you ride, and the fancy clothes you like to wear when you court the women."

"I damn well earn it all. I work like a slave in those tobacco fields."

"Yeah, you work two months out of the year. The rest of the time you're out tearing around, sniffing after any woman who will spread her legs for you."

"Are you jealous that none of them want

you?" Nate sneered. "It's not my fault that you have to go to the Shawnee village to find a woman."

The angry conversation stopped abruptly when the men caught sight of candlelight coming through an uncurtained window. "Somebody sure as hell has moved into the Barrett cabin," Matt said. "I wonder if it's his granddaughter or some stranger who's had the nerve to try and take it over."

"He'd have to be a stranger to try a foolish trick like that here in the Gap." Nate pushed his horse to walk a little faster. "He'll get a load of buckshot in his ass."

The men reached the edge of the yard and reined up with audible indrawn breaths. They sat quietly in their saddles and stared. "My God," Nate finally half-whispered, "do you think she is real or is it the fog that makes her look so airy and ghostlike?"

"I don't believe in spiritual beings, so it must be the mist. She sure is a beauty."

It was a while before Nate spoke again. When he did, however, Matt shot him a sharp look as he said, as though to himself, "She's gonna be mine and nothing this side of hell is gonna stop me."

"Are you crazy, you fool? You can't treat her like you have the other ones. Rufe Barrett will rise out of his grave and shoot you down like a dog."

"I don't intend to treat her like the other

ones." Nate's eyes narrowed in determination as he added, "I mean to marry this one. At last I'll get a farm of my own. Then you can take your big tobacco farm and go straight to hell with it."

"You'd better think twice about that," Matt advised. "The Barrett place is an all-year-round farm. It has to be worked seven days a week, twelve months a year. And you're not one to walk behind a plow."

"There's always hired help to do that."

"You won't have much money left at the end of the year if you're gonna pay another man to do your work."

"Just mind your own business and I'll take care of mine. I think it's time one of us spoke to her."

Kaitlan's uneasiness had increased as the two men didn't address her, only sat staring at her, murmuring to each other. She was ready to stand up and hurry inside when one called out, "If you're Rufe Barrett's granddaughter, we're neighbors of yours."

Kaitlan eyed the speaker warily, hesitated a second, and then said, "Yes, I'm his grand-daughter, Kaitlan."

After darting Matt an uncomfortable look, Nate said, "We own a tobacco farm a couple miles from here."

"Oh yes" — Kaitlan nodded her head — "Lish mentioned something about a tobacco farm in the area."

"We were wondering if you'd mind if we sat with you awhile until the fog lifts. Panthers slink around in this kind of weather."

"Of course. Come on up. We can keep an eye on your horses from here too," she said, letting them know that they wouldn't be invited into the cabin. After all, she didn't know them.

She watched them dismount. Both men were tall, but the resemblance stopped there. One was lean, his hair blond. The other one was large, with broad shoulders and a deep chest that tapered down to narrow hips. His hair was raven black with heavy eyebrows to match. The fair one gave her an admiring smile as he climbed the steps, but the dark one gave her a brief nod and barely even looked at her.

With a careless, masculine grace that surprised her because of his size, he crossed the floor to the corner of the porch and leaned against the supporting post. In the shadows there his face appeared to be chiseled out of rock. She knew instinctively that he was a man who would hit harder than whomever he fought with.

Kaitlan turned her attention to the handsome one. He sat down in the chair next to her and said, "I'm Nate Streeter, and the feller over there in the dark is my stepbrother, Matt Ingram."

Kaitlan smiled shyly at the large man in the shadows and received another brief nod. She looked back at the one beside her and asked,

"Is it a usual thing to get so much fog and for it to come so quickly? When I came out here ten minutes ago the air was as clear as could be."

"We get a lot of it from spring to fall, especially in low pockets. The old-timers can usually predict when it's gonna be foggy. Most of the people heed their warnings and don't venture out after dark. If they have to go out, they carry a lantern and a rifle. I'm afraid we got caught with neither one."

"I've been wondering how and when to seed my tobacco field," Kaitlan said, changing the subject. "Lish showed me where my grandfather raised his crop but he didn't tell me how to go about planting it."

Nate looked at her, amusement in his eyes. "You don't plant the seeds in the fields," he explained. "You plant them first in a hotbed. When they come up and grow into sturdy plants you take them to the fields and set them out."

"That sounds like a lot of work," Kaitlan said. "I can see I'm going to be very busy."

"Oh, you couldn't do it all by yourself. You'll need help."

"I'll have that. My friends, Peter and Hattie Smith, will help me. They're living in the small place back of the cabin. Peter claims to know a little bit about growing tobacco."

Nate frowned slightly, and Matt knew what he was thinking. He didn't like the idea that Miss Barrett wasn't on her own after all. She might not be the easy prey he thought she was.

"Where can I buy the seeds?" Kaitlan asked, "and how do I make a hotbed?"

"Folks around here save some seed from their crops, but don't worry about that. We always have more plants than we can use. We can let you have all you need."

"That's very kind of you. I'll pay for them, of course." Nate shook his head and said with a laugh, "There's only one man in the Gap who charges a neighbor for anything. That's Jacob Bradly. He makes whiskey. He'd charge you if you so much as sniffed at an open jug."

Nate looked over at Matt, who hadn't spoken a word yet, and said, "Remember that trick we played on the old miser when we were teenagers?" He didn't wait for Matt to answer, but plunged right into his story.

"One night Matt and I decided to play a trick on Jacob. We took a brown jug and stuffed it full of cotton batting, then went up to Jacob's still. 'Fill her up,' Matt said, handing over the jug. He reached into his pocket as though to draw out his money and Jacob filled the jug to the top. He held out his hand then to be paid and Matt said, acting embarrassed, 'I'm sorry, but I must have forgotten my money.' If a mean look could have killed him, Matt would be dead today.

"Jacob grabbed up the jug and poured the whiskey back into the barrel. He handed it to Matt and said that if we two ever came around

40

his still again we'd get our rumps full of buck-shot. We laughed all the way home, and when we got inside the cabin we cracked open the jug and wrung out the cotton we had hidden inside it. There was enough whiskey to give us each a full glass."

While Nate was laughing about how they had tricked the moonshiner, Matt stood up and spoke for the first time. "I'm gonna get on home now. The fog has lifted." He nodded to Kaitlan, stepped off the porch, and faded into the darkness.

"Your brother doesn't talk much, does he?" Kaitlan said, staring at the spot where Matt had disappeared.

There was amusement in Nate's voice as he answered, "He's kinda standoffish with white women."

"He is? Why is that?"

Nate gave a careless shrug of his shoulder. "He likes squaws better, I guess. He has ever since the gal he was courting took a shine to another fellow. He's not going home now. He'll go to the Indian village, pick himself a pretty young squaw, and take her out in the woods somewhere." There was a note of jealousy in his voice when he added, "The Indian maids sure like him. Maybe he doesn't like to talk, but evidently he knows how to act with them, if you get my meaning."

For a split second Kaitlan wondered if Nate had visited the Indian village and hadn't found the same welcome his stepbrother did. She couldn't imagine that being possible, though. Nate was so handsome and well mannered. Still, she found it was Matt she was thinking about once both men had left: Had he really gone to the Indian village?

# Chapter Four

Kaitlan came awake, stared at the open window, and then jumped out of bed. The eastern sky was gray. Daylight would soon arrive. Never had she been so eager for a day to begin. During the last month she had settled into her new home, and this week she and Peter had been busy breaking up her five acres of land, working with a mule hitched to a single-footed plow. The bottomland was rich from being flooded every spring. The rich, black silt was waiting for the tobacco plants to be set in the rows she and Peter had made with the edge of a hoe. Her blistered palms and aching back were testimony to the hard labor involved.

But it had all been worthwhile. This morning Nate would be bringing the tender, young tobacco plants.

"Eggs and bacon, Hattie?" Kaitlan sniffed the air as she sat down at the table across from Peter, who was drinking his coffee from his saucer. She hated that habit of his, but he would heed neither her nor Hattie's pleas in that regard.

"Are you ready to start putting out the plants?" she asked as Hattie set breakfast on the table.

Peter nodded as he helped himself to bacon

and eggs and a hot biscuit. "I just hope that sweet-talkin' Nate gets the plants to us before noon. If it's hot when we set them out, the sun will wilt them."

Peter didn't like Nate, and Kaitlan thought she knew why. Nate never talked to him. Peter liked men's talk — soil, farm animals, and the weather. But Nate liked talking to her, she thought, a little smile hovering around her lips.

"What do you think of Nate?" she asked, looking at Hattie when the black woman sat down to her right.

"Well," Hattie said as she buttered a hot biscuit, "I can't really say yet. I think he's a ladies' man and I don't think he'd go out of his way to help his own sex. I'm afraid he might be on the lazy side, because it's always near noon when he shows up here and he always looks spic-and-span, whites starched and with creased trousers."

"Maybe he gets up early, does his work, and then washes up and changes his clothing," Kaitlan said sharply, defending Nate.

Hattie shook her head as she spooned sugar into her coffee. "His nails are too clean and his hands are too soft. They're smoother than yours are now, what with grubbin' in the dirt this past week."

"Well, for someone who hasn't given it much thought, you've found a lot to cast doubt on his character," Kaitlan said smartly. "Couldn't you find one thing you like about him?"

"Now, don't go getting huffy, honey," Hattie said in her brisk way. "The fact that he's so smitten with you is in his favor. As time goes along I'm sure I'll find more things about him that I like." When Kaitlan looked away from her, Hattie rolled her eyes at Peter in denial.

Kaitlan's eyes took on a dreamy look. Nate did seem smitten with her. He had stopped by three times in the last week alone and she had enjoyed his company very much. She wasn't used to a man's compliments, his praising her eyes, her hair, how sweet her lips looked.

During the last two years many men had cast admiring looks her way. None of those men were ever allowed near her, though. Yancy had always seen to that. One time a young man had engaged her in an innocent conversation and her stepfather had seen them laughing and talking to each other. He charged at them and knocked the young man down. He marched her home, took off his belt, and as he struck her across the back with it time and again, he punctuated each stinging blow with the word *whore*. She had never dared look at another man again.

But her stepfather was no longer in her life, Kaitlan reminded herself. She could talk to any male she pleased, even try her hand at flirting a little. That should be something to watch: Kaitlan Barrett making eyes at a man. She wouldn't even know how to begin.

Hattie was pouring them each a second cup

of coffee; then she paused, listening. "I think I hear him coming now."

Kaitlan shot to her feet and hurried outside to stand on the porch. Disappointment gripped her. It was not Nate riding toward her; it was his stepbrother Matt, the dark, surly one.

As he pulled up in front of the porch and touched two fingers to his hat brim in greeting, Kaitlan got her first good look at him. He had a straight nose and firm lips above a strong jaw. He wore his coal-black hair to his shoulders and had equally black brows over the coldest gray eyes she'd ever seen. She thought to herself that she wasn't surprised that his hard looks made the young women in the Gap shy away from him.

"Good morning," she said shyly, looking past him, down the rock-strewn trail for a glimpse of Nate.

"He's not with me," Matt said, reading her searching look. "He'll probably be along later," he added. He swung out of the saddle and carefully removed a wetted-down sack from the broad rump of his stallion. "We've got to get these plants into the ground before it gets hot."

"Yes, of course. I'll go put my sunbonnet on."

"Could you also change into a pair of Peter's trousers?" Matt called after her as she was about to go through the door. "Your long skirt will drag at you as you crawl along in the soil. It will soon tire you out."

"I suppose I could." Kaitlan looked uncertain. "But I'll be awfully embarrassed if a neighbor comes along and catches me in them."

"Don't worry about that," Matt said as he pulled the saddle off his horse and then the bridle. "All the women 'round here wear their husbands' or sons' trousers when they work in the fields." He said this last as he walked off in the direction of the tobacco acres.

"I'll go see what I can find in the line of britches," Peter said, getting up from the table. "It's a good thing I'm so skinny. My homespuns are gonna fit you just fine."

"You might as well dig me up a pair too," Hattie said. "I'm going to be helping you put them plants in the ground."

"Oh, but Hattie, you don't have to," Kaitlan protested.

"Yes, I do. We need as many hands as we got if we're to get them tender shoots planted before it gets hot." She looked at the clear blue sky. "And it looks to me like this day is gonna be a scorcher."

Matt had dropped plants two feet apart halfway down one row when he saw Kaitlan and the Smiths coming across the plowed soil. Peter carried a bucket of water in each hand and Hattie had a covered basket on her arm. Their lunch, he assumed.

It was Kaitlan who had most of his attention, though. Had he known what she would look like in the trousers, he never would have suggested that she wear the homespuns.

Kaitlan hadn't taken the time to look in the mirror after donning a pair of Peter's trousers — they felt good and gave her a free stride that her skirt and petticoat didn't afford her. Consequently she didn't know how snugly they hugged her rounded hips and long, shapely legs.

Matt swore softly under his breath. He'd have to make damn sure that he didn't look at her any more than he could help. Kaitlan found him gruff when she asked what she and the Smiths should do. He handed her a carefully wrapped bundle of the tender plants, then handed one of equal size to Hattie.

"Drop one plant about every two feet. Peter and I will come along behind you and put them in the ground." The sun had been up half an hour when the four of them started working the tobacco patch.

At the end of the first row Matt managed to get behind Hattie. Working behind Kaitlan, watching the sway of her hips, was driving him crazy.

They had been working about half an hour when Lish Jones rode up on his mule. "I thought I'd ride over to see if you need some help," he said, sliding off the animal, which looked as old as its owner.

"Another hand is always welcome," Matt said. "You can walk behind her" — he motioned in the direction of Kaitlan, who was working alongside Hattie — "and give each plant a dipper of water."

"Which her?" Lish asked, a devilish look in his eyes. He seemed to be determined that Matt say the name that seemed so hard for him to utter.

After giving the old man a black look, Matt said in clipped tones, "Miss Barrett."

"Oh, you mean Kaitlan," Lish said innocently. "Didn't you catch her first name when you were introduced?"

"I guess I didn't catch it," Matt muttered, then snapped, "Why don't you stop your yapping and start putting the plants in the ground?"

"Reckon I'll just work behind Kaitlan," Lish said and got down on his knees, his old bones cracking.

When Kaitlan saw how difficult it had been for him to kneel, she urged, "Let's you and I change places. You drop the plants and I'll hill them up."

"Don't worry about me, Kaitlan. It just hurts gettin' down. But once it's done, I'm fine."

"If you're sure," Kaitlan said, doubt on her face.

She slowed her pace to make it easier for Lish, and after a while she asked, "Do you have a lot of stock to take care of?"

"Kind of. I have a couple beeves I'll slaughter this fall after a hard freeze. I'll keep some for

49

my own use and sell the rest of it. I'll do the same thing with my two hogs. And then there's the herd of sheep. I think I have about twenty head."

"That's a lot of animals to butcher."

"I don't butcher the sheep. I sell their wool."

"I expect it's a lot of work, taking care of so many animals."

"Naw. I do what everyone else around here does. You just fence in your yard and garden and let the animals graze wherever they want to. The only time you see them is about once a month when they come in for salt."

"Don't they get cold in the winter?"

"When we get freezin' weather we herd them in and see to it that they eat proper, put on fat to keep them warm. In the spring we shear them and sell the wool. Wool is the poorer people's cash crop, like tobacco is Matt's cash crop."

"I guess that tobacco is going to be mine and the Smiths' cash crop" — Kaitlan grinned — "but I imagine we are classified as poor."

"No, you're kinda stuck in the middle. You ain't poor like a lot of us, but you're not up there with Matt."

"You always refer to Matt as being the owner of the farm. Isn't Nate a half-owner?"

"No, he's not. Nate is the son of the woman Matt's paw married after his maw died. He was a young teenager when he come here to the Gap."

"It seems to me that he should have some part of the farm. He works so hard."

Lish gave her a startled look, opened his mouth to say something, then closed his lips. A minute passed, and then he said, "I'm surprised Nate's not here helpin' us."

"He's probably catching up on some work at the farm."

"Uh huh." Lish grunted and said no more.

It was near ten o'clock, and they had been working steadily for hours, when Hattie pushed the sunbonnet off her head. After swiping her arm across her face, she said, "I don't know about the rest of you, but I'm stopping for an early lunch." When she strode across the field to a big maple whose shade covered a large area, the others followed her.

Kaitlan happened to be walking alongside Matt and she looked up at him and asked, "Are you hungry?"

The hard lines around his mouth relaxed and his lips lifted into a wide, dazzling smile. "I'm as hungry as a bear just out of hibernation in the spring."

Kaitlan actually gawked at Matt for a second. His smile changed the whole appearance of his face. He didn't look like the same hard, cold man. She finally found her tongue and said, "I think Hattie has some fried chicken in her basket. Nice and crispy, southern style."

"I wondered if she and Peter were originally from the South."

"Yes, South Carolina. They were young adult married slaves on a plantation there. When their master died, his widow freed half her slaves because she didn't intend to raise as much cotton as her husband had. Peter and Hattie were among those who received their freedom papers. But after they were freed, things were actually worse for them. No one would hire them, they had no money, not even a roof over their heads. They struck out across country working for food and a place to sleep in a barn until they reached Philadelphia. There, my father hired them to work for him — Hattie as a cook and Peter to take care of anything that came up around the house. They had been with my parents a year when I was born."

"You seem awfully fond of them."

"I am. They are the only family I have left."

"Your mother and father are dead?"

"Yes," Kaitlan answered flatly and said no more.

Matt looked at her from the corner of his eye, but her stony face told him that as far as she was concerned the subject was finished.

They reached the spot where Peter and Lish were hungrily eyeing the food Hattie was taking from her basket and placing on a white cloth she had laid on the ground. There wasn't much talking going on as Hattie's chicken and biscuits were consumed. When only crumbs were

52

left, the men sat back, uttering contented sounds.

There were only two more rows left to plant, so a leisurely fifteen minutes were taken to digest their food. After Matt complimented Hattie on the chicken, he and Peter started reminiscing about other foods they favored. "Sometimes I long for crispy catfish and hush puppies and redeye gravy," Peter said.

"I'm partial to wild blackberries and winesap apples and sun-ripened wild strawberries, collard greens and sweet potatoes," Matt said.

"And white beans, corn bread, and mountain trout," Lish put in, adding his favorites.

"I'm reminded of the sun beating down on my arms and neck in a July cotton field," Hattie said sourly.

"I think what I like most is the touch of a cool wind when it has rained after a long drought," Kaitlan thought out loud.

Everyone agreed it was a good feeling when a heavy rain had cooled off a long heat wave.

Peter started to say how he thought a bunch of baby chicks was a heartwarming sight when he saw a cloud of dust coming from the wagon track that bordered the tobacco patch. He said instead, "What damn fool is ridin' a horse like that in this hot, humid weather?"

"That damn fool is Nate," Lish said disgustedly. "He always knows when to show up — when the work is practically all done. It will be interestin' to hear what excuse he gives."

Kaitlan looked at Matt, sure that he wouldn't like Lish's tone or words about his stepbrother. She was surprised to see that he looked even more disgusted than Lish. He doesn't like Nate, she thought, and wondered why. Was he jealous of Nate's good looks, his pleasing ways, which must attract the girls? Like herself, she thought.

She silently admitted that she was attracted to Nate. Very much so. And she could tell he felt the same way about her. She frowned, though, when Nate brought the sweating, foam-flicked horse to a rearing halt. She hated to see animals abused.

Evidently everyone else felt the same way. Especially Matt. His face was dark with anger when he stood up and walked over to the winded stallion. He ran a gentle hand down the horse's wet, quivering neck. Then, fast as lightning, he grabbed Nate by the arm and jerked him out of the saddle.

Nate took a couple stumbling steps backward, caught his balance, and yelled, "What in the hell do you think you're doing?"

"There's no thinking about it," Matt said coldly. "I know exactly what I'm doing, and what you're going to do now. If I ever again see this horse, or any other one you may be riding, in this condition, I'm going to beat you into the ground.

"Now take this horse down to the branch, lead him out into the water until it reaches his belly. Wipe him down, then keep him in the water for at least twenty minutes."

The fury that shot into Nate's eyes told Kaitlan that while Matt disliked Nate, Nate hated his stepbrother.

The two men stood facing each other, and it looked for a moment as if they might come to blows. Then Nate broke the eye contact and, catching up the reins of the stallion, started walking toward the nearby river branch.

Peter and Lish shot Matt approving looks, but Kaitlan ignored him. In her opinion, Matt Ingram was a bully who threw his size and strength around. She had forgotten for the moment what had brought on the confrontation between the stepbrothers.

She was disappointed when Nate didn't return to the field. When the last seedling was put into the soil, she hurried on ahead of the others to the cabin. She knew a twinge of guilt that she hadn't thanked Matt for the plants, or his help in getting them into the ground.

"He wouldn't care if I thanked him or not," she muttered, excusing her bad manners as she hurried into her bedroom to wash up and change into clean clothes.

Later, when she walked into the kitchen, however, she was reminded of her rudeness. Lish and the Smiths were sitting at the table nailing her with censuring looks.

"What?" she asked defensively, not quite meeting the three pairs of eyes.

"You know what," Hattie was quick to answer her. "Stamping off with your chin in the air, not even saying good-bye to Matt, let alone thanking him for his help. You got your nose out of joint because Matt laid into Fancy Pants for mistreating that poor horse. I was hoping he'd take his fists to his stepbrother."

"And not only that," Lish said, picking up where Hattie had left off, "Matt Ingram is a fine, honorable man, even if he does look rough. What if somewhere down the road you need his help again? Won't you be a little embarrassed to ask him for a favor after the way you behaved today?"

"He didn't have to shame Nate that way in front of everybody, treating him like a young boy who had misbehaved."

"Matt treats people the way they act. And Nate's been warned about the way he treats horses. Even old man Ingram tried to explain to Nate when he first come here that a farmer should always take care of his animals, never treat them bad. But Nate never paid any attention to him. His mother had spoiled him rotten and he didn't think he had to listen to anybody. He figured he could do as he pleased."

"Well, enough of Matt and Nate," Hattie said. "Me and Peter have some work to do at our place."

"I've got some work to do too." Lish stood up.

Suddenly Kaitlan had the cabin to herself and a lot to think about.

# Chapter Five

Kaitlan left the tobacco field with a pleased smile on her face. The seedlings that had been planted a month before were strong and sturdy. Old Lish had said yesterday that she was going to have a bumper crop.

And the garden patch Peter and Hattie had plowed and planted two days after their arrival in the Gap was doing equally well. Already they'd had green onions and lettuce and radishes, and she was pretty sure Hattie would serve their first peas tonight at the supper table.

Also, after an unexplained absence of four weeks, Nate was back in her life again. She smiled as she and the hound turned onto a wide path that ran alongside the river branch. He had come calling last Sunday night and her pulse had raced when she recognized his stallion trotting up to the cabin.

She had been sitting on the porch, counting her blessings, comparing her present life with the one in which she had been so miserable. She still had nightmares about her stepfather coming at her, his belt in his hand.

But that had all been forgotten when Nate pulled up in front of the cabin and swung to the ground.

At first he had been on the quiet side, as

though he was remembering the last time she had seen him and he wasn't sure how she might feel about him now. When she acted the same way she had in the past, he loosened up and soon became his old pleasant self.

As they sat on the top step of the moonlit porch, he told her how much he had missed her.

"I've been here all the time. You could have ridden over whenever it suited you," she gently chastised him.

"I've been . . ." He hesitated, and then said, "Matt has kept me pretty busy tending the tobacco fields, so come night all I can do is fall in bed and go to sleep."

He reached across the space between them and picked up Kaitlan's hand. "I couldn't stay away any longer no matter how tired I was."

He certainly doesn't look tired, Kaitlan thought. He looked as fresh and handsome as ever. What she could see of him, that was. He still wore his hat, which was unusual for him. The first thing he had always done before was to remove it on approaching her.

On an impulse she lifted her free hand and removed the hat from his head. When he grabbed at it she laughingly held it out of his reach. It was then she got a good look at his face in the moonlight. All playfulness left her. A circle of purple and yellow smudged his right eye, and on the same side, his cheekbone wore a red bruise, as did his chin. There was a split in his lip that was half healed.

"Good Lord." She gasped. "Who did this to you, Nate?"

Nate shrugged. "Me and Matt got into it."

"What did you do to make him batter your face like that?"

After a short, scornful laugh Nate said, "He got upset when he saw me passing the time of day with one of his squaws."

"His squaws?" Kaitlan stared at him, wondering why his words had shocked her so.

"One of his squaws. There's three or four of them."

"He lives with three or four Indian women?" Kaitlan looked horrified.

"Heavens, no. The great Matt Ingram would never have a squaw in his home. When he feels the need for a woman he goes up to their village. For some reason I can't understand, they're crazy about him."

Kaitlan thought she heard a touch of envy in Nate's voice, then changed her mind. She felt sure he could have any white woman in the area that he wanted. He would have no desire to meet an Indian girl.

She lifted her hand and laid her palm on his cheek. "Does it hurt much?" she asked.

Suddenly, before she knew what he was about, Nate had both arms around her and was crushing her lips against his. Stunned at first, Kaitlan didn't move as his kiss deepened, but when his tongue tried to force its way into her mouth, she rallied to brace her hands against his chest and push.

She was released immediately, and Nate was full of apologies. "I'm sorry, Kaitlan, but I've wanted to kiss you ever since the first time I saw you. I really couldn't help myself tonight. You look so beautiful in the moonlight."

Kaitlan held her fingers to her mouth. "I don't mind that you kissed me, Nate," she explained, "but why were you so rough?"

Nate gave her a startled look, as if he'd never imagined a girl not enjoying his kiss. Then he lifted Kaitlan's chin, and murmuring how sorry he was for hurting her, gently pressed a brief kiss on her cheek.

A loving smile tilted Kaitlan's lips now as she remembered that sweet action. Nate had come calling every night since then, and always he'd been charming and considerate.

Last night, however, he had become a little bold. He had tried to lay his hand on her breast. When she repulsed his action, he quickly dropped his hand back to her waist.

Kaitlan was wondering how long Nate would be satisfied with just talk, and what she would do when that time came, when she rounded a bend in the river road. A flock of wild ducks suddenly left the water, whirring through the air. Who had frightened them? she wondered, and hurriedly looked around in case there was a wildcat lurking nearby.

It was then she spied the old woman. She was

ancient-looking, dressed all in black with a basket on her arm. When they came face-to-face, the old lady peered at her from faded brown eyes.

"You be old Rufe's granddaughter, ain't you, child," she said, giving Kaitlan a toothless smile. "You have the look of your grandmother."

Kaitlan returned the warm smile. "I'm Kaitlan," she said, gently clasping the fragile hand held out to her.

"I'm called Granny Higgins by everyone in the Gap. Actually I'm no blood relation to any of them, but I borned most of them. That was before my fingers got all bent with rheumatiz'. Now I just help folks how I can with my herb medicines."

"It must make you feel pleased to be able to help your neighbors that way."

"Yes, it purely does. It's right good to know that God put you on earth to do somethin' worthwhile." The old lady paused, then asked, "Was you goin' somewhere in particular?"

"No, just taking a walk before it gets hot. Grandpa's hound is around here somewhere."

"Gettin' out while it's still coolish is a smart thing to do. That's why I'm out now. I'm lookin' for garden sass."

"What's garden sass?"

"It's different kinds of greens. You get yourself some sheep sorrel, dandelions, a little poke, some dock, lamb's-quarter and mustard. You wash them all proper, put them in a pot, add a little water and a ham bone with lots of meat still on it and let it all cook real slow for two or three hours. Ain't nothin' better tastin'. And real good for you too."

"It sure sounds good."

"Come along with me then and we'll pick enough for both of us."

They were gathering the tender leaves of lamb's-quarter when Granny said, "I understand you got a Negro couple livin' with you."

Kaitlan didn't answer at once. She liked the old woman and wanted to keep her as a friend, but if she was going to bad-mouth Hattie and Peter, that would be the end of any good relations between them.

"Yes," she answered tightly, "I have. They have been with me ever since I was born. They are wonderful people."

Granny grinned to herself. The young miss wouldn't allow anything bad to be said about the black couple. She liked that. Kaitlan Barrett would be a worthwhile friend to have.

"I've heard tell the woman has a sharp tongue."

Kaitlan laughed. "She does indeed. She speaks what's on her mind. I wish she didn't, though. It's difficult to be accepted by people if you're too outspoken."

"Yes, that's true. But on the other hand, a person wouldn't have to worry that she was talking behind her back."

Kaitlan agreed and added, "She has a real good heart. She will help anyone in need."

"How could she help them?" Granny looked interested.

"When Hattie was still a slave, she worked in the plantation's infirmary, helping to set broken bones, lance boils, help croupy babies to breathe. But what she did most was deliver the black women's babies. She brags that she never lost a baby or its mother."

"That's quite interestin'," Granny said thoughtfully. "Do you think she would step in and help mountain babies to be born?"

"Of course she would. She'd be happy to. I think doctoring is Hattie's real calling."

"I expect she has her own herb medicines?" Granny narrowed her eyes at Kaitlan.

"No, she was never privy to her mistress's medicines." Kaitlan waited a second and then added what she knew would please Granny. "She would have to depend on you for that." The toothless smile that lit up the wrinkled face told her she had guessed right.

"Maybe I'll come meet your Hattie one of these days."

"Please do. She always has some sweet to serve with the coffee, and we'd both welcome you. I want to get to know my neighbors. I expect to live here the rest of my life."

"There's no finer place to live than here in the Cumberland Gap," Granny said, getting stiffly off her knees by holding on to a bush.

"Sometimes our people are suspicious of strangers and it's a while before they loosen up and accept them. But I'll pass the word about how nice you are and how your Hattie can be a help to them. That last will soften them up real quick-like."

"Thank you, Granny, I appreciate that. So far I've only met Lish."

"What about Matt and Nate?"

"Oh, yes." Kaitlan blushed. "Them too."

Granny gave her a sly grin. "I hear tell you and Nate are sweet on one another."

"I wouldn't say that." Kaitlan's blush deepened. "He's awfully nice, though."

"And Matt. Is he nice too?"

"It's difficult to get to know Matt. He doesn't talk much and I've only been around him a couple times."

"I understand he spent several hours with you puttin' your tobacco plants in the ground."

"Yes, he did," Kaitlan answered, not meeting Granny's eyes. "I appreciated it."

"I expect you thanked him all proper-like."

Embarrassment flushed Kaitlan's face. Had Lish told everybody in the Gap how she hadn't spoken a word to Matt after he had rebuked Nate by treating him like a child? She was deeply ashamed of that now, for if it hadn't been for Matt her plants wouldn't have gotten into the ground that day. She hoped that an opportunity would arise so that she could correct her rude behavior and, in

Granny's words, thank him proper-like.

When Kaitlan didn't answer the old lady's question, Granny said, "It's been my experience that some men talk too much. The majority of them are just full of brag."

Kaitlan got the distinct feeling that Granny was referring to Nate. He did tend to brag a little. But Kaitlan had excused that as his trying to impress her, and she couldn't fault him for that.

"Well, Kaitlan, it's beginnin' to heat up. I'll leave most of the greens in the basket for you to take home with you, and I'll put my share in my apron. I'll pick up the basket when I come callin' on you. Whistle up your hound now and skeidaddle home."

As she walked back to the cabin, Kaitlan hummed a little tune her mother used to sing before Yancy had come into their lives. Swinging the basket on her arm, she thought that Granny Higgins would become a good friend to them if Hattie would let her.

But both women were so outspoken, she had doubts about that happening. They did, however, have one thing in common: both ladies had a bent for helping the sick and ailing. That could form a bond between them.

She was walking back down the dirt path that ran between her tobacco patch and the thick woods when Nate stepped out in front of her, his stallion trailing along behind him. The animal's beautiful hide was sweat stained, evidence that he had been ridden hard.

"Nate! You almost gave me a heart attack." She gasped, her hand going to her throat.

"I'm sorry, Kaitlan. I didn't mean to scare you." Nate took her arm and started walking.

"I wasn't scared, just startled." She smiled up at him.

"Can I come over and visit with you for a while tonight?" Nate asked, returning her smile.

"Yes, I'd like that." They came to a halt. The cabin was up ahead. When Nate would have bent his head to kiss her, Kaitlan drew back. She sensed that Hattie was watching them from behind the kitchen curtains.

"I'll be seeing you, then." Displeasure that she had refused to let him kiss her was in Nate's voice. It also showed in his actions as he mounted the stallion and viciously brought a riding crop across its rump.

Kaitlan stared after the galloping horse. She was going to speak to Nate about his rough handling of the animal, she decided.

# Chapter Six

The sun was going down as Matt approached a narrow strip of swampland known as the River Bottoms. He was halfway to his destination, a little settlement called the Village. He pulled his stallion Satan in to rest a few minutes before continuing on.

He wondered if Nate was watching the same sunset from Kaitlan's porch. His stepbrother had been over at her cabin every evening this week, getting sympathy for his black eye, no doubt.

Nate knew how to turn any situation to his advantage, Matt thought bitterly. He would be talking the sweet talk he was so good at, using smooth manners to worm his way into her heart. Of course, he wouldn't tell Kaitlan the real reason Matt had beaten him up. How he had caught him trying to rape an Indian girl near the river. Nor would he tell her how he had fathered a baby on two separate mountain girls a few years back. He wouldn't tell her how the first one had drowned herself in the river when he refused to marry her. Or how the family of the second girl had thrown her out when Nate lied and said that she had been sleeping with four other men at the same time and there was no way of knowing who the baby belonged to. When Nate tried to say the same thing to him, Matt had given him a black eye then, too. They both knew that Judy had been only with him.

Matt's big hands curled into fists. Judy Perkins had run away to Nashville. Matt had given her enough money to see her through until she delivered the baby, but afterward she'd left the Gap, unable to face the people she'd known all her life. Before she left she'd asked Matt to take her little son. "I won't be able to take care of him proper where I'm going," she said, stroking the baby's little bald head, "but I know you will, Matt."

So he had taken the little one to Ruby, the madam of a bawdy house ten miles down the river and asked her to raise the baby for him. Ruby had a heart almost as big as she was and he knew she would be good to the little fellow.

For the past three years he had visited little Samuel every chance he got. It was there he was headed now.

The June night was so hot, Satan didn't move except to twitch his hide when a fly lit on it. Matt looked up at the sky and found that it had darkened to a deep gray. Was it going to rain? he wondered. He didn't want to get caught in a storm. Touching his heels to the stallion, he urged Satan on.

An hour later a wind came up and moaned through the trees and there came a distant rumble of thunder. It was definitely going to rain.

When Matt saw the flickering lights of the village, lightning was streaking across the sky and the thunder was right overhead. He lifted the reins, urging Satan into a faster pace. By the time he had stabled the stallion at the livery, he had to dash through a hard, sheeting rain to reach the bawdy house.

He stepped into the smoke-filled room, trying to ignore the reek of stale ale and un-washed bodies. As he made his way to a door that led to the whore's quarters, men nodded to him and respectfully made way for him. Only a stranger who didn't know big "Black Matt" would have stood in his way.

As Matt walked down the narrow, candlelit hall, there came from each room he passed the sound of squeaking beds and the thump of bodies coming together. He reached the door at the end and rapped his knuckles against it. From inside he heard heels tapping on the floor, and then the door was opened.

"Matt!" Ruby Gentry's eyes sparkled with delight. "Have you come purposely to see me, or has the rain driven you in?"

"I've come purposely to see you," he answered with a warm smile as he stepped inside Ruby's office. "And to see the boy."

"I'm sorry, but he's asleep. He's going to be so disappointed he didn't get to see his uncle Matt. He talks about you all the time."

"Maybe I could look in on him," Matt questioned hopefully.

"Of course. I'd wake him up, but he'd get so excited at seeing you it would take me hours to get him back to sleep."

They stepped quietly into the small room Ruby had added on to hers. Matt walked over to the narrow bed placed against the wall and noted the high railing at the foot and side of the bed. There was no way the sleeping three-year-old could roll out of his criblike bed.

Matt longed to stroke the curly head as he looked down on the little boy, but was afraid of wakening him. "His hair is getting darker, isn't it?" he whispered.

"Yes, it is, and he's looking less like his no-good father every day. He's such a good little fellow, I have high hopes that he won't be like Nate."

"You can rest assured he won't be. I'll see to that," Matt said and turned away from the sleeping child. When they had passed through Ruby's bedroom and back again into her office, she asked as she poured Matt a glass of whiskey, "What are your plans for the little fellow? I love him and would keep him forever, but a whorehouse is no place to raise a child."

"You're right, of course, but I haven't come up with an idea yet. I know it sounds crazy, but I keep hoping that something will happen to solve everything. If I took him home, Polly could care for him, but I don't want him anywhere near Nate." Then Matt went on to tell

Ruby about the Indian girl his stepbrother had tried to rape.

"I don't know what to do for Little Wren. I feel responsible in a way, since Nate is my stepbrother. The poor girl is terrified of men now, and she's supposed to be getting married soon."

Ruby let loose a string of words that wasn't at all ladylike. "I don't let Nate in here anymore, not since I found out that he likes it rough. I won't let any man mistreat my girls. I don't think there's much you can do to help her, Matt. If her husband is a decent sort, she'll soon learn that men aren't all bastards. There are a few good ones like you around."

"Me? Black Matt," Matt scoffed. "I'm not so good, drinking and carousing all the time."

"But you don't abuse women and that's what counts in my book."

A grin creased the corners of Matt's eyes. "I can't see you letting any man abuse you, Ruby."

A hard gleam came into the madam's eyes. "One did a long time ago. My husband. The happiest day in my life was when he froze to death in a blizzard."

A silence grew in the room and Matt knew by the bleak look in Ruby's eyes that she was remembering those days of unhappiness. He stirred, cleared his throat, and when Ruby gave a start and looked at him blankly, he said, "I'm beat, friend. After I get something to eat, do you have a room where I can bed down for a few hours?"

"You mean alone, of course," Ruby teased. When he nodded with a grin she said, "There's a room next to my quarters. I keep it for the girls' use when they're not feeling well. Will I see you in the morning before you leave?"

"Not unless you'll be up at dawn. I want to get back to the Gap as soon as I have a chance to see little Sammy. I'm concerned about this rain. If it comes down much longer I could lose some of my tobacco plants." And so could Kaitlan, he thought to himself. Hers were more at risk than his. Their roots weren't very well established yet.

As Kaitlan sat on the porch, only the creaking of the old rocking chair, the murmuring of the breeze that rustled the leaves of the maples, and the droning of cicadas broke the silence. She looked often down the gravel path that led from the Ingram farm. Nate had said he'd be stopping by tonight.

She leaned forward and propped her elbows on her knees. He hadn't said what time he would be here, though. It must be close to eight, because when she and the Smiths had finished supper the clock on the mantel had struck seven. It had taken her close to an hour to wash the dishes, freshen herself up, and slip into a clean dress.

Kaitlan was beginning to believe that Nate Streeter might be the man she wanted to spend the rest of her life with. He was loving and attentive, cheerful and he was always talking about what a hard worker he was. What more could a girl want in a husband?

The clock inside struck the half hour, and Kaitlan added, a little impatiently, "And he's always late." She couldn't remember a time when he came riding up the path when he was supposed to.

"I can't expect him to be perfect, now can I, Ringer?" She patted the hound's head as he hopped up on the porch and stretched out beside her chair.

A wind suddenly came up, and high in the mountains a cougar screamed. Kaitlan shivered at the sound and, straightening up, she noted for the first time that beyond the blackness of the forest occasional flashes of lightning illuminated it.

A worried frown creased her forehead. Was it going to rain? A severe storm would slash at her tender plants, flattening them, exposing their roots and killing them.

The clock struck nine and she rose from the chair and went inside. Nate wouldn't be coming tonight.

With a prayer on her lips that it wouldn't rain, that she had only seen heat lightning, Kaitlan stripped off her clothes and slipped into her gown. But as she climbed into bed the rain came, beating against the cabin walls.

Matt left the Village in the gloom of a wet, gray dawn. It had stopped raining as he ate a hurried breakfast with Ruby. She had surprised him by getting up and making ham and eggs and fried potatoes. "You can't ride ten miles on an empty stomach," she had said when he scolded her for rising so early just to make him a meal. She slapped Matt on the back of the head and ordered, "Eat."

"I haven't been whacked in the head like that since my ma passed away," Matt said, grinning up at her.

"I'm sure you needed it," Ruby said good-naturedly as she sat down at the table with a cup of coffee.

"There's no doubt about that," Matt agreed. "I was pretty much a hellion, growing up."

"Well, you've turned into a good man and that's what —" Ruby was interrupted by the sound of pattering bare feet and a childish voice calling out, "I'm hungry, Aunt Ruby."

Matt and Ruby laughed softly at the wonder and delight that came into the boy's eyes as he spotted Matt. With a tickled laugh Sammy ran to the big man sitting at the table.

"Uncle Matt," he cried, throwing himself into the waiting arms, "I dreamed you had come to see me." Hugging Matt's neck fiercely and planting wet kisses on his cheeks, he asked, "Will we go fishing today?"

"I'm afraid not, son." Matt sat the little one

on his knee. "We had a storm last night and everything is too wet. I promise, though, that the next time I come to visit you, we'll go down to the river and catch a batch of fish for Aunt Ruby to fry up for our supper."

Sammy was disappointed, but he consoled himself by picking up a spoon and eating a good share of Matt's breakfast.

When the plate was empty and Matt had finished his second cup of coffee, he dropped a kiss on top of the curly head and stood Sammy on the floor.

"I've got to go, son," he said gently when tears brimmed in the child's blue eyes. "But I promise you that I'll be back before long."

"You promise?"

"I promise."

"Go along now, honey." Ruby gently pushed the boy toward the door. "Play with your blocks until Aunt Ruby gets dressed."

Matt watched the chubby little body disappear down the hall. It was getting harder and harder to leave him.

With a sigh he stood up, and after kissing Ruby's cheek, he let himself out.

Fifteen minutes later Matt was on the trail back home.

The rain had cooled the air, and Matt put Satan to a hard gallop that quickly ate up the ten miles between the village and his farm. He wondered if it was possible Nate would look over the tobacco patches to see how much, if any, damage had been done. If so, would he have started replacing the plants that had been lost? More than likely he's not even home, Matt thought sourly. He's probably been out all night with some woman.

But that woman wouldn't be Kaitlan Barrett, with her red-gold hair and dark blue eyes. Nate would be very careful how he behaved around her . . . for a while, that was.

# Chapter Seven

The loud clanging of a dropped pot lid awakened Kaitlan with a jerk. She sat up in bed, knuckling her red-rimmed eyes. She'd had very little sleep last night. The beating of the rain on the roof and worry about her tobacco plants had kept her wide-awake, staring into the darkness.

She became aware suddenly that all was quiet outside. It had stopped raining. She was out of bed in a flash, jerking the gown over her head and dressing herself in Peter's old trousers and shirt. As she buttoned up she heard Peter and Hattie in the kitchen, Hattie bawling her husband out about something or other.

What time had they arrived? she wondered, sniffing at the odor of frying ham. When she had shoved her feet into a heavy pair of ankle-high boots and laced them up, she went to the window and pulled the curtains apart. It was dark gray outside; there were even a few stars still shining in the sky.

But it would lighten up fast, she knew. By the time they ate breakfast it would be light enough to see what damage had been done to her plants.

When Kaitlan walked into the kitchen she saw that the Smiths didn't look any more rested than she felt. After all, they would be sharing equally in any profit they might make when the tobacco was sold. They had agreed that everything would be shared between them.

Hattie had a hearty breakfast waiting on the table, prepared purposely for the work that was sure to be ahead of them. Kaitlan hurriedly washed her face in the washbasin, and after giving her hair a few swipes with a brush, tied it back with a piece of heavy twine she took from a peg on the wall.

No time was wasted on talk as they ate breakfast, and for the first time in her life Hattie only stacked the dishes in a pan of hot water and left them to soak. Kaitlan did not make up her bed. No time was even taken to feed Ringer. When they walked outside, where it had lightened considerably, Hattie snapped at the hound, "If you're hungry, go catch yourself a rabbit."

As Kaitlan walked down the muddy, rutted wagon road leading to the tobacco patch, she dreaded what she would find there.

Kaitlan let out a low cry when she saw the destruction laid out in front of her. Hattie put an arm around her waist and together they looked at the field where at least half of the tender plants lay wilting on top of the soaked ground.

"What are we going to do, Peter?" Kaitlan wailed. "All our hard work for nothing."

Peter stared back at her helplessly. What could they do but lose half their crop? They

78

would have very little money to see them through the winter.

Hattie took charge as usual. Even if what she was going to suggest would be of little use, it would be something to keep Kaitlan busy, to soften some of the grief that had brought unshed tears to her eyes.

"We will walk along the rows, looking for plants that might be salvable, and clear out those that are dead. We can plant sugarcane in their place. We might be able to sell the sorghum we could make from the stalks."

Halfheartedly Kaitlan and Peter each picked up a wooden pail that had been left in the field and followed behind Hattie, who was already halfway down one row, every once in a while bending over and picking up a wilted plant.

The more dead seedlings Kaitlan picked up, the more hopeless tears swam in her eyes. Finally it became too much for her to bear and she dropped to her knees. Burying her face in her hands she let the tears fall freely.

And that was how Matt found her.

It cut him to the heart to see her head bent in defeat. He strode across the field to her and, grasping her elbows, brought her to her feet. He looked down at her tear- and mud-streaked face and said gently, "Don't cry, Kaitlan," as he pulled her into his arms.

Kaitlan pressed herself close to him, nudging her face into the hollow of his throat and muscled shoulder, and let her tears fall faster, soaking his shirt.

God, but she feels so good, Matt thought, unconsciously drawing her closer and dropping his black head on her golden one.

I feel so safe in his hard arms, Kaitlan thought, snuggling a little closer to the broad chest. He smells so clean and fresh, like the outdoors. She suddenly realized that she was responding to Matt's warm embrace and lifted her head to gaze in bewilderment at his clear-cut jawline, hard cheekbones, and firm lips.

Matt gazed back at her, his bland expression showing none of the feelings that roiled inside him. "Are you feeling better now?" He smiled at her.

"No, not really," she answered miserably. "I've still lost half my plants."

Matt took a clean handkerchief from his pocket and gently wiped away the tears that had run down her mud-smeared cheeks. "I need to thin some of my rows. I'm pretty sure I can dig up enough plants to replace the ones you've lost."

"Oh, Matt, do you think so?" Kaitlan gazed up at him, hope in her eyes, forgetting that she was still held loosely in his arms.

"I'll go right now and get them," he answered, then noted that the Smiths were watching them with curious eyes. He dropped his arms from around Kaitlan, and in a clipped voice he began issuing orders. "Peter, while I'm gone, you walk along the rows, and everywhere there's a plant missing, prepare a hole for the new ones. And Hattie, you do the same thing.

"Kaitlan" — his voice became softer — "you go over and sit under that tree and calm your nerves. You look ready to faint." He was astride his stallion then and racing away.

Hattie gazed after him. "That is a take-charge man," she said, approval in her voice. "It's too bad his stepbrother isn't more like him."

"Nate is a very hard worker," Kaitlan flared, coming to his defense. "He's probably at the farm checking their fields for damage."

"Why is it, then, that Matt came to see how much the rain had damaged our crop? Nate is the one who is supposed to be courting you."

"I'm sure there is a good reason," Kaitlan answered lamely. She, too, had wondered why Nate hadn't come to see how her plants had fared. She said no more, but struck off toward the tree, her chin up and her back stiff.

Hattie and Peter gazed after her, shaking their heads. "When is that girl going to take the blinders off her eyes and see that Nate Streeter is nothing but a lazy no-account?" Hattie said impatiently.

"I sure hope she does, and soon. If she should marry that man, there'll be a lot of changes taking place around here. For one thing, he wouldn't allow us to be partners with Kaitlan anymore. We'd just be hired hands, and with little payment for our work, too, if I've got him judged right."

"Let's get to work," Hattie said at the end of a long sigh. "I can't bring myself to think about such a thing happening."

Matt was back within half an hour, driving a wagon full of fresh plants. Hattie and Peter had just finished preparing the ground for them, and when Kaitlan left the shade tree, all four started right in getting the plants into the soil.

The sun was just beginning to heat up, and there was one last row to do when Nate came galloping up. Matt swore under his breath when his stepbrother slid off the horse and headed toward him and Kaitlan, who had been working side by side. When Nate reached them he took Kaitlan's hands and said in soft apology, "I'm sorry to be getting here so late, but my horse threw a shoe."

"Where and when did that happen?" Matt asked coolly before Kaitlan could accept the apology.

"Why, er, ah, when I was coming home from the Village," Nate said uneasily.

"And what time was that?"

"Hell, I don't know," Nate answered evasively. "Sometime this morning. I'd been playing cards all night with some men at the tavern. I guess it was around seven when I was putting new shoes on the stallion."

"That's strange." Matt gave a snort of derisive laughter. "When I went home around seven-thirty to pick up some plants for Kaitlan, neither you nor your horse was anywhere around. How do you account for that?"

Nate gave Matt a malevolent look and muttered, "Maybe I was mistaken about the time. It must have been around eight."

As Matt gave him a disgusted look Nate put an arm around Kaitlan's shoulders and said with a wide smile, "What difference does it make when I was in the barn? I'm here now, right, Kaitlan?"

She smiled back, happiness flushing her face. "You're just in time to help me finish this last row."

Nate looked down at his shiny boots, then, seeing Matt watching him in scornful amusement, hesitated but a second before saying jovially as he stepped into the muddy field, "Let's get it done and then we'll take a walk along the river and cool off."

Hattie, who had been watching them, frowned and said, "You can't go walking today, Kaitlan. You've got to check the cow pasture for broken limbs off the wild cherry trees. If the cows find them and eat the wilted leaves, their bellies will swell and they'll burst inside."

Nate gave the black woman a steely look, as if to say, "Who are you to give a white woman orders?" But when Kaitlan readily said, "That's right, I forgot," Nate thought it best to keep his mouth shut for the time being. He could take care of Hattie after he and Kaitlan were married. There were going to be a lot of changes then.

He said now, "I'll go with you, Kaitlan," and they began to put the plants into the soil.

A scowl twisted Hattie's features. She hadn't counted on that. When she turned around to voice her displeasure to Matt, all she saw was his broad back as he rode away. She sent her own malevolent look at Nate and stamped off toward the cabin, Peter plodding along behind her.

When they were finished planting, Kaitlan and Nate climbed over the split-rail fence that penned in the cow pasture, and walked toward a wild cherry tree in a far corner that had lost a limb to the storm. "You're awfully quiet," Nate said after they had walked in silence for a while. "I hope you didn't put any importance on what Matt tried to imply back there. Ever since I can remember, he has always tried to put me in a bad light. You'll never hear him praise me for anything. From the way he talks, you'd never know I work like a dog on a farm that I have no share of. His father, old man Ingram, was the same way, never satisfied with anything I did, always wanting more and more work out of me."

Matt's words had planted seeds of doubt about his stepbrother's character in Kaitlan's mind. But as Nate told his pitiful tale of all the wrongs done to him, her doubts disappeared. She pictured the thirteen-year-old brought to a place completely new to him, made to work at chores totally alien to him. How difficult it must have been for him, she thought, taking his hand and holding it as they walked along.

Kaitlan didn't see the sly smile that flickered across Nate's handsome face as he squeezed her hands. Her heart gave a leap when he said, "I want to marry you, Kaitlan. I want us to work your farm together, raise a bunch of kids."

He stopped walking and pulled her into his arms. "We'd be awfully happy, Kaitlan. What do you think?"

What did she think? Kaitlan asked herself as Nate held her loosely in his arms. Had she known the handsome man long enough to make such a commitment? What did she really know about him? She knew that he was an exciting part of this new life she was discovering. Her stepfather had always told her she was useless. But Nate made her feel so special when he was around.

When he was around. That bothered her. She saw Matt much more often than she did Nate.

"Let me think about it for a while." She lifted her eyes to him. "We've only known each other for a short time."

"Take all the time you need," Nate said, hiding his disgruntled feelings. "Just so you say yes after you've thought on it for a while."

Kaitlan laughed, then said, "Let's go look for broken cherry limbs."

All in all, Kaitlan and Nate found four broken limbs, which they tossed over the fence out of the cow's reach. They were walking back toward the cabin, their arms around each other's waist, and Nate making remarks that made Kaitlan's laughter peal out, when a girl stepped from behind a tree and stood in their path.

Startled by her sudden appearance, Kaitlan could only stare, thinking how wild-looking the girl appeared. Then slowly she saw the beauty that lay beneath the dirt and snarled hair. Her grimy feet were bare of shoes, and the ragged dress she wore came only to her knees. She wore nothing else beneath it, for Kaitlan could see bare flesh through the many tears in the homespun.

A grimace of pain creased Kaitlan's forehead as Nate's fingers bit into her side. She looked up at him and saw he was staring at the girl. The girl gave a strange laugh then and walked back into the woods, softly singing the sad song, "Barbara Allen."

"Who was that?" Kaitlan asked as the girl disappeared into the trees, until only her song could be heard. When Nate didn't answer at once, she glanced up at him and wondered at the beads of sweat that had popped up on his forehead and upper lip. When she nudged his side with her elbow he seemed finally to realize that he wasn't alone and looked at Kaitlan blankly. She repeated, "Who was that?"

"She's the granddaughter of an old couple who lives further back in the Gap. She's kind of fey. Whenever she can escape the old couple, she likes to wander around through the woods."

"Is her name Claire?"

"Why, yes, I believe that it is. Where did you hear her name?"

"Lish Jones mentioned it when he was telling me the names of the folks who lived in the Gap."

"Lish." Nate's tone was scornful. "You don't want to take anything he says very seriously. He sometimes makes up stories."

"He doesn't strike me as that kind of person," Kaitlan said.

"You'll see after you get to know him," Nate said stiffly. Then before Kaitlan could say anything else he said, "I'd better leave you now. I'm sure Matt has a dozen things lined up for me to do."

As he hurried toward his horse, Kaitlan stared after him, wide-eyed. He hadn't even kissed her good-bye. And he'd just asked her to marry him! She continued on toward the cabin, mulling that over in her mind. Had she stood still and kept her eyes on Nate, she would have seen that he didn't ride off in the direction of the Ingram farm, but rather turned his mount's head toward the woods where Claire had disappeared.

Hattie had a chunk of ham and a pot of

mixed greens she had picked on her way home from the tobacco field simmering on the fire when Kaitlan returned from the cow pasture. She plopped down in a chair and said, "Hattie, I don't know what to do. Nate has asked me to marry him."

When Hattie, her sleeves rolled up to her elbows, made no response, only continued kneading a large ball of bread dough, Kaitlan looked up at her.

"What do you think I should tell him?" she asked.

Hattie gave the dough a smart slap and, turning around, fastened angry eyes on Kaitlan. "Your mama would turn over in her grave if I let you marry that no-good excuse for a man."

Kaitlan blinked at the unexpected response. "Why do you say that?" she asked. "What's wrong with Nate? He's been so sweet to me."

"He's *talked* sweet to you, you mean. Matt's the one who's *been* sweet. And again you didn't bother to thank him for all he did for us today. Instead you went off with that lazy Nate, who as far as I can see has done nothing for you yet but tell you a bunch of sweet lies. I don't want no more talk about you two getting hitched until he changes his ways."

The black woman's snapping eyes warned Kaitlan not to try to pursue the topic. Anyhow, what could she say in Nate's defense? He had shown up late again and his excuse was lame in more ways than one. Matt had more or less called him a liar and Nate hadn't put up much of a fight about it, had only glared at Matt with a sullen look on his handsome face.

Kaitlan toyed with the hem of the tablecloth. She could see there was no point discussing her confused feelings for Nate with Hattie. Besides, she did feel very remorseful for having forgotten to thank Matt, for she did appreciate deeply all that he had done for them. She didn't know what they would have done if he hadn't come along, checking on their field.

"You're right, Hattie," she said quietly. "I'm ashamed I forgot to thank Matt. Do you have any suggestions of what I can do to make it up to him?"

Hattie wanted to say that she could let Matt court her instead of the woman-hungry Nate, but knew it would be a waste of words. So she said instead, "There's some winter apples in the cellar. Why don't you make him a pie and take it to him?"

"That's a good idea." Kaitlan jumped to her feet and grabbed up a basin to put the apples in. When she returned from the cellar she bustled about, peeling the fruit and rolling out pie dough.

"Bake two," Hattie said. "I feel like a slice of pie myself."

Within forty-five minutes the pies were in the brick oven built inside the fireplace, sending out a mouthwatering aroma.

As Matt rode homeward he cursed himself for a fool. When Nate had put his arm around Kaitlan's shoulder and she leaned into him, it had hurt him more than when the woman he'd planned to marry ran off with another man.

He realized now that it hadn't been love he'd felt for that girl years ago. It had been the loneliness inside him that made him seek a wife. He wanted to have children running and laughing about the farm; he wanted a helpmate to talk with at the end of a hard day's work. He wanted to share with her his hopes and dreams, his despair when a tobacco crop had been lost to a storm or a late frost.

How lucky he had been not to have married that flighty female, who now lived on the other side of the Gap and, according to gossip, put the horns on her husband every chance she got. She was not the kind of woman to be a helpful, loving companion.

But Kaitlan Barrett would be. She had all the qualities any man could wish for in a wife. Discounting her outward beauty, which dazzled the eye, she had an inner beauty as well. It showed in her lovely blue eyes, the sweet curve of her lips, the tender touch of her hands.

The pity of it was that all that would be wasted on his self-serving stepbrother. Selfish Nate would never appreciate her, never see the goodness in her. He would uncaringly take her love and trample it as though it were a troublesome briarpatch in his way. It would not bother him that she cried when he was unfaithful to her. And he would be. He lusted after women, had done so since he was fourteen and a traveling preacher's young wife had followed him into the woods one Sunday after services and taught him the delights of a woman's body. After that he had been like a rutting bull, daily seeking a woman to vent his lust on.

Matt had seen how Nate used women, with no thought for his partner's physical or emotional satisfaction. Once, he'd come upon his stepbrother coupling with a woman out in the open in broad daylight. Nate's battering thrusts had brought protests from the woman, but he hadn't paused for a moment, intent only on his own pleasure.

His release had come swiftly, with the woman complaining that he had been too fast, that she hadn't found her relief.

Matt shook his head now, remembering how he had ridden away in disgust when almost immediately Nate was once again pounding away at his companion. He knew Nate would lie with her the rest of the day, and that she would probably get no pleasure from him. He was like a jackrabbit. Hop on, hop off. There would be no kisses, no gentle stroking from him.

Matt closed his eyes as though in pain. He had no doubt that Nate would marry Kaitlan. He desperately wanted her farm, and she was so besotted with him, her love would blind her

91

to all his glaring faults. When she realized what he was, it would be too late. All the light would go out of her beautiful eyes; her wonderful spirit would be broken, her slender body worn out from the demands Nate would make of it. She would grow old much before her time.

The farm buildings came in view and Matt forced himself to shake off his painful, troublesome thoughts. There was nothing he could do to save Kaitlan from a life of misery, so he must stop dwelling on it . . . if he could.

Every fiber in Nate's being was on fire as he searched the woods for the girl, Claire. With her he could wallow in all his carnal lasciviousness. She would accept each thrust of his body no matter how hard it might be. Caught up in his own gratification, he had never even noticed if the girl found his pounding painful. All he knew or cared about was that she allowed it.

He had come upon Claire in the woods six months ago. He'd heard stories about the Tylers' simpleminded granddaughter who roamed wild, so one day he had gone looking for her and had found the girl of the woods.

His manhood had stirred and begun to grow as he looked down at her from the back of his horse. Although her face was dirty, her hair uncombed, and her feet bare, the dress of rough homespun she wore did not hide the jutting of her firm breasts or her rounded hips. The vulnerability in her eyes, the longing for something unnamed, heightened his desire for her.

Swinging from the saddle he approached, saying softly, "You know what I want, pretty lady."

She had giggled nervously, then lain down on the forest floor and pulled her dress up around her waist.

He hadn't even removed his trousers the first time they came together. He had knelt between her legs, unbuttoned his fly, and plunged inside her.

As the afternoon waned she had done to him everything he asked of her.

He had met her every day since, and had been on his way to meet her today before he got sidetracked with Kaitlan. And that was why Claire had come looking for him. He might have to slap her around a little today, to make sure she never pursued him again.

# Chapter Eight

Kaitlan placed the cooled pie in a basket and arranged a clean white dish towel over it. Hanging the basket over her arm, she said to Hattie, "I'll be off now."

"Don't stay too long. Make sure you get back before dark, and in time for supper."

Peter had saddled her grandfather's stallion, a handsome animal, solid white and appropriately named Snowy. The big horse had accepted her right off, seeming to appreciate her light touch on the reins. Peter boosted her into the saddle, basket and all. She picked up the reins, nudged Snowy with her heel, and he started off.

Kaitlan hummed a little tune as she rode down the wide, rain-gutted path. She would get to see Nate again. Probably he would ride with her when she returned home. She came to a stream of water, so clear she could see its gravel bed.

After about fifteen minutes of following the path that twisted and turned around large boulders and tall pines, she saw blue hickory-wood smoke rising from a mud-daubed chimney. As Snowy approached a good-sized cabin of peeled logs it struck her that the place had a woman's touch about it. Bright curtains hung on the two windows facing her, and a neat white picket fence surrounded the yard where pink roses and white daisies bloomed in flower beds. Even the path leading from the gate to the porch was neatly edged with rocks.

I must fix up my yard, she thought as she swung to the ground, being careful not to jostle the basket. After looping the reins over a long hitching post outside the fence, she unlatched the gate and started up the path. She had just stepped up on the porch when a round little woman, wearing an apron as white as her hair, came and stood in the open doorway, a wide welcoming smile on her rosy-cheeked face.

Dark brown eyes twinkled at Kaitlan as the woman said, "You're as pretty as Matt said you were."

"You know who I am?" Kaitlan smiled back.

"You have to be old Rufe's granddaughter. I know all the young women in the Gap and none of them are as pretty as you are." Kaitlan blushed shyly at the compliment. How she looked had never been spoken about until she moved here. Of course, no one had seen much of her back in Philadelphia. Yancy had seen to that. She hadn't put much emphasis on her mother's claim that she was beautiful. Didn't all mothers think that of their daughters?

"Well, come on in, child." The plump little woman stepped aside so that she could enter.

What a cozy place, Kaitlan thought, her fast

glance taking in the wide room that took up the entire front of the cabin. One end was the kitchen area with its own small cooking fireplace with a brick oven built inside it. A table and four chairs sat in the center of the room and a tall china cabinet sat against the end wall across from the table.

The biggest portion of the room was devoted to the living area, which had its own huge stone fireplace and a wide raised hearth. The floor was carpeted with handwoven rugs. The furniture was much like her own, simple, sturdy pieces made of pine. The settee had multicolored covers on the back and seat cushions, and the same pattern had been carried out on cushions on the three rocking chairs. A square table sat between two of them, with a candle lamp and a bowl of yellow jonquils on it. Red curtains at the wide window were the same color as those in the kitchen area.

"Everybody calls me Aunt Polly," the round little woman said, calling Kaitlan's attention back to her. "I keep house for Matt and look after him."

"I'm Kaitlan," she replied, offering her hand.

"I know your name, honey." Polly's eyes twinkled at her. "Nate speaks of you often. Sit down and we'll have a cup of sassafras tea."

"Where are Matt and Nate?" Kaitlan asked as she took a seat and placed the basket on the table.

"Matt's out in the barn doing something, and

as for Nate, I haven't seen him since yesterday afternoon."

Kaitlan lowered her lashes to hide her surprise. Nate had been lying about his whereabouts when he showed up at the farm, and Matt knew it. But how could he know that? Was Nate in the habit of lying?

"Matt will be along in a moment. He'll see your horse and come see if anything is wrong at your place," Aunt Polly said, filling two cups with tea.

Kaitlan took a spoon from a jar of cutlery sitting in the middle of the table. As she spooned sugar into her cup Aunt Polly sat down and, after fixing her tea to her taste, asked, "Have you met any of your neighbors yet?"

"Just three, besides Matt and Nate. Lish Jones, Maybelle Scott, and Granny Higgins. I've been so busy with getting settled in and getting my tobacco started, I haven't had time to do any visiting."

"We're having a church social the first Sunday in July. It would be a good time for you to meet most of them. You can ride with me and Matt."

"Thank you, Aunt Polly, but I guess you have heard I have a Negro couple living with me. It would hurt their feelings if I didn't bring them with me."

Aunt Polly was silent for a few seconds, idly stirring a spoon around and around in her cup. She looked at Kaitlan and said, "They might as well come along too. Let everyone know that they are a part of you."

Kaitlan nodded. "I think that's a good idea. The Smiths have been with me all my life."

"Tennesseans are mostly good people. They believe in the Bible, the gun, and themselves. They fear God, but nothing else. They keep the Sabbath and —"

"And anything else they can get their hands on." Matt chuckled from the doorway.

Polly and Kaitlan laughed at his remark, though Polly halfheartedly protested that it wasn't true.

"What brings you here, Kaitlan?" Matt asked as he poured himself a cup of tea and sat down across from her.

She lifted the cover off the basket and lifted out the pie. "I baked this for you in appreciation of all the help you have given me since I came to the Gap. It's apple. I hope you like it."

"Apple is his favorite pie," Aunt Polly said when it seemed Matt wasn't going to say anything. When Kaitlan hadn't thanked him, had gone off with Nate, he had decided that he had been a fool for helping her. But now he was reversing his opinion.

"It sure is," he finally said. "Cut me a slice and I'll see if it meets my standards." He grinned at Kaitlan.

Kaitlan watched him put a bite into his mouth, chew, then swallow. She giggled when he rolled his eyes and rubbed his stomach as though he had just tasted some kind of heavenly nectar.

When Aunt Polly laughed also at his tomfoolery, he said seriously, "It's really good, Kaitlan; I mean it. Thank you very much."

"What's good?" Nate stepped from the porch into the kitchen.

"Well, have you finally decided to come home?" Aunt Polly frowned at his appearance, taking in his red-rimmed eyes and beard-stubbled chin and jaw. She didn't see, as Matt did, the leaves and pine needles on the seat and back of his trousers.

"I was home," Nate answered sullenly. "You just didn't see me."

"I know your bed hasn't been slept in."

"I'm a man grown, Aunt Polly. I don't have to account to you when I come and go, or how long I'll be away." He pulled a chair around and sat down next to Kaitlan. When he leaned toward her, she drew away, wrinkling her nose. There was an odor about him that she had never smelled before.

Matt got a whiff of Nate and recognized the odor. He stood up and jerked his head toward the porch as he said, "I'd like a word with you about the tobacco."

Nate gave him a sullen stare, refusal in his look. But when a threat appeared in Matt's narrowed eyes he stood up and stalked out of the kitchen.

When they were out of hearing of the women

Matt bit out furiously, "You damn rutting bull, don't you know what you smell like? You reek of whore. It's an insult to Kaitlan and Aunt Polly. Now go stand in the doorway and say that you have to tend to your horse. When Kaitlan has left, get your ass down to the river and jump in and don't come out until all the stink has been washed off your body and clothes."

Nate glared his hatred at Matt a moment, but then his eyes settled on the bigger man's clenched fists, and he spun around. Jumping onto the porch he said from the doorway, "Aunt Polly and Kaitlan, if you'll excuse me, I have to go take care of my horse and do a few odd jobs in the barn that I have been putting off."

He gave Kaitlan a bright smile and said, "I'll see you later tonight."

Kaitlan nodded, but her returning smile wasn't quite as warm as it usually was. Nate had some explaining to do when she saw him next.

"How long have you lived here?" she asked Matt when he reentered the cabin.

"All my life," Matt said. "There's nowhere I'd rather be. The Gap is a secret, brooding place, yet beautiful with its tangled woods. We have panthers, black bears, and white-tailed deer. And rivers — the Nalichucky, Ocaee, Tellico, Hiwassee, and Sequatchie. In those streams are trout, bass, catfish, croppie, and pike."

"My goodness, everything a man could want is in Tennessee," Kaitlan exclaimed when Matt finished and leaned back in his chair.

"It surely is," he agreed with a proud smile.

Kaitlan looked across at him, thinking that he was a fixture of the Cumberlands. He was as much a part of the Gap as the tall trees, the crags and ravines. A true mountain man.

When he returned her gaze too intently, she became flustered and began talking again. Time passed swiftly as they discussed a number of topics, until Kaitlan happened to glance out the window. She gave a start. While they had talked dusk had arrived.

"My goodness." She jumped to her feet. "I should have been home an hour ago. Hattie will be beside herself with worry. I'm surprised she hasn't sent Peter looking for me for fear that I've been set upon by a panther." She gave Matt an alarmed look. "Are they out at this time of day?"

"Don't worry about it; I'll ride home with you." Matt stood up.

"Ah, Matt" — she smiled — "it seems that you're always around when I need you."

Yeah, that's me, good old Matt, he thought in self-derision as he walked to the barn to saddle his stallion.

By the time Aunt Polly picked through her many bags of flower seeds and gave Kaitlan a part of them, Matt was outside waiting for her. He helped her onto Snowy's back, then

101

mounted Satan. As they rode off at a fast clip Aunt Polly called from the porch, "Don't forget the church social, Kaitlan."

They hadn't ridden far when, to Matt's disappointment, they met Peter on his way to the Ingram farm. "Hattie is in a lather, worrying about you, Kaitlan," he started right in. "She's been holding supper and my stomach is ready to cave in, it's so empty."

"I'm sorry Hattie is worried, Peter," Matt said. "I'm afraid it's my fault. I took too long sampling Kaitlan's pie."

"Is that you, Matt?" Peter peered around Snowy's big bulk, his tone much lighter. "I thought you was that . . . your stepbrother."

"No, he's doing some chores that had piled up on him." Matt didn't add that Nate was snoring away on a pile of hay in the barn, and that he had no intention of waking him in time for him to keep his promise to Kaitlan that he would see her tonight. He had no doubt that Nate would sleep straight through until tomorrow morning.

"Well, Kaitlan, we'd better get on home before Hattie comes looking for both of us." Peter reined his horse around.

"Bye, Matt. Thanks for everything," Kaitlan said gaily, nudging Snowy to follow Peter.

Matt gazed after her until she was lost in the dimness of the evening. Then, with his broad shoulders sagging a bit, he headed back homeward.

# Chapter Nine

When Kaitlan walked into the kitchen she heard everything she had expected to hear from Hattie. "You foolish girl," Hattie started right in. "What were you thinking, staying out until dark? What if a panther had attacked you? And with me and poor Peter waiting supper for you?"

Poor Peter? Kaitlan thought with a hidden wry grin. Usually it was no-account Peter, or lazy Peter, or good-for-nothing Peter.

Every time she tried to defend herself she was cut off with more words of condemnation. Finally she stopped trying. She knew that Hattie's carrying-on came from the fear that something had happened to her, and that her friend would wind down when she got it all out of her system.

She and Peter sat down at the table and folded their hands in their laps as Hattie banged pots and pans in time with her ranting.

Finally supper was on the table and it grew quiet in the kitchen. Hattie took her chair and began passing the ham and greens, mashed potatoes, and corn bread. She looked at Kaitlan and said calmly, "Well, does Matt have a nice place?"

Kaitlan heaved a big sigh of relief, echoed by

Peter, and answered, "He has a very nice place. His cabin is big, and according to Aunt Polly, it has three bedrooms."

"Who is Aunt Polly?"

"She's the woman who keeps house for Matt. She's around your age and very nice. I think you'd like her."

Hattie's answer to that was a disbelieving "Ha."

Giving her a stern look Kaitlan scolded, "Now there you go, a chip on your shoulder before you even meet the woman. She has invited us to go with her to a church social in a few weeks."

"Are you sure me and Peter are invited?" Hattie narrowed her eyes at Kaitlan.

"Yes, I'm sure, and Hattie, I hope you won't embarrass me by not being friendly to people. And for once, will you please keep that sharp tongue of yours a little blunted when we get to the social? The people might be a little stand-offish at first. Matt said that the mountain people are skeptical of strangers until they get to know them, but that they won't say anything hurtful to you."

"All right," Hattie agreed ungraciously. "I'll treat them the way they treat me."

"Fair enough." Kaitlan looked at Hattie and said, "These greens are the best I've ever eaten."

"They are good," Peter agreed. "I haven't eaten anything like them since we left the South."

"That's because you can't find most of them in Pennsylvania. In a city, at least," Hattie said.

The meal was finished in quiet harmony.

"What's your rush?" Hattie asked when Kaitlan began to hurriedly clear the table of dirty dishes.

"Nate's coming by later and I want to get freshened up a bit before he arrives."

"Honey, I know you're flattered 'cause he asked to marry you," Hattie said as she poured hot water into a basin and dropped a bar of yellow lye soap into it, "but there's other men around that would make better husbands."

"Who? Nate is so nice and good natured, and very handsome."

"Pooh on handsome!" Hattie snorted. "Good looks don't mean nothing in a husband. Most always the good-looking ones cheat on their wives. Anyhow, he's not handsome in a man way. He's pretty like a woman."

"Oh, Hattie." Kaitlan laughed. "Where did you get such a foolish notion?"

"It's not foolish," Hattie answered stubbornly. Then as she started washing the dishes, handing them to Kaitlan to wipe dry, she asked, "What are your feelings about Matt?"

"Matt?" Kaitlan thought a minute and then said, "Matt is a dear man. Thoughtful and polite and . . ."

"Always around to help you," Hattie finished her sentence. "I can't help wishing he was courting you."

"Matt court me?" Kaitlan laughed. "He doesn't like white women. He likes Indian maidens."

"Who told you that . . . Nate?"

"Yes, he did. He says that Matt goes to the Indian village all the time."

"I don't believe that. And I bet if the right woman came along, you'd see him showing an interest in her."

"It could be," Kaitlan said, her disbelief plain in her voice as she dried the last pot and hung up the dish towel. "I'm going to get cleaned up now."

Hattie watched her leave the room, shaking her head. "Do you think she'll marry that no-account lout?" she asked Peter, who still sat at the table, smoking his pipe.

"It will be the ruination of her if she does. Old Lish told me a thing or two about him."

"What kind of things?" Hattie demanded, sitting down at the table too.

"Things that you're better off not knowing, and that's all I'm gonna say about it."

It seldom happened that Peter stood up to his wife, but when he did Hattie knew it was useless trying to make him back down.

The loud noise of baying hounds in the woodlot in back of the barn awakened Nate. "The bastards must have a coon treed back in there," he muttered. "They'll keep up that yowling until someone shoots the animal from the tree he's climbed."

He started to roll over to go back to sleep when he realized with a start that he was lying in a pile of hay out in the barn with a full moon shining through the small loft window. He fished his round, flat timepiece from his pocket and peered at it in the rays of the moon. He swore under his breath. It was after nine o'clock and Claire had been waiting for him over an hour.

Jumping to his feet he raked his fingers through his hair, brushed the hay off his clothes, and then saddled the horse. His hurrying wasn't for Claire's benefit; he knew that she would wait all night if necessary. His rush was in his own interest. The bulge in his trousers was proof of that. He couldn't move fast enough to get to Claire, to bury his aching hardness inside her.

But I can't stay too long tonight, he reminded himself as he set the horse out at a hard gallop. He'd have to get home in time to take a dip in the river before slipping into bed, where pesky old Aunt Polly could find him tomorrow morning.

As Nate rode through the bright moonlight he didn't give a thought to Kaitlan or his promise to visit her that evening. As the horse flashed past the Barrett cabin, he didn't even see her standing on the porch waiting for him.

Kaitlan had walked out on the porch shortly

after seven o'clock. She had taken a sponge bath, changed her dress again, and brushed her hair until it looked like warm honey. She wondered now, for the third time, what was keeping Nate. She did wish that he would be prompt. He was very lax in that. But she told herself that was part of his makeup. It went along with his charm, his easygoing ways. After all, she mustn't expect him to be perfect.

She couldn't help thinking, though, as a pack of hounds sounded in the distance, that if Matt had said he would be here at a certain time, she could depend on his word.

Matt wasn't the one courting her, however, she reminded herself. Sighing, she wondered once again when Nate was going to arrive.

She peered toward the path that led from the Ingram farm but saw no movement there. She shifted her gaze to the Smiths' little cabin; all was darkness there. It had been since eight o'clock. Hattie would be outraged if she knew the girl she had practically raised was sitting out in the chilly night air at this hour, waiting for a man. She would demand of Kaitlan where her pride had gone that she would wait like this for a man to keep his promise.

The clock inside the cabin struck nine and Kaitlan sighed. She would give Nate another half hour. If he didn't show up by then, she was going to bed.

An owl flew across the yard and a moment later she heard the squeak of a mouse caught in the night creature's claw. Poor little thing, she thought, envisioning the small body dangling in the air as it was brought to a nest of hungry owlets.

The lonesome call of two whippoorwills was a distant sound in the woods, and the flickering glow of lightning bugs was like tiny shimmering starlight. She looked up to the top of the mountain, where a straggely line of pines was a dark silhouette against the lighter shade of the moonlit sky.

All this was alien to Kaitlan, but she loved it and had felt she had come home from the first day she arrived in the Cumberlands.

It was near the half hour and Kaitlan was preparing to go inside, when she heard galloping hoofbeats. It was about time Nate showed up, she thought irritably. She stood up and walked to the edge of the porch, telling herself that he was going to get a dressing-down from her for being so late.

Then before her disbelieving eyes, Nate raced his horse past the path that led to the cabin without a glance in her direction.

Kaitlan pulled her curls to the top of her head and secured them there with pins. She picked up the basket from the table and left the cabin. Hattie had said that she should hunt for hen's nests hidden away in fence corners.

As she walked along she was unmindful of the birdsong, the wildflowers blooming in little patches. Her thoughts were still on Nate, her mind still bewildered by his actions last night. Where had he gone when he tore past the cabin? Why had he forgotten his promise to her?

Those questions had interrupted her sleep, put shadows beneath her eyes and a heaviness inside her. She had told herself a dozen times that he had a good reason for not keeping his word, but she had a hard time convincing herself.

She had even asked herself if maybe he had a drinking problem and had been on his way to the man who made moonshine liquor. She prayed that wasn't so. She wouldn't want a drunkard for a husband. Her stepfather had been one and he had made hers and her mother's lives miserable. But she had never smelled whiskey on Nate's breath, so she discounted that theory. Kaitlan came back now to the thought that had come to her last night as she lay sleepless in bed. Nate didn't think she was exciting to be around. The few kisses she had allowed him were short, light ones.

Then there was the touching he wanted to do. Did the other mountain girls allow him to do that? Should she give him that right because he was courting her? She didn't like the idea of his hands on her body.

Kaitlan's brow wrinkled in thought. Was there something wrong with her? Why did she find the idea of Nate fondling her repulsive?

How could she consider marrying him when she didn't want to have his hands on her body? It was a husband's right, after all.

As she moved along the fence row Kaitlan asked herself why she was in a hurry to get married. There were several reasons, she realized. She badly wanted to have children and a loving husband, to build a family life like that her mother and father had enjoyed. After those awful years with her stepfather, she longed desperately for the comfort of a family of her own.

Of course she loved Nate. Didn't she? She didn't know exactly how a woman felt when she was in love. She had read books in which the heroine always got excited when her intended came around, her heart fluttering when she was kissed.

That's only in books, she scoffed, never having felt any such emotion about Nate. She was always happy to see him, and she liked his company. And it was important to like your mate, wasn't it?

Still, she must lay down some rules of her own. He was to keep his word when he promised to come see her. And he must stop mistreating his stallion, and stop lying about his whereabouts.

Kaitlan had found two nests and had six eggs resting on the towel she had placed in the bottom of the basket when she heard a horse galloping toward her. She looked up, then took a couple of steps backward as Nate pulled his nervous stallion to a rearing halt. She frowned her displeasure at his action. Didn't he know how cruelly the bit cut into the animal's tender mouth when he did that? There were flecks of blood oozing from the poor creature's mouth. Well, there was no time like the present to confront Nate.

"Nate," she said sharply, "I wish you wouldn't saw on the reins like that. You're hurting him."

"Naw, that don't hurt him. He's tough." Nate slid off the saddle, letting the reins trail.

"Matt doesn't like you abusing your horse like that, you know."

"Who cares what he likes," Nate said negligently, putting his arms around her waist and jerking her up hard against his body. "Give me a kiss, Kaitlan, and not one of your stingy little ones."

Kaitlan put her hands against his chest and pushed, putting a little space between them. "First, you tell me where you were last night and why didn't you come by like you said you would."

"I'm sorry about that, Sugar Cake, but I got involved with some of the neighbors in a coon-running and it lasted longer than I had thought it would. By the time the blasted animal was treed, it was near midnight."

"I heard the hounds running," Kaitlan said, and dropped her hands from between them.

"I'm forgiven then?" Nate smiled down at

her, drawing her close again without waiting for a response.

Suddenly his lips came down on hers, hard, like the first time he'd kissed her. She jerked her head away, nervously explaining that she had to get back to the cabin, that Hattie was waiting for the eggs. A sulky look in his eyes, Nate pushed her away, saying harshly, "That's a poor excuse. I think you're one of those cold females who don't cotton to lovemaking. The kind who drives a man to other women who will welcome him with open arms."

"I am not cold," Kaitlan flared back, fingering her torn lips. "I told you before, you're too rough. You made my teeth bite into my lip."

"That's because you keep them closed so tightly. If you parted them a little you wouldn't get hurt. No one else has ever complained about my kisses."

"Well, I've never kissed any other man before and I don't know all of this," Kaitlan defended herself. "Right now I've got to get home before Hattie comes looking for me."

Nate gave her a mocking smile. "Yes, hurry up with the eggs. They're much more important than me." With that retort he strode swiftly to the stallion and vaulted into the saddle.

Without a word of farewell he jerked the stallion's head around and, with a slash of Nate's riding crop on the animal's rump, the stallion

113

lunged away, his flashing hooves kicking up clods of grass.

Kaitlan stared after him, wondering if she was fooling herself to think that he would ever change, or that his faults were small ones.

But a small, hurt Kaitlan hiding deep inside still wanted him to come back, still wanted Nate to make her feel special and loved, as she never had before.

Nate's face wore a smug look as he left Kaitlan. He had her worried that she might have lost him. She'd soon be coming around to his way of thinking. And she would be his wife before winter set in; he was confident of that. He mustn't rush her too much, though, he reminded himself. If he couldn't get what he wanted from her, there was always Claire. And as for that, there would be Claire after he was married to the cold little fish.

It was the first Sunday in July. The day of the church social. Three weeks had passed since Nate had ridden away from Kaitlan, displeased with her, and the only time he'd come calling since, Hattie had stayed right by them, making it impossible for them to talk privately. Would he be at the get-together today? she wondered, trying to choose which of her two better dresses to wear.

"I must stop thinking about it," she muttered, and pulled a green muslin dress over her head. This was the coolest dress she owned. Its color complemented the gold in her hair and the deep tan she had acquired from working every day in the tobacco fields.

The plants now reached her waist, and fat green caterpillars had to be picked off the leaves every morning. If they weren't, they could soon destroy every plant. So each day, with a can of water and lye soap in hand, she and Peter went to the field hunting for the pests, plucking them off the tender tobacco plants and into the can.

Of all the jobs that had to be done on the farm, that was the one she hated most.

Kaitlan walked into the kitchen where Hattie was busy filling two baskets with all the food she had prepared the day before. "You look awfully nice, Hattie," Kaitlan said. "That blue check has always been my favorite."

"It's the only one I have that's not practically worn out," Hattie said sharply.

"I know," Kaitlan said sadly. "I can't remember when either of us had a new dress. Not since Yancy came into our lives, that I know. When we sell our tobacco, the first thing we're going to do is buy all three of us some new clothes. Peter's trousers and shirts are nothing but patches."

"According to old Lish, we're not the only poor ones here in the Gap. There's some worse off than we are, with a passel of young'uns to boot."

"I can't understand why they keep having so many children, knowing how hard it is to keep food on the table."

"There's no *they* to it," Hattie said spiritedly. "It's the husband who don't care where his seed goes, then turns a blind eye to his young'uns' hunger, raggedy clothes, and bare feet."

As Hattie placed a towel over the second basket and set it aside, Kaitlan asked, "What all did you make for the social?"

"I made plenty. You won't be embarrassed that we didn't bring enough food. There's two fried chickens, two pans of biscuits, three pounds of sliced baked ham, radishes and green onions from the garden, a white cake, three apple pies, and a bag of cookies."

"My goodness, Hattie, even if none of the other women brought anything, I believe you've made enough for everybody who attends the social."

"I want to be sure those hungry young'uns get their bellies filled today. And if I see any man pushing them aside to get to what I've prepared, he'll get a clout on the head from me."

Kaitlan knew that the black woman would do just as she'd threatened, too. Hattie loved children. It was her biggest disappointment in life that she had none of her own.

A minute later Kaitlan heard the sound of a wagon's iron tires scraping on loose rock. She

116

hurried to the door and, smiling, said over her shoulder, "Matt and Aunt Polly are coming."

"Well, don't just stand there; grab one of the baskets," Hattie said sharply, nervous about meeting the white woman Kaitlan thought so highly of.

"Now, Hattie, you've got that cross look on your face already," Kaitlan scolded as she picked up one of the baskets. "Please try to look pleasant."

"Never mind how I look, missy. You just make sure you're nice to Matt."

"I'm always nice to Matt." Kaitlan looked surprised at the order.

"Yes, just like you're nice to that old hound dog of ours."

"I don't know where you come up with some of your ideas," Kaitlan muttered as she walked to the door.

As they stepped outside on the porch, Peter came walking up from the barn. He looks very nice in his Sunday trousers and shirt, Kaitlan thought.

As she and the Smiths stood waiting on the porch, Matt pulled the team of horses near to the steps. He hopped down off the high wagon seat, where Polly sat smiling down at them, and walked toward them.

There's a sort of ease and grace about Matt, Kaitlan thought, watching him approach. And how nice he looks in his black trousers and white shirt. The sleeves were rolled up to the elbows of his deeply tanned arms and the neck was open at his equally dark throat. He had brushed and tamed his longish hair until the waves lay smooth against his head. There was an aura of danger about him that warned men to step lightly around him, and made women shy away from him.

"Good morning, folks. Don't you all look chipper."

"You look pretty chipper yourself, Matt Ingram," Kaitlan called, returning his wide smile as she walked down the steps with Peter and Hattie following her. "And you look pretty spiffy too, Aunt Polly," she added as Matt helped her into the wagon bed where he had piled some hay and covered it with a blanket.

"Thank you, honey." Polly twisted her portly body around to look down at Kaitlan. "And you're looking your usual beautiful self."

When Matt had helped Hattie into the wagon and Peter had hoisted himself up behind her, Kaitlan said, "I want you to meet my dear friends, Aunt Polly. Peter and Hattie Smith."

"Kaitlan has spoken so much about you two, I feel I already know you." Polly reached down a hand in greeting.

Peter returned her genial smile and shook the hand held out to him. After a slight hesitation Hattie relaxed and followed her husband's example.

When everyone was settled in, Matt climbed up beside Polly, and, snapping the long reins over the horses' broad rumps, he set the wagon in motion.

As Peter and Matt talked tobacco and weather, worrying about the dry spell they were having, Kaitlan called out questions to Matt about the countryside they were passing. She was enthralled by the splendor of the Cumberlands. Looking downward she could see a broad, black expanse of dark pines with emerald-leaved hardwoods scattered through its darkness. What a glorious sight, she thought. She would never get tired of looking at such beauty.

Kaitlan gave a start when Hattie said nervously, "We're here." She looked around and saw that they had reached the foothills and that Matt was bringing the team to a halt where half a dozen other wagons were parked. Several yards away to their right was a crude building that she assumed was the church. The only difference between this structure and the cabins the people of the Gap lived in was the large wooden cross nailed to the peak of the roof and the bell attached over its door.

She became aware then of the men and women standing in front of the church openly staring at them. When Matt had helped Polly off the high seat, and Peter had assisted her and Hattie to the ground, Hattie muttered, "They don't know much about manners, staring at us like that. They make me nervous."

"Me too, but I don't think they mean to be

rude. They're just curious about us. Let's try not to show how we feel about it."

As they approached the knot of people, Aunt Polly began introducing Kaitlan and the Smiths. They met Elam and Grace Cook, who were somewhere in their forties, Kaitlan imagined. Then there were Harry and Alice Spencer, whose ten children played with the five Cook children behind the church. Next came Grandpa and Grandma Tyler. Kaitlan recognized the name and looked around for their granddaughter, Claire. She wasn't there.

But Granny Higgins was, and so was Lish Jones. He gave her a wide grin when she spoke to him. It wasn't the same with Maybelle Scott, though. Her long face wore a scowl, and when Kaitlan smiled and spoke to her, she barely acknowledged Kaitlan and completely ignored the Smiths.

Kaitlan's right hand became numb from all the handshakes as she met the rest of her neighbors. As they filed into church with the others, she hoped that she could couple names and faces; there had been so many. She liked the people, their open faces, their shy but friendly smiles. She felt they were good, honest men and women.

As she and the Smiths sat down on hard benches, she looked at Hattie from the corner of her eye. No one had been rude to her and Peter, but only a few of the women had smiled at them.

Nevertheless, Hattie's face didn't reflect any displeasure, and Kaitlan breathed a soft sigh. Evidently she was pleased enough with the way things were going. Kaitlan turned her head and smiled at Matt, who was sitting on the other side of her. It looked like it would be a nice day.

After all the rustling of the people quieted, Reverend Lee Turner, tall and thin, in his late thirties, started right in preaching fire and brimstone. He called on those who drank the devil's brew to stop and repent or they would go straight to hell when they died. And those who lusted after men and women who weren't their mates would follow close behind the other sinners. He then began to read off the Ten Commandments, pounding his fist on the pulpit as if to put emphasis on each one.

By the time he finished, everyone there, except for those men who had fallen asleep, was sure he or she was headed for damnation. It was with relief that everyone sang the hymn that brought the sermon to an end.

Outside again, Kaitlan breathed deeply of the fresh air, clearing her head. Then she helped Hattie put their food on the table.

Before long, everyone was gathered around the two tables made of boards laid across wooden sawhorses. Hattie's contributions to the social were attacked first. Her black eyes snapping, she kept her threat about not letting the men force their way in front of the children. She wasn't nice about it, either, as she told

Elam Cook and Harry Spencer to stand back, that the children came first. "If they leave anything and their mothers have eaten, then you can have what's left."

Both men looked a little angry, but shame-faced also, and other men making their way toward the fried chicken and ham made a swift turnabout and filled their plates with the usual plain fare they got at home. The mothers gave Hattie pleased smiles, and to Kaitlan's relief she returned their smiles.

Later when the young ones had filled their bellies, Hattie motioned the women to come help themselves. Matt, Peter, and Lish were the only men who came to sit and eat with the women. Hattie received so much praise for her chicken and cake, she grew flustered, and to Kaitlan's secret amusement she even offered to share her recipe for the cake.

When there were only crumbs left on the table and the men were sitting in a group smoking their pipes, Matt said to Kaitlan, "I'm stuffed. Let's take a walk to digest our food."

"That sounds good," Kaitlan said, "but shouldn't I be helping Hattie pack everything away?"

Matt grinned. "Take a look at her. Do you think she needs your help?"

There were so many helping hands around Hattie, Kaitlan would have only been in the way. She grinned back at Matt and said, "I'll tell her I'm going for a walk with you though."

"I'll get my long rifle from the wagon while you do that," he said, returning a minute later to lead her into the woods.

"I want to show you one of my favorite places," Matt said as they walked slowly along. "I found it when I was just a youngster out hunting squirrel with my father. I think you'll like it. It's a beautiful spot."

Kaitlan looked at him through her heavy lashes. She was struck with surprise to hear this big, rough-looking man speak of nature's beauty.

As they wound their way along a path that led deeper into the woods, the narrow trail became rocky and uneven. Matt took Kaitlan's hand to help her over rough spots and they continued to hold hands as they walked on.

"There it is," Matt said after about fifteen minutes. He was pointing to the most beautiful waterfall Kaitlan had ever seen. Framed with trees and boulders and tall ferns, it began far up the mountain, falling in lacy rivulets that sparkled like a million diamonds in the afternoon sun. As it hit the ground, the water splashed on rocks and gravel, then disappeared.

"It's so beautiful," Kaitlan said in awe, "and the area around it is so quiet and peaceful, you can hear the birdsong in the trees."

Matt nodded agreement. "Every time I go hunting I come to this neck of the woods just to spend an hour or two here."

"Where does the water go? I see none on the ground."

"It goes into a sinkhole so deep you can throw a rock into it and never hear it hit bottom."

Kaitlan was musing on that surprising fact when suddenly she exclaimed, pointing to the ground, "Are those panther tracks, Matt?"

Matt looked down and said a bit uneasily, "They sure are, and recent too."

Anxiety clouding her eyes, Kaitlan asked, "Do you think it's nearby?"

"The tracks are pointing up the mountain. He's probably in his den higher up. You stay here. I'm going to go up a piece and see if I can spot him."

"Don't go, Matt," Kaitlan cried in breathless alarm. "It's too dangerous."

"No, it's not, Kaitlan," Matt assured her. "I've got to see if it's still around. What if the children should wander up here? Or what if it should spring on a family on their way home in a wagon?"

"You're right, but please be careful."

She watched Matt disappear among some boulders, and then she crouched behind a tree, her tension almost unendurable. She felt she had been there for hours before she heard an angry cry from the panther, followed by the sharp report of Matt's rifle.

When he didn't reappear at once, she ventured from her hiding place to go look for him.

She had gone but a short distance when she met him coming down. "Matt! Are you all right?" she cried as she ran to him and threw her arms around his waist.

At first Matt was so surprised at her action, his big body grew still. Then as he felt the soft, warm flesh pressed against him, he put his arms around her. As he held her loosely, not daring to crush her against his chest as he longed to do, he slowly stroked her red-gold hair. "I'm fine, Kaitlan," he soothed. "I got him in the heart just as he sprang at me."

"I was so afraid he had attacked you before you got off a shot." She stepped away from him, rubbing at her wet eyes with the heels of her hands. Embarrassed, she said, "I guess you think I'm silly, carrying on so."

"Not at all," Matt said, remembering how she had felt in his arms. "Only a fool wouldn't be afraid of a panther. They can rip a person apart with one swipe of a paw." He waited a minute before asking, "Do you feel like joining the others now? They'll be concerned about the rifle shot."

"Yes, of course. I admit I don't feel as spry as when we started out, though."

Matt chuckled. "Neither do I."

They were halfway back to the churchyard when they met Peter and Lish and two other men who had heard the shot and started out looking for them.

"What was you shootin' at, Matt? I see you

both are all right, but Kaitlan looks a little pale."

Matt told the men what had happened, then had to repeat the story when they reached the others. Worried mothers wondered out loud if the panther had a mate hanging around, and Matt assured them he hadn't seen any others.

"You come set with us women, Kaitlan," Hattie ordered. "You look white as death."

Matt hid his disappointment as Kaitlan walked off with Hattie. He had hoped to spend more time alone with her. Today was probably the only chance he'd ever get.

As Kaitlan sat calming her nerves, her head on Hattie's shoulder, she watched the young women flirting with the single men. She noticed that they never came around Matt, but that their eyes strayed to him often. Were they like moths being drawn to a flame, the flame being a dangerous-looking man?

She remembered how tenderly Matt had held her when she was ready to collapse from fear. Those foolish young women didn't know what a gem Matt Ingram was.

Kaitlan was about to doze off when a male voice jokingly said, "I wonder if I should awaken the sleeping beauty?"

She opened her eyes and sat up straight, exclaiming, "Nate, you came after all."

"I couldn't get here any sooner. I had some work to do at the farm. There's more waiting for me, so I can't stay long." Nate held a hand down to assist Kaitlan to her feet, saying, "Let's take a walk."

"She can't walk with you," Hattie declared sharply. "She took one walk today and was almost set upon by a panther. You can go over there and sit under that big oak if you want."

Nate shot the black woman a look that would have shriveled a more timid soul, but it didn't stir a hair on Hattie's head. The one she directed at him was even more threatening than the one she had received.

Matt and Aunt Polly watched them walk toward the oak, holding hands, Nate saying something that made Kaitlan laugh. They both wanted to shout after Nate, "Liar! You haven't been home in two days."

"So, are you over your snit?" Nate asked as Kaitlan sat down and arranged her skirt to cover her ankles.

Nate frowned at the ladylike action, thinking what a prudish young woman she was. Not at all like Claire, who delighted in baring her body to him. But I'll have this one doing the same thing once we're married, he thought. If she doesn't do it willingly, I'll rip the clothes off her.

"I guess I am," she answered. "I was more hurt than angry."

"It wasn't like I asked you to go to bed with me," Nate complained. "I just wanted to kiss you."

"I know that. It's just that I have to get used

to the idea of letting you . . . well, you know. Will you be patient with me?"

Nate heaved a false sigh. "I guess I'll have to if you insist, but don't make me wait too long. You still haven't even told me when we can get married."

"I . . . I don't know, Nate."

"You might as well know now that I expect to sleep with you in the near future."

"Of course you'll sleep with me when we're married."

"I'm not talking about when we're married. I mean within the next couple weeks."

"Make love before we're married!" Kaitlan exclaimed in disbelief.

"Yes, before we're married," Nate answered impatiently. "All the other courting couples do. See those two disappearing into the woods? They'll couple before they return."

"Are you sure about that?" Kaitlan looked at him doubtfully.

"Of course I'm sure. All the couples do it every chance they get. And believe me, those chances happen often."

Nate took her hand and, kissing its palm, said, "Don't be surprised if I slip into your cabin some night and crawl into bed with you."

"Nate! Don't you dare." Kaitlan jerked her hand away from him.

They sat in a strained silence for a while, anger emanating from Nate. When a couple of minutes had passed he said coldly, "Tomorrow

I'm taking my pointer hound out to do some hunting. I'm hungry for a mess of quail. I'll be gone three weeks. While I'm gone I want you to think on this. When I get back I expect you to welcome me into your bed. If you don't, it's all over with us."

While Kaitlan stared at him, aghast, Nate rose and stalked over to his stallion. She watched him ride away, her mind wrestling with what he had demanded. Let him make love to her or lose him. She didn't want to lose him, but was she ready to surrender her body to him without benefit of marriage?

# Chapter Ten

Kaitlan sat alone beneath the tree until she noticed that Hattie was looking at her, a worried frown on her forehead. She smoothed her own brow before rising and returning to the women sitting in a group beneath a tree.

She arrived in time to hear Grace Cook saying, "If the feathers in your piller form circles, somebody is gonna die with his head on it."

As Kaitlan sat down next to Hattie, Alice Spencer said, "I've been right concerned the last three weeks because a hoot owl has come to my winder four times in a row. As you all know, that means somebody close to you is gonna die."

"What about you, Hattie?" Maybelle Scott curled her lips as she asked the question. "Don't they have omens in Philadelphia?"

Kaitlan felt Hattie's body stiffen and held her breath. What might her friend reply to the hateful woman? But after a while Hattie said calmly, "I don't like the looks of them whirlwinds. They mean more dry weather ahead."

"Oh, Hattie, are you sure?" one of the women asked, anxiety in her voice. "Our garden is dryin' up already."

"I know. Ours are too. But that's the way it looks to me."

Kaitlan hid her amusement. Hattie's talk about whirlwinds was the first she had ever heard in all her fifteen years. She felt sure Hattie had just now made it up in her anger at Miss Scott.

To change the subject to something more cheerful, she said to Grandma Tyler, "The color of your shawl is the deepest purple I've ever seen. What did you make your dye from?"

"Pokeberry roots, honey. You scrub them clean, cut them in small pieces, and put them in a large pot. Then you fill it with water and set it on the fire and let it simmer until you get the shade you want. To get this color I let them simmer for an hour."

"As soon as I find the time I'm going to dig up some roots and make the same dark color for a winter woolen dress I want to make," Kaitlan said.

"Green is my favorite color," Alice Spencer put in. "It's a simple dye to make. All you have to do is pick half a bucket of green leaves from an oak tree, rinse them off, put them in a pot of water, and let them boil real gentle-like until you get the tint you want."

"What is Claire's favorite color, Grandma Tyler?" Maybelle asked, a smirk on her thin lips. Everyone there knew that Claire didn't care what color she wore, that if it was left up to her she probably wouldn't even wear a dress.

Sympathy for the old woman showed on everyone's face as she hesitated, aware that

Maybelle was goading her. Finally she said, "When Claire was a little girl she always preferred red. I guess she still does."

"I remember how pretty she looked in her little red dresses," Alice Spencer said gently to Mrs. Tyler, then shot Maybelle a withering look.

Maybelle ignored the look and asked, "Why didn't Claire come to the social?"

"She, ah . . . she's not feeling well today. It's her time of the month."

When Maybelle opened her mouth to make another cutting remark, Hattie said, "I never noticed it before, Miss Scott, but you have a decided cast in your right eye. Did you get it from your mother's or your father's side?"

"I do not have a crooked eye." Maybelle screeched indignantly, jumping to her feet. "My eyes are just as straight as anybody's here." Her eyes swept over each woman, and when she saw them trying to hide their amusement, she half ran to her old mare, scrambled onto its back, and galloped away.

When Maybelle's ramrod straight back disappeared, everyone burst out laughing. "You shut her up right smart, Hattie," Aunt Polly said, dabbing a handkerchief at her tears of merriment. "I bet from now on she'll keep that sharp tongue in her mouth when you're around."

Hattie shrugged. "She needed to be set down, so I set her down. She has a mean disposition."

"Grandma Tyler, why are you cryin'?" Alice Spencer asked, hurrying to sit down beside the old lady.

"It's about Claire." Grandma Tyler dabbed at her eyes. "She's not home ailin' like I said. She hardly ever comes home anymore. She's met some man in the woods and mostly stays with him."

While everyone looked on, pity in their eyes for the old woman, Alice patted the aged, veined hands and said gently, "We'll send the men out to look for her. They'll bring her home. Then if you must, keep her locked in her room."

"I don't know if that's the answer." Grandma Tyler shook her head sadly. "You see . . ." Her tears increased, choking off her voice.

"She's with child," Granny Higgins said quietly.

"Yes." The gray head bent and tears dropped in her lap.

The women looked on with sympathy and anger. "What no-good man would put a baby in that fey child's belly?" Aunt Polly spoke for all of them. "It is an evil thing that man has done."

"But that's not all," Mrs. Tyler sobbed. "Paw is so upset he swears he will find the man and shoot him."

"Well, it seems to me that is what the lowlife deserves," Hattie declared.

"Oh no, Hattie. Paw ain't got many more

years to live. He won't get into Heaven with murder on his soul."

"He's got a better chance with God than the one he wants to shoot," Alice Spencer said, still holding the old woman's hand. "You stop worrying now," she said gently. "Me and the women will think of something."

"Thank you, Alice. I don't know what I'd do without my good neighbors." She pushed herself to her feet. "I'm jest plain worn out. I'm gonna go get Paw and go home and rest a spell."

The women watched her hobble over to where her husband sat with the other men. Polly broke the silence. "The Tylers are good, God-fearing people, there is no doubt about that, but they have always been too strict with Claire. They never showed her any affection when she was little, never allowed her to run and play with other children. She grew up a lonely child, looking for a smile, a kiss on the cheek. I guess when she got old enough, she found those missing things with the men she ran into in the woods."

"It's sad. Awfully sad," Alice said.

As the women agreed, Kaitlan was remembering the time she had seen Claire and the way the girl looked at Nate. It was as though she expected him to follow her when she walked away.

Her eyes narrowed a fraction. Nate had left her a short time later. Had he gone after Claire?

Shame on you to think such a thing about the man you plan to marry, she scolded herself mentally. Nate would never do a thing like that.

As the lazy afternoon wore on Kaitlan realized she had worried needlessly about Hattie being accepted by the mountain women. They liked and respected her. Relieved on that matter, she went back to worrying about her situation with Nate, coming to no conclusions.

Daylight was beginning to fade and mothers were beginning to call their children in from play when Kaitlan roused herself from her troublesome thoughts and looked up to see Matt smiling down at her. "We'd better be getting on home," he said, reaching down both hands to help her to her feet. "The sun will be setting before long."

"I hate for the day to end," Kaitlan said as they walked to their wagon. "I've had such a lovely time, getting to know my neighbors."

"And getting scared out of your wits by the panther," Matt teased.

"Yes, even that." Kaitlan laughed.

Kaitlan was waiting for Peter to help her into the wagon bed when Aunt Polly said, "Kaitlan, sit up on the seat with Matt and I'll sit back here with Hattie so we can talk."

As the wagon bumped homeward, Matt couldn't help noticing how quiet Kaitlan was. Usually she was full of questions, wanting to know about everything around them. From the way Nate had stamped away from her earlier,

Matt imagined they'd had words and that their argument was worrying her.

"Did you and Nate have a falling-out?" he asked finally.

Kaitlan sighed. "Yes, we did."

"Don't let it bother you. I'm sure you'll iron it out between you."

"I'm not sure we can. I have to make a decision that will determine whether we make up or break up. Nate will be gone for three weeks quail-hunting. I have to make up my mind about something by the time he gets back."

Matt's fingers tightened on the reins as he asked, "Is it a hard decision for you to make?"

When Kaitlan answered in a small voice, "I'm afraid so," he knew what Nate had said. Either she slept with him or they were finished. The rotten skunk, he swore silently to himself. Why did he want to debase an innocent, one he planned to marry?

His big hands clenched into fists. Even if he could convince Kaitlan that his stepbrother was rotten clear through, she would never turn to big, rough Matt Ingram. He could only stand by to console her when Nate broke her heart.

They drew up in front of the Barrett farm, and as Matt helped Kaitlan off the high seat, his hands lingered on her waist. "Think carefully on your decision, Kaitlan," he said. "When the time comes, do what your heart tells you."

"Thank you, Matt." Kaitlan stood on her

toes to kiss his cheek. "You always give me comfort." She was gone then, hurrying to the cabin. Matt touched his fingers to the spot where she had kissed him.

That night after supper Hattie and Peter sat on the porch with Kaitlan awhile, discussing the social and the people who had attended it.

"I like them all," Hattie said, "except for that Maybelle. I'd like to cut the tongue out of her mouth. But they are the most superstitious people I've ever seen. For instance, they believe if you take your ashes out between Christmas and New Year's, you'll have bad luck all year. If you eat black-eyed peas on New Year's Day you'll also have bad luck. If a rooster crows at midnight the next baby to be born will have a crooked leg."

"They're good people, though," Peter said. "They live rough, but they're proud and good hearted. Their outlook on life is that if you tend to your own business, you'll have plenty to do without tending to your neighbor's."

Peter chuckled. "That last is what old Lish said when Maybelle was mouthing off. I think everyone feels sorry for the Tylers."

Hattie yawned widely. "It's been a long day and I'm ready for bed." She stood up and said, "Come along, Peter, you're sleepy too."

Kaitlan shook her head with a small smile as she watched the pair walk toward their little house. Hattie directed every aspect of her husband's life. She wondered if Peter would know when it was time for him to use the privy unless Hattie told him he had to urinate.

She leaned her head on the chair back, and with a push of her foot set the chair in motion. She wished she had someone to tell her what to do about Nate; she knew what Hattie thought of him, but if she followed her friend's advice, she feared she would never have the husband and children she longed for.

As soon as Matt took Aunt Polly home he hurriedly unhitched the team and saddled his stallion. He was going to return to where he had shot the panther and relieve it of its beautiful hide. He would cure the pelt and give it to Kaitlan to lay before her hearth. It would keep her feet warm on a cold winter's night. There was an hour or so of daylight left, and if he hurried, he would have time to get it done before dark.

Matt had almost reached the spot where he had shot the animal when he saw Little Wren off in the trees digging roots. "Little Wren," he called softly so as not to startle her.

The young Indian woman looked up and a wide smile parted her lips. "Matt!" she cried out, coming to him. "It's so good to see you again."

"It's good to see you too." Matt dismounted and lightly kissed her forehead. "How have you been? Is everything well with your marriage?"

"Yes, everything is good. Rustling Leaves is a

fine husband. He is kind and never strikes me. Is everything well with you? You look a little thinner."

"I might have lost some weight. I've been busy tending my tobacco plants."

"The young maidens in the village wonder why you no longer come for any of them. They think that you have found a white woman more pleasing than they."

"No, nothing like that. Like I said, I've been working hard and I go to bed early."

"It's been good seeing you again, Matt. I must get back to the village now and start my husband's evening meal."

Matt nodded and said, "Take care of yourself, Little Wren."

He led the stallion the few yards to where the panther lay. As he swiftly skinned it, he dwelled on what Little Wren had said about the Indian maids waiting for him, and the answer he had given her. It wasn't true, what he had said about having no interest in a white woman. The truth was, since he had met Kaitlan he had no desire for any other woman. To lie with another woman never entered his mind. Maybe after she married Nate he could put her out of his mind and take up his previous ways. He hoped so. It was hell wanting a woman he could never have.

Matt had rolled up the panther hide and was about to mount the stallion when he heard laughter a few yards away. Recognizing Nate's voice, he walked noiselessly in that direction.

He wasn't surprised to see Claire with his stepbrother when he spotted them through the trees. They lay in front of a cave, both without clothing. Nate lay with his hands folded behind his head while Claire fondled him. Matt turned away when Claire climbed on top of Nate.

The no-good, dirty dog had no intention of going quail-hunting, he swore to himself as he climbed back into the saddle. That was his excuse to spend several weeks wallowing around with Claire. As he kneed the stallion into motion he asked himself how Nate could go from such a woman to one like the lovely Kaitlan. The thought of it made him so sick he was afraid he'd have to vomit.

Kaitlan stood on the porch. It was her habit lately to get up early in the morning and watch the east turn pink and orange over the mountain. Any minute now the sun would rise and break up the mists in the valley.

She heard the outside door close at the Smiths' place and turned her head to see Peter coming down the path. "Good morning," they called to each other. When Peter's steps turned toward the barn, Kaitlan added, "I'll be with you in a minute."

She walked back inside and put on a slatted bonnet, tied the strings under her chin, then slathered butter on a cold biscuit and washed it down with a cup of coffee she had taken time to make. She went back outside just as Peter drove up in the wagon.

Every day for the past week, she and Peter had used the wagon to haul barrels of water from the river to the tobacco patch. Once there, armed with a pail and dipper each, they walked up and down the rows giving each plant a good soaking. When the barrels were empty they would go again to the river and refill them. Their only break was at noontime, when she and Peter would stop for a quick lunch Hattie would have waiting for them.

This day was no different. Peter and Kaitlan, wringing wet with sweat and ready to drop, sighed their relief when the last plant was watered, as well as everything in the garden.

But their hard work was paying off. The tobacco leaves were firm and the plants now came to Kaitlan's shoulders. The garden was flourishing and every night they had something from it for supper.

"Do you think this heat will ever break?" Kaitlan asked tiredly as the wagon rolled homeward.

"Only if we get a big storm and a lot of rain," Peter answered.

"There wasn't a cloud in the sky today."

"Yeah, old Sol had it all to himself."

They reached the barn, and Kaitlan helped Peter unhitch the horse and lead it to the water trough, then turn it out in the penned in pasture.

At the cabin Hattie had a pail of water, a bar of soap, and two washbasins, as well as two towels, waiting for them on a bench.

When they had scrubbed up and walked inside they found fried chicken, mashed potatoes and gravy, fresh string beans cooked with a chunk of salt pork, and hot biscuits.

Kaitlan and Peter filled their plates and dug in.

Hattie watched them, shaking her head sadly. They were working too hard. Both had lost weight. But they were determined to save their cash crop.

# Chapter Eleven

In the middle of the night Kaitlan was jerked awake by a roll of thunder that shook the cabin. As she sat up, trying to gather her wits about her, lightning flashed almost constantly and the thunder was a continuing rumble.

She jumped out of bed and ran to the open window just as the rain came. It arrived in sheets, slashing through the window and onto her face. But what glorious coolness comes with it, Kaitlan thought, hurrying to close the window, but leaving it open an inch or two so that the room could cool.

She went back to bed thanking God that he had finally sent them some relief from the heat. Not only would it be cooler, but she and Peter would no longer have to haul water for the garden and tobacco patch.

The tobacco! Kaitlan sat back up. This slashing rain would cut the leaves to pieces. But even as she sat there worrying, the lightning came less frequently and the thunder became a distant sound. The storm was moving off and leaving behind it a steady, gentle rain that would saturate the soil but do no damage to plant life.

Kaitlan lay back down a second time, a smile curving her lips. Matt would be thankful for the rain too. He had too many acres of tobacco to haul water. There was nothing he could do but wait for the rain to come. He had come over three times to help her and Peter, and he had hauled water for his garden.

It, like their own, was flourishing, and she had gone to the Ingram farm a couple of evenings to help Aunt Polly string a bushel of beans on long pieces of heavy thread. They were now hanging in the attic to dry. Polly had explained to Hattie that when winter came all she had to do was take a long string of them, place them in water overnight, and they would plump up almost as fat as when they were picked. Hattie planned on doing the same thing sometime this week.

Wide-awake now, Kaitlan began thinking of the dilemma awaiting her on Nate's return. He had sent a message that he would be home that Friday and she still hadn't made up her mind about letting him into her bed. She was afraid that if she refused she would see the last of him.

If only he'd told me he loved me it would make it easier to decide, she thought as she drifted back to sleep.

The next morning Kaitlan and the Smiths were all smiles. Hattie hummed a church song as she made breakfast, and they could hear Peter whistling as he did a few chores down in the barn. She had thrown open all the windows in the cabin, and a cool breeze wafted throughout the building as she set the table for breakfast.

"Hattie," she said later as she sliced a loaf of bread, "after Peter and I have checked the tobacco, let's ride into the Village. It will do us good to get away from the farm for a few hours, and besides I want to go to the land office. I'm going to deed over half the farm to you and Peter."

"Kaitlan, you mustn't do that!" Hattie almost dropped the bowl of eggs she was carrying to the fire. "Me and Peter are real pleased with the little house you gave us."

"I want you to have some land too. I've been thinking about it ever since we got here. You and Peter are the only family I have — maybe the only family I'll ever have."

Rare tears ran down Hattie's cheeks. "You know that me and Peter look on you as our child, Kaitlan."

"I know that." Kaitlan put her arms around her narrow shoulders. "That's why I want you to own half the farm."

"What's wrong?" Peter exclaimed from the doorway, looking anxiously at his wife's tearstained face. "Did you burn yourself, Hattie?"

"No, you old fool." Hattie dried her eyes with the bottom of her apron. "You tell him, Kaitlan."

Peter looked dumbfounded as Kaitlan related

what she had said to Hattie. "Are you sure, Kaitlan?" he asked, sitting down weakly at the table.

When Kaitlan said, "I'm sure, Peter," tears glimmered in his eyes.

"I never in all my born days ever thought to own a piece of land," he said huskily. "The luckiest day in my life was when your papa hired us to work for him."

"It was my luckiest day too, Peter." Kaitlan patted his work-worn hands. "Let's say no more about it."

After breakfast Kaitlan and Peter walked to the tobacco patch, where they found every plant standing erect. Peter laughed and said, "I swear they've grown two inches since the rain. I tell you, Kaitlan, I feel reborn this morning."

"Me too. Let's get ready to go to the Village."

The sun was beginning to warm up the land as Peter sent the wagon down the rocky, uneven slope that led to the Village in the foothills ten miles distant.

Kaitlan sat in the wagon bed on a bale of straw catching glimpses of black-eyed Susans and gleaming goldenrod.

She had thought before that the mountains were beautiful, but her first sight of their glory couldn't compare with how they looked now.

She gave a happy sigh, and Hattie turned around to say, "It is a grand sight, isn't it?"

"What's a grand sight?" Peter asked, carefully

guiding the team around a sharp bend in the hard-packed road.

"Everything around you, fool," Hattie snapped.

"How in the blazes am I supposed to look at anything when I don't dare take my eyes off this thing they call a road?"

Hattie's answer to that was a snort, and nothing more was said about beauty. They soon entered the foothills and in five minutes came upon the Village.

Surprisingly to Kaitlan, it wasn't laid out in blocks like Philadelphia. But of course, she reminded herself, it was only a fraction of the size of the town she had called home for fifteen years.

The places of business were scattered about among trees, paths winding through tree stumps, leading to each building. But everything's rustic appearance appealed to Kaitlan. The Village was just like the people of the Gap — warm and friendly.

The livery was at the edge of the Village, and Peter drove the team up to it. As Kaitlan hopped off the back, and Peter helped Hattie down from the high seat, they were greeted by Lish Jones coming down one of the hard-packed paths.

"What brings you folk here to the Village?" he asked, a smile on his genial face. "It's your first time, ain't it?"

"It's the women's first time," Peter said. "I've

been here once." He was careful not to voice their real reason for the trip. "Hattie ran out of salt and she and Kaitlan decided they'd like to come with me, see the Village."

As usual Lish was full of talk, but after about five minutes of his jawing Hattie cut in, saying briskly, "We've got to get going, Mr. Jones. We've got a lot of work waiting for us at the farm."

"Of course. You folks go on about your business. Maybe I'll catch you on your way home."

"Not if we see you first, you old windbag," Hattie muttered in an aside to Kaitlan. "That man could talk the feet off a person's body."

They stood a minute, getting their bearings. The grocer lay straight ahead, the sign over the door stating VILLAGE MERCANTILE. Ten yards or so to its left and slightly behind the store was Rookie's Tavern, according to the sign over its door. And several yards to its right was a cabin, smaller than the rest. Its sign proclaimed LAND OFFICE.

Quite some distance away from the other buildings sat a long, low building, which Peter informed Kaitlan and Hattie was a fur-trading place. "The reason it sets so far from the others is because of the stench that comes off the pelts. I guess they stink pretty bad."

Kaitlan noticed a cabin that was larger than any of the others standing far back among the trees. She was about to ask what kind of business it conducted when she saw Matt step outside. He was followed by a tightly corseted female with orange frizzed hair. She laughed at something Matt said, then said something herself that made Matt throw back his head and laugh.

"There's Matt," she exclaimed happily. "Let's go speak to him, meet the woman he's talking to."

"Well . . . er . . . that might not be a good idea," Peter stammered.

"Why not?" Hattie wanted to know. "Maybe she's his lady friend."

"I doubt that." Peter looked amused.

Suspicion grew in Hattie's eyes. "Fool," she ordered, "get hold of your tongue before you trip on it. Now, who exactly is that woman?"

"I don't know her name. I only know she's the owner of the bawdy house."

"I thought as much." Hattie nodded.

"A bawdy house?" Kaitlan looked confused a moment, then said, "Oh, a bawdy house," as understanding came to her. "Do you mean Matt goes there for . . ."

"He's a man, Kaitlan." Hattie took Kaitlan's arm and led her toward the land office. "Nature seems to give them all the need for a woman once in a while, so get that look off your face."

"It's just that Matt doesn't seem to be the sort who would pay a woman for . . ."

"What's a man to do if he hasn't got a wife or a lady friend?" Hattie said impatiently. "Don't go holding it against him. What do you think your friend Nate does?"

Kaitlan didn't answer, because Hattie was opening the land office door.

It didn't take long for the Smiths to sign their names to the deed that gave them half the Barrett farm. Since they had no other business to conduct in the Village they went straight to the livery, climbed into the wagon, and headed homeward.

Kaitlan was very quiet as the wagon bumped along. She was trying to understand why it bothered her that Matt had a life that she knew nothing about. A life that included female friends. Ones that he made love to.

And why, she wondered further, wasn't she upset that Nate did the same? She planned on his being her husband someday.

A short distance down the rutted road they saw Matt riding up ahead of them. When they were almost abreast of him he guided the stallion off to the side and looked over his shoulder. His eyes lit up when he saw Kaitlan. "You folks are out early," he said, reining the horse alongside the team. "It's the first time you ladies have visited the Village, isn't it?"

"Yes, Matt, it is." Hattie smiled at him. When he looked at Kaitlan, she turned her profile to him, her chin in the air. Matt gave her a curious look, then turned his attention to Peter to talk tobacco.

An hour later the Barrett farm appeared

around a bend in the road, and when Peter pulled the team to a halt, Hattie said, as she jumped to the ground, "Matt, I'm going to fix ham sandwiches for lunch. Come on in and have some with a cup of coffee." Without a glance in Matt's direction, Kaitlan followed Hattie into the cabin.

Matt stared after them, puzzlement in his eyes. Kaitlan hadn't said one word to him, hadn't given him one smile. It was evident that she was displeased with him, but why he couldn't imagine.

For a moment he thought to refuse Hattie's invitation, but then he changed his mind. He wouldn't rest until he'd talked to Kaitlan, learned why she was suddenly so cool to him.

As they ate lunch the usual easy conversation flowed between Matt and the Smiths, but Kaitlan maintained her aloofness. When Matt tried to draw her into whatever they were talking about and she only spoke in monosyllables, he grew impatient. Always before if she had something on her mind, she didn't hesitate to spit it out.

When the meal was over Matt said he'd better get home, that he had some things to look after. He stood up and looked at Kaitlan. "Walk me outside."

"I've got to clear the table," she answered, not looking at him.

"I'm sure that can wait awhile. I only want a minute of your time."

"Oh, all right," Kaitlan grudgingly agreed and reluctantly preceded him through the door.

"Why are you walking so fast?" Matt grabbed her arm, slowing her pace. When they reached Satan, tied up under a shade tree, he swung her around to face him and ordered, "Now tell me what I've done to put that bee in your bonnet."

"I don't know what you're talking about."

"Yes, you do. You've been all huffy ever since we met on the road. Now what's bothering you?"

Kaitlan took a deep breath. "I saw you at the Village today talking to a woman."

Everything became clear to Matt. She had seen him with Ruby and had leaped to the wrong conclusions. How was Kaitlan to know he'd been visiting little Sammy? "I wasn't at the bawdy house for the reason you think, Kaitlan."

"What other reason could a man have for going to such a place?" Kaitlan asked sharply.

"Look, Kaitlan, believe it or not, I don't have to pay for a woman."

Kaitlan knew by his sharp tone she had angered him. Her voice softened as she asked, "Why were you there, then?"

"I was there strictly on business. I can't tell you about it now, but someday the whole Gap will know."

Kaitlan looked into his earnest eyes and knew he wasn't lying. To lie wasn't his way. She laid a hand on his arm. "Forgive me, Matt. I

152

believe you. At any rate it's none of my business what you were doing there. I don't know why I got so upset when I saw you talking to that painted-up woman."

"Her name is Ruby and she's not a bad sort. She has a soft heart, softer than most of the women in the Gap."

Kaitlan gave him an impish grin. "Since you think so highly of her, if I ever see her in the Village I'll stop and chat with her."

Matt laughed and gave one of her curls a tug. "You're getting pretty sassy now."

"Oh am I? What are you going to do about it?" she laughingly asked, darting out of his reach.

"I'll think of something." A slumberous look came into Matt's eyes as he reached for her again and this time caught her.

Holding her loosely in his arms, he grew serious. "Kaitlan," he said, "don't be in a rush to marry Nate. I know he's handsome and all that, but with him things aren't always what they seem to be. I don't think he would make you happy."

Kaitlan drew back to gaze up at him. "You're mistaken, Matt. I am happy when I'm with Nate."

Matt looked into her earnest blue eyes and didn't know which he wanted to do more: shake some sense into her, or kiss her pink lips until she was dizzy.

"When you're with him," he repeated her

153

words. "In all truthfulness, how often have you been with Nate? Altogether, how many hours have you spent with him? Have you had enough time to really get to know him? Have you learned how he reacts to anger, irritation, when things don't go his way? It's very important that you know all these things before you give yourself to him in marriage. To any man, as for that."

"I've seen Nate aggravated," Kaitlan said slowly, remembering how cross he always got when she held herself away from his rough kisses or when he tried to put his hands where he shouldn't. He did act like a spoiled little boy at those times. "Every man has a temper."

"Oh, Kaitlan." Matt sighed. "You are so innocent, so trusting." He stroked a finger down her cheek. "That's why I want you to take your time about marrying Nate. There are a lot of young men in the Gap who would break a leg in their hurry to come courting if you would give them a signal."

He playfully clipped her on the chin with his loosely balled fist. "I've been thinking that maybe I'll come calling on you."

"Oh, I'm sure you would," Kaitlan laughingly scoffed, pulling away from him. "You're not the sort to come sparking a skinny girl like me. I'm sure you like your women full bodied."

Looking at her bodice, which was amply filled, he said, "You're not so skinny." He grabbed for her again, and this time Kaitlan laughingly eluded him.

They were both laughing when Peter, who had come up unnoticed, asked with a grin, "Are you two playing tag?"

"I'm trying to get hold of her to give her a whack on her behind, teach her not to sass her elders," Matt said with a grin.

Peter laughed. "It won't work. She's been sassing me ever since she learned how to talk."

Matt made one last lunge at Kaitlan, missed and then climbed into the saddle. Grinning down at them he said, "I guess she's a little old for a spanking anyhow. I'll have to think up another way to curb her sharp tongue." He gathered up the reins and sent the stallion off at a gallop.

"He's a fine man," Peter said as they watched him ride away.

"He's so different when he horses around a bit," Kaitlan thought out loud. "It's almost like he's someone else. He should do that more often."

"He probably does when he gets to know a person real good."

Kaitlan wondered about Peter's remark as she walked back to the cabin. Matt had said that he didn't have to pay for a woman's company and she could believe it. When he loosened up he was charming. With strands of his coal black hair falling over on his forehead, and that devilish glitter in his gray eyes, he looked rather rakish. She could understand how he'd have no trouble getting into a woman's bed.

That thought got her to thinking of Nate. He would be coming home tomorrow and would want her answer. Would he be welcome in her bed or not?

She sighed as she walked into the cabin. She still hadn't made up her mind. If Nate loved her, he ought to be willing to wait until they were married. But the idea of marriage made her remember Matt's cautionary words. Perhaps she *was* hurrying into things with Nate. Oh, how she wished they could just go back to those friendly visits on her porch, when Nate had made her feel so special, so wanted.

Kaitlan was venting some of her exasperation by sweeping the floor when someone reached inside and knocked on the open door. "Well, hello, Grace, come right on in," she invited with a friendly smile. "It's so nice of you to come visit me."

Grace Cook smiled shyly as she stepped inside and handed Kaitlan a small pail. "I brung you some sourwood honey. Ain't none better than sourwood."

"Thank you, Grace. I love honey and use it in place of sugar whenever I can."

"We do that too. We'uns also like sorghum molasses. The young'uns like sorghum cause they can make taffy out of it."

Kaitlan set a plate of sugar cookies on the table and then poured them each a cup of coffee. "These are real good," Grace said, biting into one. "I'll bet you're a fine cook."

Kaitlan shook her head with a small laugh. "I can't take credit for the cookies. Hattie does all the baking. Actually she does all the cooking."

Grace looked at Kaitlan, disbelief in her eyes. "Don't you know how to cook?"

"Not very much, I'm afraid."

"What are you gonna feed your husband when you get married?"

"When that time comes I'll have to have Hattie teach me."

"You're lucky to have her, with your mother gone and all."

"Yes, I am. I thank God for her every night. Peter too."

"Granny Higgins said that she's right smart about doctorin' too."

Kaitlan nodded. "She knows a lot about curing ailments."

Kaitlan discovered that when Grace got over her shyness she could talk a blue streak, as Lish would say. The sun was close to setting before Grace left, after making Kaitlan promise to come visit her.

As soon as she disappeared in the woods, Hattie came hurrying from her little house. "I thought that woman would never leave," she grumbled as she poked up the fire in the cooking fireplace. "Peter will be coming in here any minute, hungry as a bear."

"I sure am." Peter walked into the kitchen and laid two good-sized bass, scaled and gutted, on the workbench. "Fry them up,

157

woman" — he grinned at Hattie — "and make some hush puppies to go with them. Can't eat fish without hush puppies."

"Then get out of the way, fool." Hattie took an iron skillet off the wall and placed it on the fire.

"Have I got time to go down to the river to take a bath?" Kaitlan asked.

"Yes, if you don't lollygag about. Peter, go with her and keep an eye out that no men come along to gawk at her."

"Dad rat it, I just came from there," Peter complained, but he waited while Kaitlan went into her room to get clean clothes and bath linens. "It gets boring sitting there with my back to the river just staring into space."

"Then stare up at the sky," Hattie said as she rolled the fish in cornmeal.

An hour later Kaitlan and the Smiths were telling each other that they had never eaten fish any better.

"It's because they're fresh from the river and not from a store, like we used to get in Philadelphia. No telling how old those were."

As soon as Hattie helped Kaitlan clean up the kitchen, she and Peter went home to bed. Kaitlan sat a few minutes on the porch to catch a cool breeze, then she, too, retired, keeping only her petticoat on.

As she fell asleep Nate was on her mind. What was she to tell him when he asked that all-important question?

# Chapter Twelve

The glowing tip of a cigarette was the only evidence that a man leaned against the trunk of the large beechnut tree. Matt had been watching Kaitlan's cabin for over an hour, trying to make up his mind whether he should do what he was contemplating. It wouldn't be a manly act, but he felt driven to do it. It would be the one thing he would always have to remember in the long years ahead. Something he could recall to ease the pain of losing Kaitlan.

There was something else equally important. Kaitlan was undoubtedly a virgin and should be initiated into the act of lovemaking with care and tenderness, things that Nate knew nothing about. He would take her as he did all his women, caring only for his own satisfaction. She would be torn and bleeding when he finished with her.

Still, it would almost be like rape if he made love to her when she thought he was Nate.

The interior of the cabin grew dark and Matt ground out his cigarette. He walked out of the shadows, still undecided. To his right lay the trail to his farm, and straight ahead was the path that would take him to the girl who made him hurt, he loved her so much.

A cloud passed over the moon, and in the

total darkness it was impossible to tell which direction Matt took.

Only a short time had elapsed after Kaitlan fell asleep when she was awakened by the embrace of strong yet gentle arms. She stiffened and held her breath. Nate had returned a day early and wasn't even giving her a chance to say no to him. Hadn't he meant to when he left her nearly three weeks ago?

She raised her hands to push them against his chest, but grew still. His work-roughened hands were stroking her face, smoothing the hair off her forehead. She could feel his heartbeat beneath the coarse material of his shirt, and a comforting warmth spread through her. She dropped her hands and unconsciously snuggled a little closer to him. In wonder, she felt his lips on her forehead, then on her cheeks, her eyelids, until finally they settled on her lips.

She braced herself for the onslaught of his kiss and was surprised. His lips were soft and gentle when they moved over hers. He has changed his roughness for me, she thought joyfully. When his tongue probed her lips, coaxing her to open to him, she unhesitatingly did so.

Kaitlan was surprised that she didn't feel repulsed as his tongue roamed the inside of her mouth. In fact, she liked it and felt its loss when he removed his mouth and began planting kisses up and down her throat.

She stiffened a bit when she felt his fingers at the ties of her gown. But his lips closed over hers again and she was barely aware when the neckline parted. She became very aware when a warm palm was placed on one of her breasts. She lay perfectly still and caught her breath when eager fingers began to slowly massage there, and a thumb was drawn across her hardened nipple.

When a long, softly drawn sigh escaped her, he removed his lips from hers and settled his mouth on her other breast. A jolt like a streak of lightning spread from his mouth to the inner core of her being. And when his teeth nibbled on her aroused nipple, she moaned low in her throat. As if it were a signal, his lips began to pull on her pink, puckering areola like a hungry suckling baby.

Kaitlan lay in a state of bewilderment, her mind reeling as she experienced sensations she had never known existed. She never felt that Nate had taken advantage of her. She knew now by his loving actions that he did care about her. This gentle side of him assured her that she wouldn't be wrong in loving him back.

She gave a small sound of disappointment when his mouth and hands deserted her breasts. It had all felt so good, she wished it could go on forever. But he had only freed his lips in order to trail little kisses up her throat to claim her lips in a hot, searing kiss. She cupped his head in her hands and hungrily returned the pressure on her mouth.

The kiss went on and on, his tongue slipping between her lips, flicking and sparring with hers, until he gathered the hem of her petticoat, removed his mouth, and pulled it over her head. And as she lay there, naked, he began stroking his hands down her body, pausing to kiss each curve and valley.

Her body stiffened when he parted the golden curls at the apex of her thighs and slid a finger inside her. She gasped as he began to massage the little nub there, bringing her a pleasure she hoped would go on forever.

He removed his hand after a while and, to her disbelief, his mouth took its place. "Nate, what are you doing?" she whispered. She started to sit up, but was gently pushed back down. As she lay there, her whole body throbbing, she felt him kneel between her legs. What now? she wondered as he lifted her thighs and settled them on his shoulders. She moaned in helpless passion then as his tongue darted inside her, his teeth nibbling at the little nub that had grown pebble hard. She moaned low in her throat when his mouth closed over her and sucked her as he had her breasts.

But as good as it felt, it wasn't enough. There was a void inside her that must be filled; filled with that hardness she had felt nudging her side when he had planted kisses on her body.

She reached down to where he knelt and unbuttoned his trousers. Her hand went immediately to what she wanted. His large size startled her, but she knew that she wanted this man, needed him. She knew instinctively what to do. Her fingers closed around his sex and she began stroking her palm up and down its length in time to his working mouth.

As she had hoped, her caressing was too much for him to bear for very long. He lifted his head, removed her legs from his shoulders, and then took off his clothes. He stretched his body over hers then and in the darkness urged her legs apart. As she waited she felt him take his hardness in his hand in preparation to enter her. She spread her legs farther apart, anxious to welcome him.

A sigh feathered through her lips as she was filled, his throbbing male part stretching the walls of her femininity. At last she felt complete. She wound her arms around his neck, whispering his name. Then simultaneously his mouth came down on hers just as he gave a hard push of his hips.

A searing pain went through Kaitlan and she would have cried out had his mouth not been on hers to stop the cry. He had broken her maidenhead and had known that it would hurt when he did. He slowly smoothed a palm over her body until she relaxed. He then dropped his head and took her breast into his mouth.

It had the effect he desired. Kaitlan was soon straining her hips to nestle in his again. He cupped her small rear in his hands and, lifting her slightly, held her steady as he began to move slowly inside her. Her body stiffened a moment; then she was clutching his shoulders, silently urging him on.

With a relieved sigh he removed his hands from her bottom. Sliding one arm under her waist and the other around her shoulders, he held her close as he thrust in and out of her.

It took but a short time before Kaitlan almost panicked, afraid of what was happening to her as her body seemed to spiral upward in a release of passion that seemed to leave the rest of her behind. "Nate!" she cried out, "what is happening to me?"

Her only answer was an earth-shattering kiss. A moment later his body grew rigid and he was withdrawing from her, spilling his seed onto the bedcovers.

Kaitlan held him close, threading her fingers through his hair until his heavy breathing returned to calm. When he would have moved off her, she whispered, "No, not yet."

He gave a low chuckle, and guided his ready shaft back inside her.

This time they didn't reach the crest of sublime release so quickly, and Kaitlan reveled in each drive of his hips. Their bodies bathed in sweat, they climbed the mountain of passion together.

Feeling as fluid as water and completely drained, Kaitlan was barely aware of her lover leaving the bed, and only vaguely heard the rustle of his clothes as he got back into them. When a light kiss was placed on her lips, her only response was a soft smile. She was sound asleep before his footsteps ceased to sound as he left the cabin.

Kaitlan awakened to the sound of Hattie making breakfast. She lay a moment, wondering why she felt so relaxed, yet sore in all her muscles. Even her breasts felt sore and swollen.

It all came back to her in a rush, in vivid detail. Nate had visited her last night and had made such wondrous love to her, he had turned her into a wanton.

Smiling as she remembered, she stretched her slender body. She couldn't wait to see him today, couldn't wait to feel his naked body against hers tonight. She had never dreamed that making love could be so wonderful. How odd it was that she had never responded to Nate in that way before. Why had his earlier kisses been so harsh? It was as though he'd been a different man altogether last night as he made love to her so tenderly.

No longer did she have doubts about their marriage. Nate had cherished her body last night, making words unnecessary. Never had she felt so sure that they belonged together.

Kaitlan became aware of her naked state and, leaving the bed, she scrambled into her clothes. Hattie certainly wouldn't approve of her sleeping bare and would ask a hundred questions if she discovered her without her gown on.

Kaitlan hurriedly poured water from a pewter pitcher into a matching basin and dropped a piece of flannel into it. She soaped it well with a bar of scented soap Hattie had learned to make when she was a slave on a big plantation. Her mistress had taught her how to crush dried rose petals until they were powdery fine and mix them in with the lye and ashes as they simmered over a slow heat.

She washed her face and arms; then, lifting her skirts, she sponged her private parts, ridding herself of all traces of her and Nate's spent passion. Crossing the room to stand in front of the wall mirror, Kaitlan attacked her tangled hair with a brush.

She had just brought the curls to their usual smoothness when Hattie called from the kitchen, "Are you up, Kaitlan? Breakfast is about ready."

Kaitlan felt uneasy on entering the kitchen. Would Hattie be able to see that she had been made love to? Would her eyes show that she had lost her innocence?

To Kaitlan's relief, when she said, "Good morning," Hattie barely glanced at her.

"Don't you and Peter dawdle over breakfast this morning," Hattie said. "There's at least a bushel of string beans waiting to be picked in the garden."

"Do you want me to help you?" Kaitlan asked as she sat down at the table and transferred three batter cakes from the platter in the center of the table to her plate.

"No, I won't need you. Peter is going to help me. The yellow rose is in bloom. Why don't you pick a bouquet and bring it to your grandparents' graves like you've been talking about doing?"

"I think I will." Kaitlan slathered butter on her batter cakes, and then spooned some of Grace Cook's honey on them. She was thinking that maybe she would run into Nate. She knew he didn't like coming to the farm because of Hattie. Those two simply did not like each other, which made her feel bad. She knew there would be a lot of problems once they were married.

Peter came in from outside, and as he took his place at the table, he looked at Kaitlan's high stack of batter cakes, and the way she was digging into them. He grinned and said, "You got quite an appetite going there, girl. You're eating like a farmhand. Did you have a dream last night where you were working hard?"

A light blush tinged Kaitlan's cheeks. She had worked hard last night, but not in the sense that Peter meant.

Peter didn't seem to require an answer, so she didn't give him one.

An hour later Kaitlan had cut a large bouquet of sweet-smelling roses. She wrapped them in a wet cloth and carefully laid them in a basket. When she had added a tin can of water to the reed container, she set off, walking toward the church and cemetery. It was a two-mile walk, but the morning was cool and the mountain air brisk.

When she arrived at the burial grounds it took Kaitlan a little time to find her grandparents' grave markers. She would have visited their graves on the day of the social, but she had known she would be followed by some of the women and she wanted to be alone the first time she went there. She wanted to tell her grandparents that she wished she had known them, and how thankful she was that they had provided her with a home when she needed one so desperately.

The cemetery was a serene, peaceful place with a few trees scattered about, and crape myrtle climbing over the headstones.

When she had set the can of roses between the two graves she began to speak softly to the old couple, saying all the things she wished she could say to them in person.

Tired from her long walk, she sat down under the tree that shaded her grandparents' resting place. Settling her skirts around her she looked up and smiled. Matt had just come from behind the church and was walking toward her. He had a rifle slung over his shoulder and a pair of squirrels dangled from his hand. He had been out hunting. As usual she was struck by his hard muscular grace.

"I see you're visiting your grandparents' graves," he said, laying the rifle and his kill on the ground and sitting down beside her. He brought up a knee and rested his elbow on it. "They were a nice old couple, well liked by their neighbors. Rufe was kinda rough, but everyone in the Gap knew they could come to him when in need of anything. He and Lish were close friends and Lish misses him."

There was a slight silence. Then Matt said, "Have you seen Nate yet?"

"Seen him?" Kaitlan turned her head to hide the flush rising to her face. "I haven't seen him," she answered, thinking with a stirring of her blood that she had only felt him.

"He'll probably stop by your place sometime today."

"Yes, I'm sure he will," Kaitlan said, eager to get home and freshen up before Nate dropped in on her. She rose to her feet and, brushing off the back of her skirt, smiled down at Matt as she said, "I'll be getting on home now. Are you coming?"

"Not just yet. I'm going to visit my parents' graves, then go home by way of my special waterfall."

"Well, I'll be seeing you, then."

Matt watched her walk away, her hips gently swaying, and he cursed himself for a fool. Why had he asked her about Nate? He should have known that she would want to hurry home.

He heaved a sigh, wishing for the first time in his life that he stood in his stepbrother's shoes. He got up. It was important that he find Nate before the scoundrel pressured Kaitlan into allowing *him* to make love to her.

# Chapter Thirteen

Arriving home an hour later Matt found Nate bathing in the horse trough. The water had been piped into the long wooden vessel from the spring that flowed beneath the cabin. He walked over to Nate, and asked in a barely civil tone, "How long are you planning to stay home this time?"

"Oh, I don't know, a week at least, I guess," Nate answered indifferently. "What's it to you how long I stay? There's no pressing work on the farm right now."

"I don't care how long you stay. You can be gone for a month, for all I care. But I'm warning you, don't pressure Kaitlan to go to bed with you. And don't try talking her into marriage right away either. If I find out that you have done either one, I'll geld you."

When Nate only glared at him through hate-filled eyes, Matt said, his voice harsh, "Do you understand me?"

"Yes, dammit, I understand you!" Nate dropped the bar of soap and stood up.

Matt turned on his heel and walked to the cabin. If Nate heeded his threat he had bought a little time, for he had made up his mind that he was going to be the man who would marry Kaitlan.

After Kaitlan arrived back at her farm, hot and sweaty from her fast walk, nothing went as she had planned. It was near lunchtime and Peter had just driven the mule into the barnyard. He had been out tilling a piece of land to plant some late corn. Lish had told him that it made excellent fodder for the farm animals in the winter. As he unhitched the gray mule, he handed Kaitlan the long reins and said, "Take him down to the branch for a drink of water, then turn him into the pasture. It's getting too hot to work any more today."

Kaitlan wanted to refuse, to say that she had something else to do, but Peter looked beat. He took off his old hat and mopped his sweaty forehead with a piece of rag he took from his back pocket.

By the time she brought the mule back from the river and turned him out to pasture, lunch was on the table. She promised herself that as soon as the meal was eaten, she would wash up and change her clothes. But she had barely swallowed the last bite of her berry cobbler when Hattie spoke.

"Kaitlan, we'll spend most of the afternoon stringing the green beans me and Peter picked before he went off plowing. Let's get the dishes washed up and start right in."

"But, Hattie, I wanted to take a bath now. I feel so hot and sticky."

"There's no use bathing now. You'll only be

in the same condition after we're finished with the beans. Take it after supper. Then you'll be clean and fresh when you go to bed."

Hattie's advice was logical, Kaitlan knew. How could she say that she expected Nate to drop in and she wanted to look nice for him? Hattie didn't like or trust him.

She held back a sigh. Maybe she could hurry the chore along and still have time for an early bath.

When she and Hattie went out onto the porch where it was cooler, Kaitlan soon learned that one could not hurry the stringing of green beans. They were very firm, and if the needle wasn't carefully and slowly pushed through them they would snap in half and lose their juices. When this happened to the first eight ones she tried to do in a hurry, Hattie impatiently chastised her.

"You're not stitching a piece of cloth, Kaitlan. Stringing these vegetables is a slow process. Slow down and be careful how you use the needle."

The sun was well westward when at last the basket was empty and there were yards of thread strung with beans piled around Hattie's and Kaitlan's feet.

"While I take them up in the attic to dry out, go out in the garden and cut us some lettuce for supper," Hattie said, standing up and carefully looping their work over one arm.

Kaitlan gave a sigh of hopelessness. There

would be no bath until after supper. She picked up the basket that had held the beans, stepped off the porch, and unlatched the gate to the garden.

And that was where Nate found her, down on her knees in the dirt of the lettuce bed, her face all sweaty, and her hair straggling down the sides of her cheeks.

Kaitlan heard the crunch of footsteps and wished she could disappear in a puff of smoke. Just when she wanted to look her best, she was looking worse than she ever had in her life.

Her face an embarrassed red, she scrambled to her feet, wiping an arm across her damp brow to push most of the hair off her face.

"Nate!" she exclaimed. "I must look awful."

"You could never look awful, Kaitlan Barrett." Nate said with his usual charming smile. "You could have mud all over your face and your hair could be a rat's nest, and you would still be the most beautiful woman I've ever seen."

Memories of last night swept into her mind and, blushing, she said, "It's so good that you are back home again."

"I'm happy to be back. I've missed you." After a pause he added, "I'm afraid I'll only be staying a week, though. I found a job over on the other side of the Gap helping a man build a barn. So I'll only be able to see you on the weekends."

The disappointment Kaitlan felt showed in

her eyes. "Why did you do that? What about the tobacco farm? Aren't you going to help Matt anymore?"

"I'll help him when it comes time to cut the tobacco and hang it in the drying sheds, but until then I want to make some money and lay it aside for you know what."

"For when we get married?"

"That's right." Nate took her by the arms and pulled her up to him. "I don't want to marry you with empty pockets. It's bad enough that through you I'll be getting a fine little farm."

"But, Nate," Kaitlan began, then was stopped as he lowered his face and covered her lips with his. When the kiss ended, leaving her feeling somehow disappointed, she looked up at him and said, "I want to talk to you about setting a date for our wedding. I've decided that I don't need any more time to think it over. We can get married anytime you want to."

Elation shot into Nate's eyes, then quickly faded as he remembered Matt's threat to him.

He stroked a hand down Kaitlan's smudged cheek and said softly, "That's sweet of you, honey, but there's no need to rush. Like I said, I want to put some money by before I make you my wife."

As he released her Kaitlan nodded and said, "I expect you're right, but I wish you weren't. I long to be your wife, Nate."

"I know. I wish that too, more than you know.

But it will be better if we wait."

Kaitlan reluctantly agreed.

"I've got to go now. Aunt Polly is expecting me to eat supper with her and Matt."

Kaitlan wished that he would kiss her again, the way he had the night before, but it didn't look as though he intended to. "Will you be over tonight?" she asked shyly.

He lightly pinched her nose. "If I can get away."

She watched him leave the garden, swing onto his stallion's back, and race away. The blood seemed to hum through her veins at the possibility that another unbelievable night of lovemaking awaited her.

Kaitlan couldn't see a single star in the sky as she sat on the porch. The dark clouds that had begun to gather at twilight had apparently grown larger. Occasionally she heard the distant rumble of thunder. The close, humid air said plainly that a summer storm was on its way.

She leaned her head on the chair back and sighed. Nate wouldn't ride through lightning and a downpour to visit her tonight. "I shouldn't be surprised that it's going to storm tonight," she muttered. "Everything else has gone against my wishes today. Hattie has seen to that, so why not the weather tonight?"

It still bothered her that Nate hadn't been as excited as she about her decision that they should get married right away. He had been at first. She had seen his pleasure in his face. But it had faded so fast, for a moment she questioned if she hadn't been mistaken about the gleam in his eyes.

It was right, the way he was thinking about their future, and she was grateful that he wanted to save some money. Nevertheless she wished he hadn't decided to be so thoughtful now. It didn't seem his nature to wait when he wanted something.

Inside the cabin the clock struck nine. A light wind came up and the tiny tree frogs ceased their chirping. Kaitlan could see patches of the mountains light up when heat lightning flashed above them. She noticed that the thunder came more frequently now and was much closer. She began to count the lapses between each rumble. When she could only count to five before the next one she knew the storm was only five miles away. Before she could count anymore it was upon her, the rain beating against the cabin walls.

Almost in tears, she jumped to her feet and hurried inside. The old hound nearly knocked her over in his rush to get in where it was dry. She ordered Ringer to go lie under the table and then she ran through the rooms, closing the windows and pulling curtains across them. She didn't like storms, didn't like to see the lightning streak across the sky.

In the total darkness she felt her way to the

bedroom. She fumbled her way to the bed, turned down the covers, then pulled her single garment over her head. She stood a moment wondering if she should grope her way to the dresser and fumble for a nightgown, or crawl into bed naked.

The decision was made for her. Suddenly, familiar arms had wrapped around her and hot kisses were searing across her mouth. "I'd given up on you coming tonight, Nate," she whispered when the long, hungry kiss finally ended. "Get out of your damp clothes and hang them over the footboard to dry." Her fingers went to his shirt buttons. "I'll help you."

Kaitlan took her time sliding the shirt over his shoulders, surprised at how much wider they felt now than they had looked this afternoon. She paused to plant little kisses on his chest, flicking her tongue over his nipples, making him gasp the pleasure he was feeling.

When the shirt lay on the floor, thoughts of hanging it on the footboard forgotten, Kaitlan unbuckled his belt and unfastened the buttons on his fly. His body went still when she pulled his pants down over his hips. His hard erection seemed to jump into her hand. She caressed it, stroked and fondled it a moment. He caught his breath when she went down on her knees and begun running tiny kisses up and down its long length. He was in agony when finally she closed her lips over him.

He sensed that she didn't know what to do

next, so he gently pushed her head down so that her mouth covered more of him. A long sigh of relief whistled through his teeth as she began to slide her lips on his hardness.

He groaned deep in his throat. To deepen his pleasure he stroked his fingers around her mouth, wishing he could see her lips on him. Finally he could stand it no longer and gently lifted her head away from him. As she stretched out on her back, he tore off his boots and stripped the pants over his feet. They landed on top of the shirt. His hands found her in the darkness then, and, bending her knees and spreading them apart, he adored her as she had him.

When Kaitlan began to moan and thrash her head about, he lifted his head and raised his body over hers. He suckled one breast and then the other for a moment; then, covering her lips in a searing kiss, he took his aching member in his hand and guided it inside her. He groaned when her feminine walls closed around him and flexed. His body stilled as her sheath squeezed, then released, then squeezed again around his throbbing maleness. This caress had never happened to him before and he wished that it could last forever.

But when Kaitlan's whispered plea urged him on he gave a shove of his hips that plunged him deep inside her. Her fingers grasped his shoulders as she dug her heels into the bed and met each thrust with cries of delight.

The storm blew itself out as twice more they made slow, sweet love. When the clock struck midnight, Kaitlan, feeling drained and fully sated, turned over on her side and fell instantly asleep.

For the rest of the week, each night was spent in the same way. Kaitlan went about her chores in a daze, causing Hattie to give her many curious looks.

But inevitably, the day that Kaitlan had been dreading arrived. Nate would be leaving, going to his new job on the other side of the Gap. She would miss him dreadfully. She hadn't seen all that much of him in the daytime, but he had come to her every night. She had grown used to the ecstasy his body brought her, and as much as she hated to admit it, the nights of love-making would be missed as much as — or more than — Nate's company. They never talked all that much when they saw each other in the day-time, and certainly there were few words spoken when in bed. Nate was a silent lover, letting his actions speak for him.

Kaitlan waited for Nate down by the river where it was cool, and out of sight of Hattie's disapproving eyes. He had asked her to meet him there, adding, "If I see that look she always gives me one more time, I don't know if I can keep from hitting her."

Kaitlan thought about those words as she waited. Something had to be done about the hard feelings between the two people she loved so dearly. She hoped she never had to choose between them.

Kaitlan saw Nate's stallion coming down the river road then. As usual he was keeping the animal at a hard gallop. The August sun shone on his blond head, and her pulse stirred as she thought how very handsome he was. When she married him she would be the luckiest girl in the Cumberlands. She couldn't believe that some girl hadn't already coaxed him into marriage.

As he pulled his horse to a rearing halt, Kaitlan saw a canvas bag strapped to the saddle, and her joy at seeing him faded a bit. His clothes were in the bag, clothes that he would need for his week away from her.

She stood up and ran to him as he swung out of the saddle. He swept her into his arms and held her tight. "I'm going to miss you," he said, the hard ridge of his arousal pressing against her stomach.

"I wish you weren't going," Kaitlan replied. "Don't go, Nate. Let someone else help the man build his barn."

"A man doesn't go back on his word, Kaitlan. Besides, you know why I took the job in the first place."

"I know, but it's not necessary. Money isn't that important. Just marrying you is enough for me."

"It does my heart good to hear you say that,

but I would feel better bringing more than my-self to you."

When Kaitlan would have protested more, he sealed her lips with a long kiss. When he lifted his head he said, "I'm going now. I'll see you next Friday,"

Kaitlan could only nod and watch him ride away. It was going to be a long week.

Less than an hour after leaving Kaitlan, Nate was back at the cave he and Claire shared whenever he could find an excuse to get away from the farm. He unsaddled the stallion and set aside the satchel that wouldn't be opened until he needed clean clothes to change into before returning home.

He found Claire asleep on her back. He stripped off his clothes and, straddling her, plunged inside her before she was fully awake. After he had taken her a second time, he pulled on his clothes and stretched out on the forest floor to take a nap.

Claire came and sat down beside him and, touching his shoulder, said shyly. "I have your babe in my belly, Nate."

"I'm aware of that," Nate said carelessly. "I've known about it for a couple months. Do you think I'm blind?"

"No." Claire giggled. "I just wanted to make sure." After a few seconds of silence passed, she said, "I can't wait until we're married and have our own little family. I'll play with the baby,

182

hug and kiss it. And when it gets older, I'll let it play with the other children in the Gap."

Nate grunted and turned his back on her, saying indifferently, "I can't marry you. I haven't got any money to take you anywhere."

"What about Matt's farm? Me and Aunt Polly would get along fine."

"Are you crazy? Matt would never allow it. You'll have to get rid of the brat."

A silence grew between them. Nate was ready to nod off when Claire spoke. "I know where there is some money," she said.

"You do?" Nate turned over and leaned up on an elbow. Looking at her doubtfully he asked, "Where?"

"Grandpa has a cardboard box full of greenbacks. If you was to get it from him, we could leave the mountain and get married."

"Are you sure the old folks have money stashed away?"

"Yes. I've seen it. The last time I was home Grandpa caught me lookin' at it. He got mad and took the box away. He told Grandma that the money was for my baby. He said he'd have to find a new hidin' place now that I knew where the old one was."

"Do you think you could find it?"

Claire shook her head. "They watch me like a hawk when I'm in the cabin. You'll have to find it."

"I'll think on it." Nate lay back down and turned his back to her. But he wasn't thinking about their conversation. He was thinking it was time to stop coming up the mountain. It was time to start distancing himself from the stupid girl who no doubt was planning their wedding as she sat beside him. If she pointed the finger at him as the father of her baby he would be in big trouble. Everyone at the church social had heard Grandpa Tyler swear that he would shoot the bastard who had ruined his little girl.

# Chapter Fourteen

Her face glum, Kaitlan moped about the cabin, restless, heaving deep sighs. When she plopped down at the table where Hattie was cutting up beef for a stew, the black woman gave her an impatient look.

"Can't you settle down to something, Kaitlan? You're making me nervous with your pacing around. If you can't find anything to do, why don't you go visit someone? A lot of our neighbors have asked you to come and visit them. Maybe a chat with someone will take you out of your doldrums."

Kaitlan doubted that. Nothing could lift her spirits until Nate came home for his weekend visit.

"Why don't you go spend a couple hours with that nice Aunt Polly?"

Kaitlan perked up a bit. She hadn't seen Matt for over a week. He hadn't been around when Nate was home and he hadn't come to see her since Nate had left two days ago. She had missed him. If anyone could lift her spirits, it would be him. He had a way about him that made a person think of nothing but the present.

"That's a good idea, Hattie," she said, standing up.

"Fine." Hattie nodded her approval, thinking to herself she would be rid of the moody girl for a while. She sliced into a piece of meat with a fierce chop of the knife. It was that no-account Nate Streeter who had Kaitlan brooding all over the place.

Kaitlan held her grandfather's stallion to a slow walk on her way to the Ingram farm. It was the dog days of August now, much too hot to make him run.

Nevertheless, not too much time lapsed before she arrived at Matt's home and tied Snowy up in the shade of a large maple just outside the weathered fence. Feeling better already, she walked up the flower-bordered path and knocked on the open door.

Aunt Polly saw her standing there and called out cheerfully, "Come on in, honey."

The pleasant-faced woman was dipping candles in a container of tallow when Kaitlan entered the neat kitchen. "You'll have to forgive me for not stopping this chore right now, Kaitlan, but I have to work fast before the tallow cools. I only have three more to do."

"Go right ahead." Kaitlan sat down at the table to watch how deftly the other woman dipped the candles, then hung them on a little wooden rack to dry. "I'd hate to run out of them too."

"Oh, I'm not about to run out of them. I have plenty stored away. It's just that I like to

186

keep busy. It's doing things that keeps a body content."

"I can never find anything to do," Kaitlan complained. "Hattie does everything."

"Yes, I noticed she's a take-charge woman. But before long you and Nate will be married and you'll be doing all the things Hattie does now."

"That's true." Kaitlan brightened up. "I can't wait to run my own household." She gave a small laugh. "Nate will have to be patient with me for a while when it comes to my cooking, though. The only things I know about a kitchen are how to wash the dishes and sweep the floor."

"I'm sure Hattie will be around to teach you how to cook." Aunt Polly grinned.

"Oh, there's no doubt about that." Kaitlan smiled. "She'll probably want to continue running my house like she always has." When she and Polly laughed about that Kaitlan said, "I don't know if you're aware of it, but Hattie and Nate don't get along at all. I know there's going to be a lot of trouble once we're married."

Aunt Polly didn't voice an opinion on that, and after a while Kaitlan asked, "Where is Matt today?"

"He's down at the tobacco sheds seeing that they are in good condition for harvesttime. Why don't you go on down there and visit with him for a while. Bring him back with you a little later and we'll have some cookies and cold milk."

187

Kaitlan found Matt on the roof of one of the sheds, sweat pouring down his face as he hammered at a new shingle to replace one that had rotted. It was important that once the tobacco was cut and hung up to dry out, it never got wet.

He had removed his shirt and Kaitlan was fascinated by the play of the muscles on his arms and wide back as he brought the hammer up and down. Always before, his shirts had hidden his broad shoulders, his lean waist and flat stomach and narrow hips. She visualized what his long legs would look like minus his pants, and decided that they too would be firm and muscular.

She grew flustered when suddenly she wondered how it would feel to be in Matt's arms, both of them bare to the waist. Would the light pelt of hair on his chest excite her as it rubbed against her breasts the way Nate's did?

Matt called down to her, "How long have you been standing there?"

Kaitlan blushed a fiery red. She had to swallow a couple of times before she lied and said, "I only just got here."

Matt climbed down the ladder that was propped against the wall and reached for the shirt hanging on a nail. When he had shrugged into it, he ran his fingers through his unruly hair, pushing it off his forehead, and then mopped his face with a red handkerchief.

"I haven't seen much of you lately." He

smiled down at her. "Maybe now that Nate is gone for a while we can correct that."

"I like that idea, Matt. I miss Nate and can't wait for him to come home Friday."

"Is that when he's returning to this side of the Gap? He never told me or Aunt Polly."

"He said he'd come back every weekend until the barn was finished. Aunt Polly is waiting for us to come up to the cabin for milk and cookies," she said, changing the subject.

As she started walking away from the sheds, she didn't see the look Matt gave her. He had serious doubts that his stepbrother was helping to build a barn. He was too lazy to do hard labor. It was most likely he was up in that cave with Claire.

"Is he still pressuring you to get married soon?"

"No. He decided that it would be best to wait awhile."

A cynical smile twisted Matt's lips. Like hell he had decided. It had been decided for him. He wished he could ask her if Nate was pestering her to make love, but didn't have the nerve.

Matt fell to watching the gentle sway of Kaitlan's hips as she walked ahead of him. He'd like to take them in his hands and pull them up against his body. When they approached the cabin he stuck his hands in his pockets so the bulge in his trousers wouldn't be noticed.

Aunt Polly had the cookies and milk waiting,

and as they ate the gingersnaps and drank the milk, which was refreshingly cold from sitting in the spring that ran beneath the cabin, Aunt Polly asked what Hattie and she had been doing these days.

"Stringing beans, mostly, and sun-drying tomato slices for the winter. I think she has stored away enough to feed half the families in the Gap," Kaitlan said with a laugh. She changed the subject then. "Aunt Polly, I have noticed that your furniture always looks shiny. How do you keep it that way?"

"There ain't that much to it, honey. I just boil honeycomb for its beeswax and rub it into everything."

"I must remember to do that when I start keeping house."

Matt, not liking to think of Kaitlan keeping house for Nate, changed the subject this time. "Has Peter started topping your tobacco yet?"

"No," Kaitlan answered.

"That has to be done or seed stalks will develop and will rob the plants of energy. I don't imagine he knows about suckers either."

"What are suckers?" Kaitlan looked puzzled.

"They're little tobacco plants that grow alongside the mature stems. If they aren't pinched off they'll also rob the plants of strength."

"Oh boy, I see I'm going to be busy the rest of the summer." Kaitlan made a face. "Are you doing all those things now?"

"Yes. I started a couple weeks ago."

"You've got so many acres to cover." Kaitlan frowned. "Shouldn't Nate be helping you instead of building a barn?"

Matt only shrugged. "I hired the Cooks' two oldest young'uns, Abigail and Edward, to help me."

"That's not right. I'm going to speak to Nate about it," Kaitlan declared.

"No. Don't. Let him do what he wants," Matt said, thinking to himself that he got more work out of twelve- and thirteen-year-olds than he did from his stepbrother. They didn't sneak off the first chance they got.

"All right, I won't say anything to him, but it doesn't seem right that he's not helping you."

Matt and Polly looked at each other, their eyes asking the same question. Was Kaitlan beginning to get a peek into Nate's real character?

Kaitlan helped herself to another cookie. After biting into it, she asked, "How are our neighbors? Is everything well with them?"

"I haven't heard any complaints, so I guess everything is all right with them," Aunt Polly answered. Then she said, "Come to think about it, poor old Grandpa Tyler came by this morning, right after you had gone down to the sheds, Matt, worn out from tramping through the woods lookin' for that granddaughter of his. He said she hasn't been home for weeks and he and his wife are worried sick that something has happened to her. That maybe a panther has got her."

Anger sparked in Matt's eyes. He knew where Claire was but he hesitated to tell. He might be furious with Nate, but he didn't want to get him shot by Grandpa Tyler. He decided he'd go see the elderly couple later today. He would pretend that he had only stopped by for a visit, then casually mention that he had seen Claire on his way to their place. At least they would know that she was still alive.

"Something has to be done about that wild girl," Aunt Polly was saying. "I think she should be put away somewhere. It ain't right the way she acts, chasin' through the woods lookin' for a man. She's been doin' that since she was thirteen. It's a miracle she doesn't have four or five children by now."

"I agree she should be put into some kind of institution, but I don't know where we'd take her."

"There's got to be someplace," Aunt Polly insisted stubbornly. "The next time I go to the Village I'm gonna ask around."

And I'm going to have a serious talk with Nate, Matt thought. He's the reason that simpleminded girl never goes home anymore.

When the clock struck eleven, Kaitlan said that she must get home. "Hattie wants me to go berry-picking with her after lunch."

Matt and Polly walked with her out onto the porch. "Come visit us again, Kaitlan," the plump little woman said, kissing her cheek.

"Bring Hattie with you the next time."

"I'll try, but she's always busy doing something."

Matt walked with Kaitlan to where she had tied Snowy. When he helped her to mount, his hands lingered on her waist. She smiled down at him, then dug her heels into the stallion and cantered away. Matt stared after her, thinking morosely that his touch didn't mean any more to her than Aunt Polly's would.

But he was mistaken in thinking Kaitlan hadn't been aware that his hands stayed on her longer than necessary. She had been hard-put not to show it. She could still feel the warm imprint of his fingers on her waist as she rode up to the cabin. They had relayed his desire and her body had responded. Bewildered at her reaction, she asked herself what kind of woman she was. Was she loose-moraled like that girl Claire who was always looking for a man? Nate's lovemaking was totally satisfying, and yet when Matt held her waist in his hands, for a split second she wished that he would pull her out of the saddle and make love to her right there in the grass.

A disturbing thought niggled at her brain. What if Matt discovered how his touch affected her? What would he think of her? Would their friendship be broken, or at least strained? She would be devastated if he lost his respect for her. She never stopped to consider Nate's reaction.

Matt heard Nate's and Claire's voices as he bypassed their cave. After he visited the Tylers he'd stop there and have his talk with Nate.

Grass was growing on the path that led upward to where the elderly couple lived, proof that few people traveled it. That shouldn't be, he thought. It was true Grandpa was hard of hearing and that trying to hold a conversation with him was trying. But that was no excuse for neglecting them.

Matt made up his mind that he was going to talk with his neighbors and remind them of the old couple living up the mountain.

When the Tyler cabin came into view Matt wondered what made it still stand. Another winter would surely see the roof cave in. The door hung on one hinge and most of the glass was missing from the single window facing him. Grandpa Tyler sat on the porch, which had several boards missing and its roof completely gone. When the old fellow saw him climbing off his horse he removed the corncob pipe from his mouth, his lips spreading in a pleased smile.

"Come on up, Matt; sit a spell," he called, then went to the door and yelled, "Marthie, come out here. Matt Ingram has come visitin'."

The old man and woman were so pathetically pleased to have company, Matt was swamped with guilt again. He vowed to himself that he was going to make it a habit to look in on them more often. Furthermore, he was going to get some of the men to help him chop enough wood to see them through the winter; to fix the roof and tighten the hinges on the door. There was too much glass missing from the window, so it would have to be boarded up in order to keep the winter cold out. Also the neighbors must donate some of the food they'd raised in their gardens so that the old people wouldn't starve this winter.

Matt spent half an hour with the Tylers, bringing them up-to-date with what had been happening with their neighbors. From having to almost shout at them, his voice was hoarse by the time he managed to make them understand that he had seen Claire on his way to their cabin. When he took his leave disappointment was on their wrinkled old faces. Climbing back in the saddle, he muttered angrily that the granddaughter they had raised could make such a difference in their remaining years if only she were like the other young girls in the Gap.

The stallion picked his careful way down the twisting mountain path, and as Matt guided him toward the cave he heard no sound coming from within. It wasn't hard to imagine what was going on inside. He made a lot of noise as he drew nearer and called out Nate's name as he halted the stallion.

A full minute passed before Nate came through the cave's dark opening, buttoning up the fly of his trousers.

"What are you doing up here?" he asked, giving Matt a suspicious look. "Are you spying on me?"

"What are you going to do about Claire?" Matt asked in a low voice. The girl had come outside and sat down on a large rock.

"I'm not going to do anything about her."

"In other words you're going to drop her like you did the other two girls after you got them with child."

"Look," Nate said with a growl, "I'm not taking the blame for her big belly. Half a dozen men in the Gap could have got her that way."

"You're lying, and you know it."

"Prove it."

"It will be proof enough if that baby looks like you."

"It will be too late then," Nate said, sneering. "I'll already be married to Kaitlan."

Controlling the urge to fling himself at Nate and beat his handsome face into a pulp Matt pinned Nate with narrowed eyes and asked, "Will you still go sniffing around after other women when you are married to Kaitlan?"

Giving Matt an insolent smile, Nate shrugged indifferently. "It will depend on how Kaitlan pleases me in bed. If I can teach her to be as good as Claire there, I'll be a good boy and stay home all the time. If she's stingy with her lovemaking, don't give it to me often enough, I'll look elsewhere."

Matt's lips curled in cold contempt. "You

know damn well Kaitlan will never become the kind of slut you like. Most women wouldn't, so what you're really saying is that you have no intention of changing your ways."

"Don't be too quick in judging what Kaitlan can do in bed," Nate said slyly. "There's a lot of fire in her."

Murder looked out of Matt's eyes. "How would you know about that?"

"I don't know from experience." Nate backed off at the threatening look. "I can just tell."

Matt so wanted to smash his fist into Nate's leering face he couldn't speak for a moment. When he had collected himself he said, "Claire's grandparents haven't seen her for weeks and are worried about her. Some of the folks in the Gap are mad as hell about that and are going to see about putting her in some kind of institution."

Dark rage came over Nate's features. "Claire," he barked, "get your ass over here." When Claire came over to stand in front of him, her lips curved in a vacuous smile, he rasped, "Didn't I tell you to go home every time I left you to go back to the Gap for a few days?"

Claire gave a twitch of her shoulders and whined, "I don't like to be around them. They preach at me all the time."

Matt couldn't follow the movement of Nate's hand as it slapped across Claire's mouth. The blow was so hard it knocked her to the ground, and she lay there, her trembling fingers on her bleeding lips. When Nate moved to stand over her she started scooting fearfully away from him, and Matt knew from her action that this wasn't the first time Nate had struck her.

Matt maneuvered his horse between them. "Don't touch her again," he ordered.

"Go on," Nate shouted at her.

"Get your worthless ass up that mountain and spend some time with your folks. If you cause the law to come looking for you, I don't intend to be involved in it."

After giving Nate a hurt look, Claire took off in the direction of her grandparents' cabin.

Matt gave Nate a hard look. "I live in the hope that Kaitlan will discover what your true character is before she marries you."

He nudged Satan with his heel and rode off down the mountain, Nate's jeering laugh following him.

# Chapter Fifteen

Hattie had finally succeeded in nagging Peter to take the cow to visit Matt's bull. Kaitlan, needing a respite from the constant work in the tobacco field, was accompanying him. As Peter led the cow on a rope she walked alongside it. The tinkling bell tied around Bonnie's neck was a soothing sound as her thoughts turned to Nate.

It was Friday and he would be home this afternoon. Her heart beat a little faster, thinking that tonight he would slip into the cabin and make love to her.

At first she had worried that Hattie, or one of the neighbors, might see him entering or leaving the cabin. Sometimes it was near dawn before his desire for her was sated. Evidently, though, Nate had been very careful not to be seen, for no rumors were floating about. And certainly if Hattie knew of his visits, she'd have raised the roof with a tirade of scolding.

When Matt's cabin came in sight Peter brought the cow to a halt and said, "This is as far as you go, Kaitlan."

"Why so?" she was quick to protest.

"You ain't got no business being around when Bonnie is put to the bull."

"For heaven's sake, I don't intend to watch,"

Kaitlan said indignantly.

"I didn't think you did, but sometimes it takes a while before a cow will accept a bull, so you just scoot on home."

"But, Peter —"

"No buts about it, Kaitlan," Peter said in his no-nonsense tone. "You leave me right here."

"Oh, all right." Kaitlan stamped away, retracing her footsteps. However, she didn't feel like going home yet.

She recalled Matt's waterfall. She remembered how to get there and turned to her right. It was the perfect place to relax and dream of Nate.

Kaitlan hadn't walked far when she heard a woman singing. The singer had a beautiful voice and she wondered which of her neighbors could sing like that. She turned her steps in the direction of the song.

She stopped and gaped when she came upon Alice Spencer. Alice was in her early forties but looked much older from having borne ten children in quick succession. She and her two oldest sons were dragging a large fallen tree limb across the forest floor toward a pile of dry, twisted limbs that had already been accumulated.

"Hey, Miss Kaitlan," called one of the children as she approached them. Alice broke off her song and, brushing leaves off her hands, gave Kaitlan a wide, welcoming smile.

"Me and the young'uns was just gonna have

a bite of lunch." She nodded her head toward a tin pail sitting on a stump. "Come eat with us."

Kaitlan was about to refuse, recalling talk she'd heard about the Spencers having hard times. She remembered then how proud the mountain people were and knew that Alice would feel insulted if she didn't partake of their lunch.

"I just ate a large apple," she fibbed, "and I'm not too hungry, but I'd like a bit more to eat."

When Alice took the lid off the lunch pail, the only food inside was five slices of corn pone with honey spread on them. When she had given each of the four children a share, she broke the remaining piece in half and handed it to Kaitlan.

"Oh, goodness, I couldn't eat this much, Alice," she exclaimed, breaking her half into another half and handing it back to Alice. "Like I said, the apple pretty much filled me up."

As everyone settled down to eat the meager meal, Kaitlan looked at the wind-break Alice and her children had been working on.

"Where's Elam?" she asked.

"I guess he's down at the Village passin' time with his friends. That's where he mostly is."

"Shouldn't he be helping you and the children gather wood? Those tree limbs look much too heavy for the five of you to handle."

"Yes, he should." Alice sighed. "But Elam is a dreamer. He never seems to see what needs to be done."

"A dreamer, ha!" The oldest boy snorted. "He's lazy, that's what he is."

"Johnny Spencer, you hesh up," Alice ordered sharply. "Women do more thinkin' ahead than men do. Your pa would have gotten around to rememberin' that it was time to start choppin' wood for the winter," she defended her husband.

"Yeah, and then he'd cut down young trees." Johnny's lips curled in disapproval. He looked at Kaitlan and added, "Green wood in a fireplace is dangerous. It don't give off much heat, what with the sap runnin' and puttin' out most of the flames. And it could set a place on fire the way it pops out live sparks."

"Why would your father use that kind of wood if it's so dangerous?"

"Cause it's easier to walk a few steps and cut down a tree than hunt through the forest for deadwood."

"Now, Johnny, I ain't gonna tell you again to hesh up." Alice glared at her son.

When young Spencer went stamping over to the fallen tree and started chopping a large limb, Alice sighed and said, "He just don't understand how his pa is different from most men. He never seems to see how kind Elam is to all of us, never a cross word out of his mouth. He's never once lifted a hand to any of the young'uns."

Kaitlan had the same opinion about Alice's husband as her son had. The man was probably too lazy to lift a hand against his children.

"Do we have bad winters here?" Kaitlan asked to get off the subject of Alice's husband.

"Sometimes we do. Had us a blizzard last winter. The young'uns sleep up in the loft under the shingle roof and lots of mornin's when they woke up, snow had sifted on top of them while they slept."

As Alice finished the last of her pone Kaitlan asked, "How have you been passing the summer?"

"The usual. Tendin' the garden and corn-fields, puttin' up food for the winter. It takes a lot of vittles to feed this brood of mine. In be-tween that I've been preparin' wool for cardin' and spinnin'."

"How do you do that?" Kaitlan was curious.

"Ain't much to it. You wash it in warm water with lye soap. When it's nice and clean you dry it in the sun, then put it away for later use. I spin in the winter when there ain't nothin' else to do."

"I didn't know you raised sheep."

"We only have a few. Just for our own use. We had a couple black ones this year for which I was grateful. I need to knit some socks and sweaters and the wool won't have to be dyed." Alice smiled at Kaitlan and asked, "What have you been doin' this summer?"

"Like you said, the usual things that need to be done on a farm. Mostly I've been helping Peter with the tobacco. I'll be glad when it's cut and hanging in the barn to dry."

"That won't be long off. Latter part of this month it's ripe enough to be cut."

"Do you raise any tobacco?"

Alice shook her head. "Elam always says that he's gonna raise some, but he never seems to get around to it."

Kaitlan could believe that. Raising tobacco took a lot of hard work.

"I've enjoyed visiting with you, Alice," Kaitlan said as she slid off the rock she'd been sitting on, "but it's time I was getting home. Hattie plans on starting a batch of pickled cabbage today. She has a gunnysack full of cabbages waiting to be sliced up."

Alice grinned. "Your cellar is gonna smell somethin' awful for a while."

"So we've been told." Kaitlan grinned also. "But it will taste good this winter cooked up with some smoked sausage." After Alice agreed that it would, Kaitlan called good-bye to the children, who had joined their brother, then took leave of Alice.

A night breeze puffed at the drapes as Kaitlan lay in bed waiting for Nate to come to her. It was a hot, sultry night and she was naked. If she hadn't been expecting him she wouldn't have closed the window coverings that prevented any trace of breeze from reaching her. She would most likely be sleeping on a pallet in front of the kitchen door. Wearing a nightgown, of course.

She hadn't known that Nate had returned to the Gap until near twilight. Her spirits had been low, but they lifted when at the supper table Peter said, "I saw that Nate person riding toward the Ingram farm when I was putting the mules in the barn."

It had been too late to take a bath in the river, but she had taken a thorough sponge bath. The scent of roses was still on her skin.

Kaitlan didn't have to wait long before she heard the soft, familiar sounds of someone feeling his way through the darkness. She listened to the rustle of clothes being removed and held her breath as she waited for Nate to join her.

She felt the mattress give as his weight came down on it; then a moment later she was being drawn into his hungry arms. Her heartbeat increased and her pulse raced as their bodies seemed to fuse together. His lightly furred chest rubbed against her sensitive breasts, her nipples puckering into hard little nubs. And if that weren't enough to set her on fire, his long, thick arousal throbbed against her stomach.

They wanted each other so badly, little time passed before her legs were being nudged apart and her impatient lover was positioning himself between them. She moaned his name as he plunged himself inside her.

It took but two long drives of his hips and his body was shuddering its release. She felt the warmth of his spent desire flow inside her and smiled. This was the first time he hadn't spilled his seed onto the bedcovers. His desire for her had been so strong he had forgotten that usual precaution.

That thought, and everything else, was driven from her mind as her hips were lifted and held. Then his large manhood was stroking in and out of her, creating a frenzy of desire.

However, every time she was about to reach that peak of total satisfaction, the narrow hips stopped pumping against her. Then hot lips began to suckle her breasts, first one and then the other until she was squirming and begging him to put her out of her pain.

Twice more she was teased before finally his hips moved faster, his engorged shaft plunged deeper into her. Together, their bodies tensed and they exploded in a burst of sensation that left them weak with its force.

Completely spent, they both napped for a while, regaining their strength. Then, rejuvenated, Kaitlan took the lead. She climbed on top, whispering, "I'll do the work this time, Nate darling."

She reached between their damp bodies, found his stiff rod, and slowly slipped it inside her. When she leaned forward and started to ride him, he raised himself up on his elbows so that his lips could suckle her breasts as she moved up and down on him. I can't bear it, Kaitlan thought. The stimulating pull on her breasts and the slide of her sheath sucking on his hardness was making her weak.

But her partner seemed to sense her dilemma and his hands grasped her hips and moved them up and down; all the while his mouth was tugging at her nipples, making her complete the joy that awaited them.

When that joyful release came, Kaitlan sobbed her relief on his broad chest.

When Kaitlan regained her composure and would have removed herself from that male part that had given her sublime pleasure, he held her fast. She wasn't sure she could bear going through that storm again, but once hot lips closed over a swollen nipple she found herself responding as before.

After a rest of a few minutes he lifted her up and laid her down on her back. Then he made slow, tender love to her. This time her release was sweet and relaxing, and as usual, she was in an exhausted sleep when her lover's careful footsteps left the cabin.

Late the next morning when Kaitlan awakened, her breasts tender and her nipples swollen, she worried that her cries and Nate's groans had carried all the way to the little house where Hattie and Peter lived.

A surprisingly cool breeze blew through Kaitlan's window, and a soft smile curved her lips. Nate had opened the heavy window coverings before leaving her last night. The room had been stiflingly hot as they made love.

She forced her tired body off the bed and again gave herself a careful sponge bath before entering the kitchen. Hattie looked up from the big pan into which she was slicing cabbage, and Kaitlan relaxed when she smiled and said, "Good morning sleepyhead. Your breakfast is keeping warm on the hearth."

Kaitlan had a voracious appetite, and Hattie didn't interrupt her until she had wolfed down half the bacon and eggs.

"Nate was here before," Hattie announced. "When I told him you were still sleeping he said he'd be back in about an hour."

"Hattie! You should have wakened me."

Hattie gave a small twitch of one shoulder. "I figured that if you were still in bed you needed more sleep."

It was a lame excuse and both of them knew it, but Kaitlan let it pass. She had yet to win an argument with the black woman. So she hurriedly finished her breakfast, washed her plate and fork, then went to her room and made up the bed, which took a while since the sheets were all twisted and rumpled from two bodies rolling around in them.

When she had put on a fresh dress and brushed the tangles out of her hair, she went outside and sat on the porch, waiting for Nate. She hadn't expected to see him until much later today, so it was a pleasant surprise that he wanted to see her so soon after last night.

When she saw his stallion galloping toward the cabin, she rose and stepped off the porch just as Nate pulled the animal to its usual rearing halt. He looks as tired as I feel, she thought in amusement as he swung from the saddle and she saw the dark smudges under his eyes.

"How are you this morning, Kaitlan?" he asked, smiling at her.

"I feel just fine, Nate." She smiled back and tilted her head for his kiss. After a cautious look at the cabin, he gave her a quick peck on the cheek.

"Now what kind of kiss was that?" she teased. "That's the kind of kiss I get from Hattie."

"And because of her, that's the kind of kiss I just gave you," Nate grumbled. "I can feel the old witch watching us. Let's go sit under that oak over there." He nodded his head in the direction of a gnarled tree that was reputed to be over a hundred years old. When they had settled themselves beneath its large branches Kaitlan waited to be kissed properly. Nate, however, made no move to take her in his arms, only sat in stormy silence.

"What's wrong, Nate?" Kaitlan finally questioned. "Something seems to be bothering you."

"It's that damn black bitch that's bothering me. Can't you see she runs your life?"

"That's not true." Kaitlan's voice was sharp. "She's a bit bossy, I admit, but I do as I please if it's important to me. I do listen to her advice a lot because she's very wise."

"Get used to not taking her advice." Nate looked angrily toward the cabin. "Once we're married she's not going to be around to give you orders."

"What are you talking about? Even though she won't be telling me what to do once I'm your wife, she'll still be around."

"No, she won't. The day we tie the knot, she and that henpecked husband of hers are getting off this farm."

Shocked speechless, Kaitlan could only stare for a moment at the man she planned to marry. After a while she said, "I could never ask them to leave."

"You won't have to. I'll tell them to get the hell out." Nate's tone said that he'd enjoy ordering them off the land that would soon be his.

Kaitlan couldn't believe what Nate was saying. How could he be so cruel? Her disillusionment made it easier for her to say, "You can't order them to leave. They own half the farm."

"Ha!" Nate snorted contemptuously. "You might have told them that, but I can untell them."

Kaitlan shook her head in denial. "You can't. It's all legal. It's on the deed. We went to the land office in the Village and had the papers drawn up. Hattie and Peter are equal partners with me."

She thought that Nate was going to strike her, his face was so contorted with rage. When she ventured to lay a hand on his arm, to assure him the black couple wouldn't interfere with their lives, he struck it aside and jumped to his feet. Glaring down at her he ground out, "For all your beauty, you're only an empty-headed fool. I would never tie myself to a feather-headed, harebrained female like you. You've seen the last of me, Kaitlan Barrett," he ground out and stamped away.

Kaitlan wished for a minute that he had struck her. It couldn't have hurt more than his scornful words. She had acted the wanton with him last night, giving herself up to him completely, and it hadn't meant a thing to him. If he truly loved her, he wouldn't demand that she turn out the couple who were like parents to her.

She bent her knees and, laying her head on them, sobbed brokenheartedly.

# Chapter Sixteen

Nate's stallion was flecked with foam and blood from the many whiplashes on its magnificent body. As usual, when there was no one else around Nate took his rage out on the animal.

There was a demented look in his eyes as he stretched over the horse's neck. In just ten short minutes a dream had been shattered: his big plans of owning a farm and marrying the most beautiful girl the Gap had ever seen. Having to share the small farm with the black couple, he'd be no better off than any of his other dirt-grubbing neighbors, and he aspired to something better.

He thought of his stepbrother and the large farm he had inherited from his father and the whip came down more sharply on the helpless animal.

The stallion was wild-eyed and heaving when the cave and Claire came in view. Claire jumped from the log she'd been sitting on and ran to meet Nate as he brought the horse to a cruel halt, the bit cutting into its tender mouth.

There were no fond embraces, no welcoming kisses exchanged as they met on the gravel-strewn ground. There was only the flurry of Nate's impatient hands as he tore off her clothes. When Claire lay beneath him, Nate took out the rest of his rage by plunging himself in and out of her.

When Nate finished with her, his rage spent, he was able to think more logically. He heaved himself off her, pulled up his trousers, and sat down on the log Claire had left in such a hurry. When she came and sat down beside him, he ignored her. He was preoccupied with questions of what course he should take now to satisfy his driving need to someday have more than Matt Ingram had.

His body relaxed suddenly and a wide smile brightened his face. It had just come to him where he could find money to make a fresh start. To hell with them all down at the Gap. He didn't need any of them.

Kaitlan cried until her eyes were swollen and her face was blotched. She wiped her eyes and wet face on the hem of her skirt when her inner voice scolded, "Why do you waste tears on a man who is not worthy of your love? Ask yourself these questions. Has he ever really acted like he is courting you? Has he ever escorted you to a social, to church on Sunday? Taken you on a picnic, canoeing on the river, done all those things that other courting couples do? Have you ever spent more than half an hour with him at a time? Isn't he always in a hurry, with an excuse that he has to be somewhere else? Does any of that say he loves you?

"Admit it, you foolish girl, it was your farm

he was in love with.

"But what about —" Kaitlan stopped short. Not even to her inner voice was she going to speak about the long nights of lovemaking. Those hours had meant nothing to Nate. What she had given him, he could have gotten from any number of women.

Feeling like the world's biggest fool, used and tossed aside, Kaitlan lifted her head and vowed that never again would she lay herself open to such pain and shame. If ever she should love again, she would be sure of the man's character first.

She lingered a while longer under the tree, hoping that the traces of tears would vanish and that Hattie wouldn't know she had been crying.

But she had cried too hard, felt her shame and heartbreak too deeply to keep eagle-eyed Hattie from seeing its aftermath. As soon as she stepped inside the cabin Hattie demanded, "What's wrong, child? Why have you been crying? What did that devil say or do to you?"

Kaitlan averted her face as she choked back the lump in her throat and blinked away fresh tears. "Nate has decided he doesn't want to marry me," she managed to blurt out.

"*He* has decided that he doesn't want to marry *you!* What brought on that miracle?"

Not for the world would Kaitlan tell Hattie the real reason for her and Nate's breakup. As much as the black woman despised and mistrusted Nate, she would nevertheless insist that her and Peter's names be stricken from the deed. So Kaitlan shrugged and answered, "He claims he's not ready yet to settle down to marriage."

"Whatever the reason, thank you, dear God, for answering my prayers." Hattie looked upward.

"Now, child," she said, turning her attention back to Kaitlan, "count your blessings and bathe your face in cold water, then do whatever it pleases you the rest of the day. You can lie around, or find something to do. Everybody has their own way of coming to terms with hurt and disappointment."

After showing the two Spencer children where he wanted them to work that day, Matt walked toward the cabin to have a midmorning cup of coffee. Halfway there he stopped, as he often did, to look across the distance to the Barrett farm. He was sometimes able to catch a glimpse of Kaitlan as she worked in the garden or fussed with the flower beds she was raising from the seeds Aunt Polly had given her.

He narrowed his eyes against the sun when he saw Nate's stallion streak away from the farm. Even at this distance he could tell that his stepbrother was in a rage from the way he was laying the whip on the horse.

Anger sparked Matt's eyes at his stepbrother's cruelty. Nate must have had a run-in with sharp-tongued Hattie. He decided that after he had his coffee, he'd ride over to Kaitlan's and find out what had riled the mangy dog so. He wasn't surprised to see Nate take the fork that led to the cave a mile or so from the Tyler place. He would soothe his anger with Claire for a few hours.

Matt had almost reached the Barrett farm when he saw Kaitlan riding toward him. Her face looks strained, he thought, when they met on the trail. "Are you on your way to visit me and Aunt Polly?" he asked, smiling at her.

"No, I wasn't." Kaitlan smiled back. "I'm on my way to your favorite waterfall."

"Do you want company, or would you rather be alone?"

Kaitlan hesitated a moment, then answered, "I think I need your company."

"Lead on then; I'll gladly lend you my company."

His gaze never left Kaitlan's small rear as it moved with the horse's gait. It wasn't long before he became very uncomfortable. He was thankful that Kaitlan had eyes only for the waterfall when they arrived there and dismounted. Had she looked at him, his feelings for her would have been impossible to deny.

Kaitlan stood and looked in awe at the lacy waters tumbling down the mountainside, landing with a musical splash on stones that were polished to smooth perfection over the years.

Finally she sensed that Matt stood beside her, and, looking up at him, she said, "I could look at this all day. Wouldn't it be wonderful to have a home up here so that you could look at it every day? It soothes a person, promises that something wonderful lies ahead."

Matt took her arm, led her to a moss-covered rock, and guided her down on it. Sitting down beside her he said, "We can watch the waterfall from here while you tell me what is troubling you."

"What makes you think something is troubling me?" Kaitlan gave him a startled look.

"I know all your moods by now, Kaitlan. Has it anything to do with Nate? I saw him riding away from your place earlier. I knew he was mad as a disturbed hornet's nest the way he was riding."

"You're right. My mood does have to do with him. He flew into a rage when I told him I had deeded half the farm to Hattie and Peter, and that I have no intention of changing it."

"I didn't know you had done that."

"Nobody knows but the man in the land office, and he promised not to tell anyone. The Smiths want it that way."

"That was a thoughtful thing for you to do. Lucky for Hattie and Peter too. Nate had plans that as soon as he got a ring on your finger he was going to kick them off the farm."

"Why didn't you tell me that?"

"And take a chance of losing your friendship?

You know the story about the bearer of bad news. And I wasn't sure you would believe me. Would you have?"

Kaitlan looked into his hard, chiseled features, his gray eyes, and wasn't sure if she would have or not. Had he told her before Nate made love to her, she felt sure that she would have believed him. But after those night hours spent with Nate, when she felt with all her heart that he loved her, she probably would have thought Matt was lying to her.

Since she couldn't explain all this to him, she answered, "I truly don't know. However, I'm sure I would have questioned Nate about it. Whether or not I would have credited his denial, which I'm sure now he would have uttered, I'm not sure."

Matt laid a comforting arm across her shoulders. "Do you think Nate will be back when he has cooled down?"

"I don't want him back. He called me an empty-headed fool, a featherheaded and hare-brained female."

"That was anger talking. I'm sure he didn't mean it."

"Hattie says that the truth comes out when a person is angry."

Matt's eyes gleamed. "I always heard that the truth comes out when a person is drunk."

"Well, whichever way it is" — Kaitlan half laughed — "Nate meant every word he said, and his words cut deep. If I married him I'd always be afraid of doing or saying the wrong thing and his ridiculing me for it."

Nate would do that, Matt thought angrily, not that he'd have cause to ridicule Kaitlan, but putting her in a bad light would make him feel superior, even though he knew that she was far above him in all ways.

"There are several nice young men in the Gap who would love to court you with marriage on their minds." Matt gave Kaitlan's shoulder a squeeze. "And they wouldn't mind sharing the farm with Hattie and Peter. Just having you for a wife would be enough for them."

Kaitlan stared unseeingly at the waterfall tumbling down the mountain. She was so ashamed that she had given in to Nate's lovemaking, had enjoyed it so. Worse yet, she was more ashamed that Matt might find out about it.

"What are you thinking now?" Matt gave one of her curls a playful tug.

"I was thinking that it will be a long time before I'll be interested in a man again. I may just become an old maid like Granny Higgins. I'll wander over the mountains, gathering bark and digging up roots."

Matt threw his head back and gave a throaty laugh. "I can just see you doing that. First of all, you're afraid of panthers and bears. How would you gather your herbs and dig your roots?"

Kaitlan had to laugh too. She wouldn't make a very good herb medicine woman. "At any rate," she said, "I'm in no hurry to meet any young men, so don't go pushing any of them at me."

"I guess I should be getting home," Kaitlan said after Matt promised he wouldn't push any young men at her. "I've been gone from home quite a while and Hattie will begin worrying about me."

Matt walked Kaitlan to her horse and, putting his hands on her waist, easily lifted her up and set her in the saddle. She looked down into his dark gray eyes and thought sadly, If only you had come courting me first.

When they had ridden to the place where the path split three different ways, and Kaitlan turned her horse in the direction of the Barrett farm, Matt said, "I hope you don't mope around too much. Nate is not worth it."

"I don't intend to mope at all. But I'll probably give myself a good tongue-lashing more than once for being fool enough to think that Nate ever loved me."

Matt watched her ride out of sight, praying that if Nate changed his mind and wanted her back, she'd have nothing to do with him. For he, Matt Ingram, fully intended to start courting Miss Kaitlan Barrett.

Matt started to take the path home, then decided he'd ride up to the cave and see if he could learn what Nate planned to do now. Did he really mean the words he had lashed out at her, or had he said them in hopes of scaring her into taking back what she had deeded to the Smiths? He was capable of doing that.

He found Nate sitting alone in front of the cave. His stepbrother's features were relaxed, showing none of the rage that had consumed him when he raced away from the Barrett farm. He was almost pleasant when he greeted Matt.

"You're making quite a habit of coming up here," he said. "What brings you calling this time?"

"I just left Kaitlan. She tells me that you don't want to marry her after all. That can't be true, can it?"

"The hell it can't. Did she tell you why?"

"She said something about you getting mad about the Smiths owning half of her farm."

"You're damn well right it made me mad. I'm not going to marry a featherhead who would give away half her property to a couple negroes and expect me to be partners with them."

"I don't see why not," Matt said in order to draw him out. "The farm consists mostly of bottomland, good rich soil. Peter is a hard worker, and even sharing with him and Hattie, you could make a nice living."

"I don't intend to spend the rest of my life making a *nice living*." A virulent gleam shot into Nate's eyes. "You'd like that, though, wouldn't you? Seeing me grubbing out a living like a slave."

"So you're not planning to make peace with Kaitlan?" Matt asked, secretly delighted.

"I have no intention of crawling back to that one. I have other plans. I'm clearing out of these mountains."

"Are you taking Claire with you?"

"That slut? Hell no."

"By the way, where is she?"

"I sent her to look in on her grandparents. I don't need the law to come nosing around before I can get out of here. Pass the word around that she is taking care of the old folks, will you?"

Matt nodded and gathered up the reins. "In your mother's memory, Nate, I wish you good luck. She was a fine woman." He nudged the stallion with his heel and sent the animal down the rocky, twisting path. He could feel Nate's hatred boring into his back, and wondered what kind of plan he had hatched up in his evil mind.

One afternoon several weeks later, Hattie said to Kaitlan as she finished ironing the last piece of clothing in the laundry basket, "Let's go visit Grandma and Grandpa Tyler and take them some stuff from our garden."

Ever since Nate had left, Kaitlan had kept as busy as possible to take her mind off her hurt and humiliation, so she readily agreed. "We can bring them a loaf of your bread and one of the pies you baked yesterday. Matt said that he's not sure they're getting enough to eat."

"It's a shame how that granddaughter of theirs neglects them," Hattie said, wiping off the irons and storing them in the bottom of a cupboard.

Forty-five minutes later, after leaving a note for Peter on the kitchen table, Hattie and Kaitlan set out, each carrying a basket filled with fresh vegetables, a loaf of bread, and a blackberry pie.

It was a pleasant day; the heat of summer was giving way to the coolness of September. A light breeze lifted Kaitlan's curls off her forehead and flipped the corners of Hattie's white apron.

"The leaves will start changing color soon," Kaitlan said, walking ahead of Hattie on the narrow, twisting path that led upward through the trees.

Hattie nodded, remembering Lish Jones's predication yesterday. He had shaken his head and said dolefully, "I heard the first katydid holler last night. It's just six weeks till frost."

She had said to him, "You sound sad about that."

He had answered, "Snow will soon follow after, and freezing weather. My old bones won't like that."

Hattie was beginning to puff a little when Matt overtook them, astride his black stallion. "Where are you ladies off to?" His smile included them both as he swung down from the saddle.

"Carry our baskets," Hattie commanded, pushing hers at him. "We're taking some food up to the Tylers."

"They'll appreciate that," Matt said, taking Kaitlan's basket from her. "I don't think they've been eating properly for a long time."

"Now that we know of their plight, it's up to us neighbors to take care of that." Hattie nudged Kaitlan to start forward again.

Walking behind the black woman, with Satan following him, Matt grinned in amusement. Hattie Smith was a no-nonsense, take-charge woman if ever he had seen one. He glanced at Kaitlan, who was stepping gracefully along, and thought how surprising it was that none of Hattie's dictatorial ways had rubbed off on her through the years.

She did have some of Hattie's more admirable traits. She was always willing to help others. She was a hard worker and very honest. It was still a mystery to him that such a level-headed girl could have fallen in love with a man completely her opposite. He wondered if she still loved Nate despite the hurt he had given her. He hoped with all his being that she didn't.

They rounded a bend in the path, and the old Tyler cabin stood in front of them. There was something forbidding about the run-down building, and Kaitlan and Hattie stayed close to Matt as they approached it.

"That's strange," he said, concern in his voice. "By now Grandpa Tyler should be coming through the door to greet us."

Matt stepped up on the rotting porch, but Kaitlan and Hattie hung back now. They were reluctant to step inside the dark cabin.

"Grandpa, Grandma Tyler, are you home? It's Matt Ingram and two of your neighbors come to visit you," Matt called out from just inside the door.

The eerie silence was suddenly broken by a wild-eyed Claire bursting into the clearing behind them. "Oh, Matt," she said, panting. "Thank God you are here. Something terrible has happened to Grandma and Grandpa."

"Calm down, Claire." Matt took the frantic girl by the arm. "What has happened to the old folks? Where are they?"

"In the bedroom." Claire pointed a shaking finger. "They . . . they're dead."

Matt rushed toward the bedroom, Kaitlan and Hattie at his heels now. Inside the room he stopped abruptly, and Kaitlan and Hattie gasped and cried out in horror.

On a bed of tumbled covers lay the old man and old woman, dead from multiple stab wounds. Their twisted features told of a painful death.

"Who would do such a thing to these nice, harmless people?" Kaitlan asked, tears brimming in her eyes.

Matt could only shake his head as he picked up a cardboard box lying beside the bed.

"That's the box Grandpa kept his money in,"

Claire cried. Matt jerked his head up to stare at the girl. Watching her closely, he asked, "How many people knew he had money? I always thought the old folks were poor as could be."

"Just us three," Claire answered; then after a slight pause, she added, "I told Nate about it. The money was for our young'un."

Matt and Hattie looked at each other, suspicion in both their eyes. "Where is Nate, Claire?" Matt asked quietly.

"I don't know. I just come from looking for him. We were at the cave last night, but when I woke up, he was gone. I come home and found my folks. . . . Oh God! I didn't know what to do. I just wanted Nate, so I run looking all over the mountain, but he ain't there."

"Do we have any law enforcement to notify, Matt?" Hattie asked.

"We'd have to go all the way to Nashville to report it," Matt answered. "Anyway, we always handle our own affairs up here. Bad deeds have a way of being found out and the guilty party punished. Nate will pay for this horrendous deed."

"What are you saying, Matt?" Kaitlan exclaimed, aghast. "Surely Nate wouldn't —"

"I'm afraid he would, Kaitlan." Matt looked at her white face. "He told me he was leaving the Gap, that he had no intention of marrying Claire even if she was carrying his baby. He would need money when he left. What easier way to get it than to steal it from the old

226

people? Even if it meant murdering them."

With a small cry, Claire stumbled to a chair and sat down, tears running down her cheeks. "No, it can't be true!" Kaitlan gasped. She covered her mouth and ran outside to vomit. As she lost her breakfast, she loathed herself for letting Nate make love to her.

When Matt saw Claire wiping her eyes, he asked softly, "Do you feel like tolling the church bell, Claire, to let your neighbors know that your grandparents are dead?"

When she nodded and started to walk outside, he called after her, "Make sure you ring it seventy-two times, so everybody will know where to come."

When Hattie looked questioningly at Matt, he explained, "Both the Tylers are seventy-two years old. The oldest couple in the Gap. The neighbors will know who died by how many times the bell tolls. Of course they won't know that both of the old people are gone."

"And after you do that, what then?"

"Everybody will come here. People travel great distances to attend wakes. They'll help dig and fill the graves, make the coffins, wash and dress the bodies."

Once she recovered from the shock of finding the dead couple, Hattie took over running things. "Kaitlan," she said, "let's try to straighten up the place a little before the neighbors get here. I'm sure Grandma Tyler wouldn't want them to see her home in such a state. Matt, you go build a fire under the wash pot outside and fill it with water to heat."

Kaitlan, following Hattie's orders in a daze, found a meager stack of linens on a shelf. She took a yellowed sheet off the pile and helped Hattie spread it over the Tylers.

During all the hurrying about, the bell sent out its mournful message to the people. When Kaitlan and Hattie finished setting the house to rights, Kaitlan went outside and leaned against a tree. She looked up at the sky, which was fast clouding over. It's going to rain, she thought, trying to fix her mind on anything other than Matt's shocking words about Nate and Claire, the two old people, and the tolling of the bell.

# Chapter Seventeen

Matt had left Kaitlan and Hattie to look for Nate. He'd found Nate's stallion and some of his clothes missing from the farm. After finding the cave empty, he scoured the nearby area, calling Nate's name loudly. "He's left the Gap," he thought out loud. "I thought as much when I found the stallion gone."

With a resigned sigh he turned Satan in the direction of the Tylers' home. It's going to rain any minute anyhow, he thought.

When he rode up to the old cabin, the yard was crowded with wagons, while horses and mules were tied up in the woods. The wagons told him that whole families had come to pay homage to the old people.

Matt climbed out of the saddle and tied Satan some distance from the other horses. If there was another stallion tied up with the other horses Satan would want to fight him. As he walked toward the cabin, he wondered why the rotting porch hadn't collapsed from the weight of all the people. At least fifteen men stood on it, talking in quiet voices.

When he had returned the greetings called out to him, Matt took a seat on a stump, far enough away so that if the roof fell in, he'd be out of harm's way. He saw Lish step off the porch and walk toward him.

"Hattie told me you've been looking for Nate. I can see by your face that you didn't find him," Lish said, sitting down on a rock.

Matt shook his head. "He's probably in Nashville by now."

"How in the hell could that numbskull make a livin' there?"

Matt gave a short, hard laugh. "He's got the old people's money, remember? When he runs through that, he's slick enough to figure out a way to make money."

"Do you intend to go there and try to find him?"

Steel determination blazed in Matt's eyes. "As soon as the funeral is over, I'm riding to Nashville. If Nate's there I'll find him."

Both men turned around when Kaitlan spoke behind them. "Matt?" she said hesitantly. "Did you find him?"

Shaking his head, Matt scanned Kaitlan's face. She looks ready to drop, he thought. "Where were you just now?" he asked.

"Back behind the building at the burn-pile. I was burning the old people's bedding. Hattie said that it was all so dirty it could never be washed clean again. They've laid the bodies out on Claire's bed. It's in surprisingly good shape."

"Ha!" Lish snorted. "It should be. It ain't hardly been slept in since Claire was thirteen, or there about."

Lish opened his mouth to add something more, but before he could speak, the rain was upon them. Since the porch roof leaked like a sieve, the men jumped off it and ran toward the shelter of the heavy woods a few yards away. When Kaitlan would have dashed to the cabin, Matt grabbed her arm.

"You'll be better off with me and Lish under a tree. From what I can see through the door and window, the cabin is packed tight with women and children and it's going to be hot in there."

They ran behind Lish until they reached the fringe of the forest. Matt paused there long enough to unsaddle Satan and grab the blanket off his back, then struck out after Lish and Kaitlan.

Lish led them deep into the woods, stopping finally when he came to a large pine whose bottom branches swept the ground. "We'll hardly get damp under here," he said, dropping down on all fours. "I took shelter under this tree a couple years ago when I got caught out in the rain."

When Kaitlan and Matt had crawled behind Lish onto the dry ground beneath the tree, Matt spread the blanket out, bringing it up close to the trunk. As Lish had promised, no rain penetrated the heavy foliage. But cold air had come along with the rain and it was finding its way under their shelter. When Matt took Kaitlan's arm and eased her down on the blanket where she could rest her back against the trunk, she was shivering. He sat down close beside her. Lish noticed Kaitlan's condition and sat down on the other side of her.

Within ten minutes the men's body heat had warmed Kaitlan, and her teeth had stopped chattering. The shock and horror of the day slipped from her mind. She grew drowsy and her head dropped. Almost immediately she was asleep.

Lish gave Matt a sly grin when he eased Kaitlan's head to rest on his shoulder. "She was going to get a crick in her neck in that position," Matt said self-consciously.

"Yeah." Lish grunted and turned his head so that Matt couldn't see his wide grin.

Matt, however, knew the old man too well. Lish didn't believe his explanation and was amused by it. *I don't care how entertaining it is to the old devil to see Kaitlan sleeping on my shoulder. I'm not giving up the chance of having her there,* he thought.

In her sleep Kaitlan nestled closer and closer into Matt's warmth, and before long her head had slipped between his shoulder and chin, her slightly parted lips only inches from his, her breast pressing against his arm. *Oh, Lord.* Matt squeezed his eyes shut as he grew large and hard. *What am I going to do now? If Lish looks over here and sees my state, I'll never hear the end of his teasing.*

He tried to put his mind on other things. . . .

Would the recently dug grave fill up with water, or maybe cave in and have to be dug all over again? Would it still be raining tomorrow when they laid the old people to rest? And where was that mangy cur, Nate?

Nothing worked. Kaitlan seemed to draw closer to him, and he seemed to grow larger and harder. He gave Lish a sideways look and sighed softly when he saw that his old friend's eyes were closed. Maybe he was having a nap too. He looked down at the blanket then and saw the solution to his predicament. One corner of the blanket was large enough to pull up and lay across his lap.

With that done, he relaxed and enjoyed the feel of Kaitlan's soft body to the fullest. Before he knew it, he too was asleep, dreaming that he was making love to her. He was on the verge of reaching a climax when Lish shook him awake.

"It's stopped rainin'," Lish said. "I hear the men leavin' the woods."

Kaitlan came awake at the sound of Lish's voice, and straightened up. Pushing the curls off her forehead and freeing one that had caught on her lips, she gave Matt a sleepy smile that made him want to groan. "I guess I dozed off," she said.

"Dozed off, ha!" Lish snorted. "You slept for almost two hours." A mischievous glint glimmered in his eyes. "I would have liked to sleep too, but your snorin' was too loud."

"I was not snoring!" Kaitlan jabbed Lish in

his skinny ribs. She turned to Matt. "Was I snoring?"

Matt smiled at her, half amused, half indulgent. "What kept Lish awake was his own snoring."

"Is that right?" Lish retorted. Then giving Matt a sly look, he asked, "What kept you awake?"

"I slept," Matt answered, helping Kaitlan to her feet and then quickly grabbing up the blanket to hold in front of him.

"I'm not all too sure about that." Lish grunted and groaned as he heaved his stiff bones up straight.

"Have it your own way," Matt said as he held up the wet branches for Kaitlan to crawl under.

An early dusk had set in because of the rain. Dark clouds hovered in the sky, threatening that they were not yet finished visiting water on the land and its people.

Candles had been lit in the two rooms and shed an unearthly, wavering light on everything when Kaitlan stepped into the Tylers' cabin. All available seats had been taken, and the rest of the women sat on the hearth or floor. The only space big enough for her to sit was beside Maybelle Scott. Kaitlan had no desire to talk to the sour spinster. While she was wondering if she should just lean against the wall, Miss Scott smiled at her and patted the space beside her.

After Kaitlan settled down beside her, Maybelle kept such a friendly conversation going, Kaitlan couldn't help wondering at the woman's changed demeanor. She noticed that the other women were giving Maybelle curious looks and she wondered if they, too, were surprised at the softer side she was showing.

Later, the men and children would go to the barn, where the adults would pass a jug of whiskey around and the young ones would fall asleep on a pile of hay.

Each wife had brought a dish, and before long everyone's appetite was sated. Matt thought to himself that the old couple lying in the other room hadn't had that much food in their home for a couple of years. He said to Peter now, "Hattie looks exhausted and Kaitlan is weary to the bone. Take them home. Don't let Hattie say no to you."

"I'll do it, Matt. I know when to be firm with that woman."

And so he was. Fifteen minutes later he was bundling Hattie and Kaitlan into the wagon. For once his wife was too tired to argue with him.


It was gloomy and drizzly as the procession of wagons and horses wound their way to the church and cemetery. Reverend Turner led the way, with Lish following him in the wagon in which the two coffins rested.

The Smiths' wagon was farther back in the line; then came Matt and Aunt Polly in a buggy. Those on horseback brought up the rear of the slow-moving cortege.

It was a wet, bedraggled group that arrived at the church and hurried inside. As they found seats on the rough benches, the pallbearers placed the coffins on wooden sawhorses. When the rustling of clothing settled down, the preacher stepped up to the simple pulpit and opened his frayed Bible. He read a couple of passages from it, then began to speak of the long life the Tylers had spent with their neighbors and that it was heartwarming to see that they had all gathered to pay homage to the old folks.

As he talked of their goodness, their honesty, and the way they'd always been ready to help those who needed it, Kaitlan was suddenly overwhelmed by the horror of it all. Images of the old couple at the church social, Nate's smiling face, Claire's burgeoning belly, whirled in her mind. She was sure that if she didn't get some fresh air, she would vomit. She whispered to Hattie, "I can't seem to breathe. I'm going outside a bit."

She stood on the small porch, breathing deeply of the fresh pine air. When she noted that the fine, misty rain had stopped, she walked over to the cemetery, passing the two raw, open graves as she made her way to where her grandparents were buried.

Looking down at the crape myrtle climbing over the two mounds, she tried to keep her mind on her relatives, but she kept remembering what Lish Jones had said this morning when he stopped by on his way to the Tyler place. She had learned from him that it was almost certain that Nate had killed the old couple. His bloody hunting knife had been found in the woods behind the Tylers' cabin. And while her heart seemed to jump into her throat, he had gone on to say that he knew for a fact that Nate and the old couple's granddaughter had been meeting at a cave all summer. So Matt's words had all been true.

After Lish had gone, she went to the river and almost scrubbed the skin off her body, but she still felt unclean. How many times, she wondered, had Nate left Claire's arms to come make love to her?

No, she amended, there had been no love in his possession of her body. There had only been lust. She would never feel clean again.

The turmoil in Kaitlan's mind was diverted by the pallbearers coming through the church door. The preacher followed behind them. When the church had emptied and the mourners had gathered around the open graves, she went to stand between Matt and Hattie.

"Why did you leave the services?" Matt asked in low tones.

"It was so stuffy in there, I thought I might faint."

Matt nodded in sympathy.

As Reverend Turner began his last prayer

237

over the two coffins, the sky became dark and overcast again, promising more rain. He made the prayer a short one, for which everyone was thankful. Almost before he said, "Amen," they were hurrying to their conveyances. The four men left to fill in the graves looked longingly after them as the mourners left the cemetery. The men knew they were in for a soaking.

Good-byes were called to those who had come a long distance as the wagons turned off at the different forks that would take them home. Some neighbors might not be seen again until the next funeral or wedding.

When Peter was about to turn the team onto the rocky way to the Barrett farm, Matt drove his buggy up alongside them. "Peter," he said, "will you look in on Aunt Polly for a few days? I'm going to Nashville to hunt down Nate."

"I sure will." Peter smiled at Aunt Polly. "It will be my pleasure."

"Are you sure that's where he's gone?" Hattie asked.

"Yes, I'm sure," Matt answered with conviction.

Three days later Matt wondered if he'd been mistaken about Nate being in Nashville. He had scoured the town from the dark, littered streets of saloons and whorehouses to the respectable neighborhoods filled with fashionable town houses. No one he questioned had seen a handsome blond man fitting Nate's description.

# Chapter Eighteen

It was a couple of hours before sundown when Nate reached the run-down section of Nashville that was his destination. He had been hiding out in the woods long enough. Now it was time to find lodgings, and they had to be cheap. After beating the old man to learn where he kept his money hidden, Nate had been infuriated to find the box contained only forty dollars. In his rage, he'd killed both the old people. Forty dollars. A man couldn't go far on that. It would behoove him to find a poker game in progress. The one thing he was good at was cards. His father, a well-known cardsharp, had taught him all the tricks of the trade.

Nate didn't linger on the fact that his father had been shot dead for cheating at cards.

He struck off down the street and found what he sought in the middle of the block. The building, like the others lining the cobblestones, was run-down, with peeling paint on the doors and window frames. A big sign on the window read, ROOMS FOR RENT UPSTAIRS. He tied the stallion to an iron hitching post and knocked on the flimsy wooden door.

After a few minutes a slattern opened the door and stared at him through drink-blurred eyes. "What can I do for you, dearie?" she asked, giving Nate a loose-lipped smile.

"I'd like to rent one of your rooms. One that looks out on the street."

"I have one" — her eyes narrowed speculatively — "but it's my finest and will cost you more."

"How much money are we talking?"

"Two dollars a night."

"What if I want it for a week . . . maybe a month? Would it be cheaper then?"

"The same price, dearie. I get fifty cents every time one of the street girls brings a gent up here. Once in a while I'll rent the room six times a night. That's three dollars."

"If it's only once in a while that you make three dollars on the room, wouldn't you end up with more money at the end of the week by letting me have a cheaper rate?"

"Two dollars a night," the landlady repeated stubbornly.

Nate heaved an impatient sigh and ordered, "Show me the room. I'll decide if I want it or not."

Nate wondered what the other rooms looked like if this was the old soak's best. A sagging bed stood in one corner, covered with a stained blanket. A small table stood beside it holding a stub of a candle in a cracked saucer. There was one rickety chair, a battered dresser with a cracked mirror, and on a narrow washstand was a chipped basin and pitcher.

It will do until I can get my hands on more

money, Nate thought, and handed over fourteen dollars. That didn't leave much of Claire's grandparents' money for food, so he'd better find a game as soon as possible.

Matt had risen early. The crew who came every year to help cut the tobacco would be arriving in the Village any day now, and he wanted to make sure all was ready for them. They would spend the night in the Village, camped out under some trees. Then they would arrive at the farm with the first light of the sun over the mountain. Some of the workers would slice the tall, sturdy plants free of the soil; then men following them would string the tobacco on slender poles. Another group of men would stack them on a wagon and drive them to the long drying shed to cure. When the long, broad leaves turned a golden brown color, buyers would come from Nashville and bid against each other for some of the finest tobacco in the country.

"Do you still plan on searching for Nate again when you finish with the tobacco?" Polly asked as she poured Matt a cup of coffee.

Matt nodded. It had been two weeks since he'd returned from his fruitless search for Nate, but he hadn't given up. "As soon as I get the tobacco sold. I haven't forgotten for a minute the dastardly thing he did. He's gotten away with a lot of things in his lifetime, but he's not going to get away with murder."

"I saw Claire with Granny Higgins in the Village yesterday," Polly said as she cleared the table of their breakfast dishes. "I hardly recognize the girl since Granny took her in. She was nice and clean, her hair combed neatly, and," Polly added laughingly, "she had on a pair of shoes."

"They're good for each other," Matt said. "Granny has someone to lavish love and care on in her old age, and Claire, starved for affection, will lap up all that Granny will give her."

"I just hope her baby is all right when it's born. You know what I mean, brighter than its mother."

"Chances are it will be. I just hope it's not a boy who might turn out like his father."

"Amen to that," Polly said fervently. "We don't need —" She was interrupted by a knock on the door.

Matt immediately recognized the redheaded, freckle-faced boy who hung around Ruby's place. He ran errands for her and helped her in small ways. Matt looked at the old mule the boy had ridden and guessed from its heaving sides that Danny had pressed it hard in his hurry to get to the farm.

"How's everything at the village, Danny?" he asked.

"Not too good." The boy shoved a folded sheet of paper at Matt. "It's from Miss Ruby."

Matt's face paled as he scanned the short note:

Matt, me and the girls are down with ty-
phoid fever. I'm afraid you're going to have
to come get Sammy. I'm not up to caring for
him right now and I would like for him to
be away from here before he comes down
with the sickness too. Your friend, Ruby.

"What is it, Matt?" Polly asked, alarmed.
"Your face has lost all its color."

"I haven't got time to explain now, Aunt
Polly. I'll tell you later. Come on, kid, let's go."

Matt had saddled his horse, and he and
Danny were racing out of the barnyard when
Kaitlan came trotting her horse toward them.
"I'll talk to you later," he called to her. "I have
pressing business to take care of in the Village."

Kaitlan tied Snowy at the hitching post as
she stared after Matt's rapidly retreating back.
Why was he in such a hurry, and why that
strained look on his face?

When she put the question to Polly, the bewildered woman answered with a shake of her
head. "All I know is that a young'un called
Danny brought Matt a note. He read it, then
tore out of here like a fire was singeing his rear
end."

"Did the boy say anything about what was in
the note?"

"All he said was that the note was from Miss
Ruby."

Kaitlan felt as if she had been hit in the
stomach by a hard fist. She recalled the day she

had seen Matt talking and laughing with Ruby Gentry on the porch of her bawdy house. When she had asked him about the woman, he had convinced her that the madam was only a friend.

Doubts about their relationship rose in her mind again. If they were only friends, why was he rushing to the flashy woman with that panicky look on his face?

"Did you want to talk to Matt about something?" Polly asked, setting a cup of coffee in front of Kaitlan.

It took a minute for Polly's question to register. "Yes, I wanted to ask him when it was time to start harvesting the tobacco."

"His plans were to start cutting as soon as possible. The crew he always hires should be showing up any day. I would say that you can start on your crop whenever you feel like it."

Kaitlan had gotten the answer she had come for, but still she sat, reluctant to leave until she learned why Matt had rushed off to the Village. Besides, Aunt Polly seemed to want her company, for she had, without asking, stood up and poured a second cup of coffee for her.

"Are you going to the harvest dance?" Polly asked as she stirred sugar into her coffee.

"I haven't heard anything about it. When is it happening?"

"This comin' Saturday. We have it every year in somebody's barn come late September. This year it's being held in Maybelle's barn. It's a lot of fun. Everybody comes and we dance until we give out."

Kaitlan halfheartedly agreed that it sounded like fun, and that she imagined she and the Smiths would attend. She sneaked a look at the wall clock in the kitchen. Matt had been gone for over an hour and there was no telling how much longer he would be gone. She should be getting home. Hattie had several small jobs she wanted her to attend to.

She stood up and was about to make her excuses for going home when she saw Matt's stallion cantering toward the cabin. She stared, blinked her eyes, and stared again. Sitting in front of Matt, in the protection of his arms, was a tot, three or four years old. Who was the child? she asked herself. And was he the cause of Matt's mad dash to the Village?

Something told her to leave, that she didn't want to hear the answers to her silent questions. After Nate's crushing betrayals, she didn't think she could stand to discover that Matt had not been completely honest with her. She thanked Polly for the coffee and was near the door when Matt, a wide smile on his face, walked through it, the little boy riding in the crook of his arm.

"Who's little boy is that?" Polly asked. "I don't believe I've seen him before."

"Well" — Matt sat Sammy on the table — "I guess you could say that he's mine. Ruby has been taking care of him ever since he was born."

Kaitlan didn't stay to hear any more. Numb, she quietly left the cabin, unnoticed. She climbed onto Snowy and galloped away, disillusionment gripping her. She would have bet her life that Matt was an honorable man, that he would never father a child on a woman and then hide it from his neighbors.

Meanwhile, Matt was explaining to Aunt Polly how Sammy had come into his care, how he had been paying Ruby to keep him until he decided the little one's future. It wasn't until he turned around to introduce Sammy to Kaitlan that he discovered she had left.

"When did she leave?" He turned back to Polly.

"I don't know. She was standing beside the door when you walked in."

"Hell." Matt slapped his hand on the table in frustration. "She probably only heard me say that Sammy was mine. I'll have to ride over to her place later and explain Sammy's heritage to her."

"It shouldn't be too hard to convince her who fathered the boy. He looks just like Nate."

"But he's not going to grow up like his father. I'll see to that."

"Then you'll be keeping him with you from now on? Before the sun goes down, everyone in the Gap will know of his existence and put two and two together."

Matt shrugged his shoulders. "It can't be helped. Now that Nate's gone, I intend to keep him. I hope it won't be too much for you to look after him while I'm working."

"It will be no trouble at all." Polly ruffled Sammy's golden curls. "I'll love taking care of this little fellow. But don't you think he'll miss Ruby? He probably looks on her as a mother."

"He'll miss his aunt Ruby, but he's awfully fond of his uncle Matt, so I don't think he'll have much trouble settling in with us."

"Are you going to start on your tobacco tomorrow?"

"Yes. I ran into the workers just as they were arriving in the Village. They'll be here early tomorrow morning."

But before he could get started on the harvest, Matt knew he needed to straighten things out with Kaitlan.

# Chapter Nineteen

Matt found Kaitlan in the woodlot in back of the cabin. She didn't hear his silent approach and he stood a moment watching the movement of her body as she loaded her arms with wood for the fireplace. She's as graceful as a young deer, he thought, deliberately stepping on a dry limb to alert her to his presence.

She straightened up from her stooped position and turned around to look at him. For a split second a welcoming smile curved her lips, then just as fast disappeared. She glanced up at the sun fading westward, trailing scarlet sashes across the sky, and asked coolly, "What are you doing here at this hour, Matt? Did you come to have supper with us?"

"No, I didn't come for supper and well you know it." Matt's tone had an impatient edge to it. "I'm here to explain Sammy to you."

"What's there to explain?" Kaitlan said stiffly. "You said he's your son, so that just about covers it, wouldn't you say?"

"No, it does not. I didn't say that he was my son. I said he was mine. If you hadn't left in such a hurry, I wouldn't have to be explaining everything to you now. I'd appreciate it if you'd get rid of that wood and sit on that chopping block and listen to what I've got to say."

"Oh, all right." Kaitlan dumped the wood on the ground and plopped herself down where Matt had indicated. Matt hunkered down on his heels beside her and was thoughtful for a moment.

"Some of my story may hurt you," he said finally, "but it can't be helped if I'm to tell it all."

When Kaitlan said, "I'll be the judge of that," he plunged into his explanation, telling her who Sammy's father was and how the child had come into his keeping. He told her also how the first young woman Nate had fathered a child on had jumped off a bridge and drowned herself out of shame.

"I guess I didn't have to tell you that last part. It's just that I want you to know what kind of man Nate is and how lucky you are to be rid of him."

A small, happy breath slipped from between Kaitlan's lips. She told herself that she should have known better than to think that Matt would do such a dishonorable thing as to father a child and refuse to marry its mother.

She laid a hand on his shoulder. "I'm sorry I didn't stay and listen to your whole story. I'm ashamed of what I've been thinking these past hours."

"Are you ashamed enough to make it up to me by going to the harvest dance with me?"

Kaitlan looked up at Matt, a teasing in her eyes. "Are you courting me, Matt Ingram?"

"I'm trying to." Matt smiled at her as he

braced a foot on the chopping block and leaned an elbow on his bent knee. "I guess you can tell I'm pretty rusty at it."

"Well . . . I wanted to be sure. A girl hates being made a fool of. Especially if it's happened to her before."

"Kaitlan, don't compare me to Nate. We are not alike in any way." There was a hint of anger in Matt's voice.

"I know, Matt. I shouldn't have said that."

"I can't honestly blame you for feeling cautious, after Nate. But, Kaitlan, I'll never hurt you."

Oh, but Matt, Kaitlan thought, I might hurt you. You don't know all that went on between me and your stepbrother.

"So, will you go with me to the dance?"

"Yes, Matt, I'd love to go with you."

"Fine." Matt's white teeth flashed in a smile. He dropped his foot to the ground and, bending over, began to gather up the wood that Kaitlan had tossed down. As he added more to it, he said, "I'm going to be cutting my tobacco tomorrow morning. If you and Peter intend to do the same, I'll come over and help you for a couple hours, show you how to cut your tobacco."

"Thank you, Matt. Peter and I know nothing of how to go about it."

"I'll be over around nine o'clock."

"We'll be ready."

The next morning at nine, Matt found that

Kaitlan and Peter were ready in spirit, but lacked the tools they needed to harvest their cash crop. They didn't have the slender, razor-sharp knife to slash through the top of the plant, nor did they have the heavy, long-handled knife that could cut through the heavy stalk, freeing it from the roots. He didn't see a pile of four-foot-long poles to support the split stems once they were cut, either.

He had suspected that might be the case, however, and lying in the wagon bed was everything they would need.

"You don't look too chipper this morning, Kaitlan," Matt said, noticing the dark circles under her eyes as he jumped from the wagon.

"I didn't sleep well last night." Kaitlan shrugged away her wan look.

Peter chuckled. "Hattie made chicken and dumplings for supper last night and our Kaitlan made a pig of herself. She had a belly-ache last night."

A pink flush spread over Kaitlan's face. Peter's remark didn't make her sound very lady-like, but what he said was true. She had eaten way too much and her sleep had been restless because of it.

Peter was embarrassed when Matt pulled from the wagon the poles and tools they would need. He and Kaitlan were only armed with a sicklelike knife to cut the heavy plants. And as for the long poles, it hadn't entered his mind that they would need them.

"We'll be better prepared next season," he promised Matt.

The sun grew so hot Kaitlan thought she would faint as Matt showed them how to bring down the heavy tobacco and hang it in the barn loft.

All three were sweating freely when Matt prepared to return to his own tobacco field a couple of hours later. He looked at Hattie, who had brought them a bucket of fresh, cool springwater, and asked, "Are you and Peter going to the dance Saturday night?"

"Yes. We're looking forward to it."

"I was wondering if you would pick up Aunt Polly . . . and young Sammy. I'm going to need some support, facing all the questions that will be put to me about the boy." He grinned wryly. "Maybe if you and Aunt Polly told the women how it came about that he's in my care, they'll leave me alone."

Kaitlan looked up at Matt, her eyes twinkling, and said, "I can't believe that a big man like you is afraid of a few nosy women."

"I'd rather fight a panther bare-handed than be cornered by them." Matt grinned.

"Why don't you sic Hattie on them?" Peter was grinning also. "She'll straighten them out in short order."

"Well, Hattie, what do you think about me taking on Sammy's rearing? I don't imagine you approve of it. You probably think it is Nate's duty."

"I sure would, if Nate was a decent sort, but as it is, I wouldn't trust him to take care of our old hound. I think it's a fine thing that you're giving the little one a home."

"It's more than giving him a home. At first, when he was just a few days old, I took him because his mother begged me to. I felt a sense of obligation toward the little fellow, since his no-good father was my stepbrother. Then, as I spent time with him, I grew to love him as if he were my own flesh and blood."

Matt's lips twisted in a crooked grin. "He's probably my only chance at fatherhood."

"Why do you say that?" Kaitlan scolded. "You talk like you're an old man who will never get married."

"I most likely won't ever get married. The young women shy away from me."

"That's your fault. You always look so hard and brooding, you scare them away. I've seen them peeking at you."

"You're crazy in the head, woman." Matt laughed and tugged one of her braids. Gathering up the reins, he said, "I'll stop by after supper to see how you and Peter made out."

Kaitlan and Peter worked all day bringing in the tobacco, stopping only once to eat the lunch Hattie brought out to them. The hours of daylight were growing short when the last stalk of tobacco was cut, hauled to the barn, and hung up in the loft.

"Well, Peter, we've done it," Kaitlan said, a happy but tired smile curving her lips. "We've brought in our first cash crop. What are you going to do with your share of the money we'll get for it?"

"Danged if I know. In all my life I've never had more than ten dollars to spend." He gave a short laugh. "I don't think that will change a great deal. Hattie will take charge of the money."

Kaitlan echoed his laugh. "She'll probably take charge of mine too."

Peter agreed, adding, "Do you suppose she'll ever let us grow up?"

Hattie stood on the porch, her hands on her hips, thinking that Kaitlan and Peter had been out in the sun too long. They were roaring with laughter as they came in toward her. She frowned. When they laughed like that she always suspected that she was the butt of their hilarity. She had long since stopped asking them what was so funny. She always received an asinine answer.

Nate walked his stallion up and down the streets of a respectable section of town. He had been unusually lucky at cards since coming to Nashville and had amassed quite a bit of money. He was now able to move out of the rat-infested building and leave the drunken landlady behind. He could afford better clothes also, and enjoy the services of more attractive whores.

On one of the clean, shaded streets he spotted a FOR RENT sign on an attractive wood-framed house. He dismounted and knocked on the bright white door. An elderly woman cracked it open and peered out at him. Giving her his most winning smile, he said, "Good afternoon, ma'am. I might be interested in renting your house."

The old woman hesitated a moment, then invited him inside. Walking ahead of him with the aid of a cane, she said, "I'll show you through, although I must tell you that I have it up for sale. The place is too much for me to keep up and I'm moving to Memphis to live with my daughter."

Nate barely looked at the kitchen, but he found the parlor and two bedrooms well furnished. He rented it on the spot. He would entertain his new set of friends here, meet their sisters, and in time marry one of them. In the meantime there were always the fancy whores to while away the time with.

Life was being very good to him, he thought as he rode back to his room to collect his clothes.

It was the morning of the harvest dance, but Kaitlan awoke still feeling tired from the hard work of cutting the tobacco. Peter felt the same way, and it was a lazy day for them. Hattie seemed to understand and didn't have a long list of things she wanted them to do.

After lunch Kaitlan went out onto the porch and sat in one of the chairs. With a shove of her foot she set it to rocking and breathed deep of the honeysuckle climbing up one end of the porch, and of the newly cut hay waiting in the field to be raked up and stored in the barn for the livestock to munch on during the winter.

She turned her head and looked at Hattie when the black woman walked out onto the porch. "Aren't you feeling well?" she asked Hattie, seeing the pained look on her face as she sat in the chair next to her.

"I have one of my awful headaches." Hattie leaned her head back and closed her eyes.

As Kaitlan tried to remember ever hearing her friend complain of headaches, Hattie went on to say, "I'm afraid me and Peter won't be going to the harvest dance, after all. I just couldn't bear to have that loud music beating against my ears."

"But, Hattie, I couldn't go off and leave you when you're feeling so poorly."

"No, no, you go. There's nothing you could do for me. I've been drinking some of Granny Higgins's headache tonic. You just be ready when Matt comes for you."

"But you promised to help Matt explain about Sammy," Kaitlan reminded her.

"You'll have to do that. Now, hadn't you better wash your hair? It will take a couple hours for that mop of yours to dry."

The days had grown shorter lately, and full darkness had arrived at seven o'clock, when Kaitlan heard Matt talking to Peter and Hattie. She finished brushing her red-gold curls and, giving herself one last look in the mirror, picked up the lacy shawl Hattie had knitted for her years before, and walked into the family room.

Matt broke off his conversation with the Smiths and simply stared at her. What a picture she made, he thought, taking in her sparkling eyes, her glowing face. He wanted to fold her in his arms and never let her go. He swallowed a couple of times, and then managed to say in a reasonably normal tone, "You're looking real nice, Kaitlan."

"Thank you, Matt." Kaitlan smiled at him. "You're looking real handsome."

A faint red crept over Matt's face. "Aunt Polly insisted that I wear this white shirt."

"I'm glad she did." Kaitlan's eyes moved over the snow white shirt, open at the throat, baring the dark column of his strong throat. He had rolled the sleeves midway up his equally tanned muscular arms, and a little flutter of excitement ran through her as she remembered the strength in them. She looked up at his face and was glad he hadn't had time to get his hair cut. She liked it long, almost to his shoulders.

She dropped her gaze to take in the snug fit of the trousers on his lean waist and narrow hips. Her eyes fastened a moment on his fly and the noticeable bulge there. Her face grew warm and she looked away, but not in time to stop the fluttering that stirred in her lower body.

What kind of woman am I? she asked herself. A month ago I made wild love with Nate, and now, this short time later, I'm wanting to go to bed with Matt.

Kaitlan left off her inspection of Matt and stared at Hattie when she said, "Isn't it too bad that Polly can't go to the dance either?"

Before Kaitlan could ask why not, Matt was saying, "Sammy has been sneezing and she's afraid he might be coming down with the illness that put Dolly and her girls in bed."

"I guess she would be afraid of that," Kaitlan had to agree, but she was still reluctant to be alone with Matt.

"When I saw Peter earlier this afternoon," Matt said, "and he told me that Hattie wouldn't be going to the dance either because of a headache, I thought you and I might as well go on horseback."

"I'll go saddle your horse, Kaitlan," Peter said, hopping off the porch and hurrying toward the barn.

As they waited for him to return Hattie seemed miraculously cured of her headache. Kaitlan eyed her suspiciously as the skinny woman kept up a running conversation on inconsequential subjects, laughing and giggling

like a young schoolgirl. What is that old har-
ridan up to? she wondered.

Peter arrived with her grandfather's stallion,
and as Matt swung her up and onto the saddle,
his hands lingered on her waist and she dis-
missed Hattie's strange behavior.

It was a beautiful night as Kaitlan and Matt
took the rocky path to Maybelle's farm. A full
moon shone down on them, so bright every
rock and tree was clearly defined in its light.
They did not talk, so there was only the sound
of rattling bits and the creaking of leather. Occasionally there was the hoot of an owl. Kaitlan
and Matt heard the laughter and music before
the Scott place came in sight. The harvest
dance was in full swing.

"I guess we're the last to arrive," Matt said as
they rode up to the lantern-lit barn.

When they entered the building, everyone except the elderly and the children was dancing.
A dulcimer, banjo, fiddle, and French harp
were playing rollicking music, and couples
stamped and swung around the dance floor,
making the loose boards pop. The children
chased each other in a game of tag, their
squeals adding to the noise. The old folk sat on
bales of hay, watching the merrymakers and
possibly remembering when they were young
and doing the same thing.

Matt removed Kaitlan's shawl from around
her shoulders and hung it on a peg with others.
He grinned then and said, "Let's join them."

Her eyes sparkling with excitement, she went into his arms. With natural grace Matt swung her around the makeshift dance floor, her feet scarcely touching the boards. She became caught up in the moment and returned the smiles directed at her and Matt from friends and neighbors.

Everything went well until the musicians slowed their pace, giving the dancers a chance to catch their breath and letting them get closer to each other. This created a problem for Matt, and also for Kaitlan. Each became too aware of the nearness of the other. Kaitlan felt the urge to get closer still to Matt, and he wanted to crush her in his arms. He had to squelch that thought, for he was rapidly getting aroused. If he held her any closer she would feel his condition, and Lord knew what she would think of him.

Instead of holding her closer the way his body cried out to do, he firmed his jaw and held her farther away. He pretended not to see Kaitlan's confusion at his action.

Everyone was sweating freely when the musicians stopped for a rest. Matt and Kaitlan went with the others to crowd around the keg of sweet cider and platters of cookies the wives had brought.

Kaitlan and Matt took their drinks and found a seat on a bale of hay, sharing it with Elam and Grace Cook. Grace leaned across Matt and whispered to Kaitlan, "Look how cozy

Maybelle and Stokes the grocer are. They ain't left each other's side since he arrived. Maybelle is all pink and fluttering around like a teenage girl."

"Do you suppose there's a romance building there?" Kaitlan whispered back, her eyes twinkling.

"It sure looks like it, but I can't believe that sanctimonious Maybelle would let a man touch her."

"Hell," Elam cut in. "She's human. She's got a right to get itchy like the rest of you women."

"Elam Cook." Grace slapped her husband on the arm. "I've never . . ."

"Oh, yes, you have." Elam put his own ending on her sentence. The four of them laughed, and then Elam said, "Ol' Stokes better not get too close to Maybelle's bony hips. He'll get a few good cuts, that's for sure." And again their laughter rang out.

The music started up again, and it seemed to Matt that every single man there swooped down on Kaitlan. He was jealous of every man who claimed her for a dance.

As Matt sat alone on the bale of hay, trying not to watch Kaitlan and her partner, he gradually became aware that the single young women were flashing him smiles and coy looks. Were they flirting with him? he asked himself in surprise. He was sure of it when one, bolder than the others, walked up to him and, smiling, asked, "May I have this dance, Matt Ingram?"

His eyes searched for Kaitlan as though for help. But she was being whirled around by her partner, her laughter ringing out with the others. There was nothing he could do but stand up and swing the girl in among the other couples.

Once he came face-to-face with Kaitlan and the gaiety on her face died. She looks displeased, he thought, missing a step and treading on his partner's toes.

It was almost daylight when the exhausted dancers and musicians decided it was time to go home. Mothers roused sleeping children and herded them out to the wagons they had arrived in. Those who had come on horseback hurried to mount and get ahead of the wagons and the dust their wheels would stir up.

Kaitlan was practically asleep on her feet when Matt swung her onto her grandfather's stallion. "You're not going to fall asleep and fall out of the saddle, are you?" he joked, handing her the reins.

"No, I'm not," Kaitlan answered crossly, her tone telling him that for some reason she was still displeased with him.

"Kaitlan," he said as he climbed onto his own horse, "you're put out at me for some reason. Do you want to tell me what it is that I have done?"

Kaitlan gathered the reins together and, leading off, said curtly, "You're imagining things. Why should I be put out at you?"

Why indeed? Matt wondered, but watching her stiff back, he knew he hadn't imagined anything. Was it possible she was jealous? If so, his plan was working even better than he'd hoped. With Nate gone, he might yet convince Kaitlan to marry him.

# Chapter Twenty

It was a raw and wet day when Kaitlan awakened. She pulled the blanket up around her shoulders and lay listening to the rain patter on the roof and the soft noise it made as it ran off the eaves and hit the ground.

She wondered how Matt and Peter were faring. Three days ago they had received word that this year the buyers wouldn't be coming to the farms to bid on the tobacco. That meant they had to make a trip to Nashville. They had loaded their wagons last night so they could get an early start this morning.

The men would get wet, but the tobacco would be fine. It had dried beautifully in the weeks since the harvest. Matt and Peter had covered it with canvas tarps and tied the heavy material securely to each wagon bed. Matt had said that the dark clouds gathering in the north meant it would start raining sometime that night. And, as in most things, his prediction had been right.

Kaitlan slid out of bed and padded over to the window. She pulled the heavy curtains aside and looked outside. The ground was saturated and pools of water stood all over the yard. She told herself that it must have rained all night because the flowers she had tended so carefully all summer were now beaten into the ground, and the sweet-smelling honeysuckle at the end of the porch hung heavy and limp with water.

Sighing, she slid her feet into the scuffed, soft slippers she wore inside and left the bedroom. It was going to be a long, gloomy day.

When Kaitlan walked into the kitchen, she found Hattie squatting in front of the small cooking fireplace, frying bacon and batter cakes. "Umm, that smells good," she said and began setting the table. That done, she took a platter over to Hattie to put their breakfast on. "I hope Peter and Matt are keeping dry," she thought out loud.

"Me too," Hattie said, standing up. "You know how easily Peter catches cold."

Kaitlan paused in picking up the coffeepot and gave Hattie a startled look. In all the years she had known Peter, she couldn't remember his ever having a cold. It was true Hattie caught one every winter, but never Peter. She shrugged her shoulders. It would be useless to point that out to the stubborn woman, however. She would argue all day that she was right.

"What are we going to do all day?" Kaitlan asked as she spread butter on a batter cake.

"If it ever stops raining, I want you to ride down to the Village and buy me some yarn for the loom I saw out in the barn. There was also a bag of wool sitting beside it. When I was a young girl on the plantation, the mistress taught us all how to weave. I'll be busy all winter making us bedcovers and rugs."

Kaitlan wondered glumly how she would pass the cold days when they arrived.

The rain finally ceased in midmorning, but when Kaitlan stepped out onto the porch she found that a cold wind had blown in. "Put on your heaviest jacket," Hattie ordered when she came shivering back into the kitchen and prepared to ride to the store.

"As if I didn't know to do that," Kaitlan muttered under her breath.

A few minutes later as she rode down the rain-gutted trail, Kaitlan loosened the reins and let the stallion choose his own gait. He took off at an easy lope, giving her time to view the passing scenery. A few mahogany-colored leaves still clung to the oak trees, but the rain had beaten off the leaves of the other trees, and they now stood bare and stark against the gray sky.

When Kaitlan entered the small settlement she was at first surprised to see so many horses and mules tied up in front of the store. On second thought she imagined that others had been as anxious as she to get outdoors as soon as the rain stopped. When she dismounted and walked into the establishment, the women were all achatter about the old Tyler place, which now stood empty, overgrown with weeds.

"Last night my two oldest young'uns saw Grandpa and Grandma Tyler plain as day walkin' around in the cemetery. They was cryin' out to Claire. Them boys scooted out of there real fast, let me tell you," Grace Cook said.

"And my Harry," Alice Spencer broke in, "saw a light in the old cabin a few nights back and there was wailin' and cryin' goin' on inside it. The place is hainted, that's what it is."

Kaitlan looked at Lish, who stood beside her. "Is that true? Is the house haunted?"

"Hell no," the old man answered in a low voice. "Them young'uns were either imaginin' things or they was makin' it all up to sound important. As for Harry Spencer, he was probably drunk when he passed the place."

"If you ask me," Granny Higgins said on the other side of Kaitlan, "somebody ought to burn the place down and stop all this crazy talk. The little ones are gonna start havin' nightmares, hearin' such nonsense. And it don't help poor Claire either."

"They ought to for a fact," Lish said after a while, then walked away.

Grace Cook took his place beside Kaitlan and, her eyes glittering in amusement, murmured to her and Granny Higgins alone, "Maybelle was here when I arrived, but I don't see her horse outside. Do you reckon she spent the night with Mr. Stokes?"

Granny started to let loose one of her high-pitched cackles, then smothered it with her hand. But her eyes showed her mirth as she said from the corner of her lips, "Do you suppose some sheet-shakin' went on in Stokes's bedroom last night?"

Kaitlan's lips twisted as she tried to contain her laughter. "Wouldn't that be something to watch?"

"It sure would," Grace agreed. "Fat ol' Stokes and skinny Maybelle goin' at it. You don't have to speculate on who would be on top."

The three couldn't hold back their laughter any longer. It rang out, making everyone look at them.

"What's so funny, ladies?" Maybelle asked, appearing from the back room.

It was Kaitlan who thought fast enough to come up with a believable lie. "I was telling Grace and Granny how Hattie walked out onto the porch and tripped over our old hound. She went flying out into the yard and landed facedown in a puddle of dirty water." When everyone laughed at her fictitious story, she prayed that none of the women would ever mention it to Hattie.

The women began to leave the store, and Kaitlan purchased the yarn for Hattie and said good-bye to those few who remained. She thought she hadn't heard right when Maybelle called after her, "Come visit me one day next week, Kaitlan."

"Thank you, Maybelle, I will," she managed to say before stepping outside.

All the way home she puzzled over the

change that had come about in the sour disposition Maybelle had once shown to the world.

Dispirited by the weather and by a weariness of bone and muscle, Matt and Peter rolled down the muddy main street of Nashville.

Hungry, tired of eating the cold meals Aunt Polly had packed for him, Matt whipped up his team, leading the way to the livery stable at the other end of town. When they pulled the mules up in front of the big building, they saw long lines of wagons, loaded with tobacco, waiting for a stall to pull into.

"You reckon we'll find a spot for our wagons?" Peter asked anxiously.

"We'll find room," Matt answered confidently, then smiled when he was hailed by a big man carrying a buffalo gun.

"Matt Ingram! How are you, you son of a gun?" The man's loud voice rang out.

"Couldn't be better, Jake." Matt hopped down from the wagon and shook the big hand held out to him. "What about you? How have you been this past year?"

"Fair to middlin', can't complain. I got me a new baby boy." The big man laughed proudly. "A new one every spring. That Lucy of mine is a fine breeder."

"Congratulations. How many boys does that make for you?"

"Seven. But don't forget the pretty little daughter squeezed in among them. She looks just like her mama. She don't have Lucy's bossy ways and sharp tongue, though." He chuckled.

It was well known by those who knew the Formans that the wife ruled the household and everyone who lived in it, even though she was barely over five feet tall and weighed about a hundred pounds.

"Has she hit you with her rolling pin lately?"

"Naw, I've learned how to dodge it. Sometimes, though," Jake added with a smug grin, "I let her hit me. She's always sorry later, and when we go to bed she spends a long time showin' me just how much she regrets thumpin' me."

Matt jokingly threatened, "I think I'll tell Lucy what a sly dog you are."

"If you do that I'll tell her that you're the one who gets me drunk all the time," Jake retaliated. "Then you'll get a taste of the rollin' pin."

"Lord save me from that." Matt threw up his hands in defeat. "Not only would I get a knot on my head, I wouldn't get the pleasure of making up."

Both men laughed; then Matt said in a more serious vein, "Do you think you could find me two stables this year?"

"Sure thing. Down at the end of the livery where I always put you."

"Do you still have that big dog prowling around?"

"Yeah, Bruiser will be right there keepin' an eye on your wagons."

"Only one wagon is mine. The other one belongs to a friend and neighbor of mine." Matt
motioned to Peter, who had been standing
back, enjoying the banter between the two big
men. "Meet Peter Smith, Jake. He raised his
first crop of tobacco this summer."

"Howdy, Smith." Jake stuck out a hand twice
the size of Peter's. "Don't worry about anyone
drivin' away with your tobacco. Between my
gun and my hound, ain't nobody comin' near
your wagon."

When Matt and Peter had backed their
wagons into their designated spots, a young
teenager appeared and began unharnessing the
mules. On their way out of the livery, Matt
stopped to have a few last words with Jake.

"Jake, I was here in Nashville sometime back
looking for Nate. We in the Gap are pretty sure
he murdered an old couple for their life savings. Have you seen him?"

"You don't say!" Jake's face grew dark with
anger. "I saw the bastard a few weeks back. At
a distance."

"Where was that?"

"Two or three blocks down. Where the riff-
raff hangs around the saloons and gamblin'
halls."

"Thank you, Jake. I'll see you in the morning
at the auction."

A moment later, as Matt and Peter walked
down the water-soaked wooden sidewalk, Matt
said, "There's this boardinghouse where I al-

271

ways spend the night when I'm in Nashville. The woman provides a good hearty supper and breakfast, and a comfortable bed to sleep in. After we've settled in and we've eaten, I'm going to leave you for a while."

"To look for Nate?"

Matt nodded. "I think I'm close on his trail this time."

An hour later Matt left Peter and went searching for his stepbrother.

He hadn't gone a block before his attention was caught by the painful squealing of a horse and the loud swearing of a man. He looked down the street and saw the animal in question. Painfully thin, the horse was hitched to a wagon so loaded with firewood that it was impossible for him to pull, no matter how hard he struggled to do so. The sting of a whip flayed his back and haunches. Swearing furiously under his breath, Matt ran forward and snatched the whip from the brutal, bearded driver. When he dragged the man off the wagon, the driver let out an angry roar.

"What the hell do you think you're doin'?" the man yelled, taking a threatening step toward Matt.

Clapping a hand on the handle of the wicked-looking knife stuck into his belt, Matt ground out, "I'm taking this poor animal off your hands. How much do you want for him?"

Eyeing the knife and sensing that his opponent knew how to use it, the driver said slyly, "He's not for sale. He's a good worker."

"A good worker, ha! The animal is dying on his feet." Matt stalked after the man, who was backing away from him. "You'll sell him to me or I'll take him away from you."

"All right, you can have him for fifty dollars."

"I'll give you ten and that's five dollars more than he's worth. Now unhitch him. Gentle-like."

Muttering under his breath, the loutish man freed the horse from his burden. It was then that Matt recognized the once-handsome animal. At one time it had belonged to Nate, who hadn't even bothered to give it a name.

Matt shook his head, for a moment blinded by rage. It was hard to believe that any man would be so uncaring that he would sell a beautiful animal to a man who would turn him into a workhorse.

He threw a ten-dollar bill at the man's feet, then called to a boy across the street who had been watching them. "Hey, kid, do you want to make a dollar?"

"I sure do, mister." The boy loped across the street. "What do you want me to do?"

Matt took a piece of paper and a short pencil from a jacket pocket. He wrote, "Jake, this stallion needs immediate care. If possible I would like to take him home with me tomorrow. Give this kid a dollar for me. Matt."

He folded the piece of paper and handed it to

273

the youngster. "Take this to the livery stable down the street. Do you know the owner, Jake?" When he received a nod, he said, "Jake will give you a dollar when you hand the horse over to him. Go slow with the beast; he's about dead."

He ignored the malignant look the driver shot him. The man was stuck with a loaded wagon and no horse to pull it. Pull it yourself, you heartless bastard, Matt thought as with long strides he began walking down the dirty streets looking for Nate.

# Chapter Twenty-one

Before returning to the boardinghouse that evening, Matt went to the livery to check on the black. "How's he doing?" he asked of the teenager currying the rib-thin stallion.

"He's coming along pretty good, considering the abuse he's had."

"Has he had anything to eat?"

"Jake gave him a small ration of oats. Said he was afraid the poor animal might get sick if he ate too much right off. Said his stomach was shrunk from hardly having anything in it. He had me wash the poor beast down; then he rubbed some salve in the cuts on his hide."

Matt moved to stand in front of the horse and gazed into his brown eyes. The previous beaten look in them was gone, replaced by the spirit of his fine breeding. "How are you feeling, fellow?" he asked.

He was answered with a soft whinny. Matt rubbed the soft spot between the animal's intelligent eyes, promising, "You'll never have a whip laid on you again."

"God knows he's had that happen to him often enough," Jake said as he entered the stall. "Some of the scars on him are years old."

That's another thing Nate will have to answer for when he tries to get into Heaven, Matt thought grimly. He looked at Jake and asked, "Do you think he'll be able to go home with me tomorrow after the auction?"

"If you go slow. He won't be up to runnin' for some time. He's pretty weak."

Matt returned to the boardinghouse just in time for supper. Peter was already seated at the long table and had saved a place for him. After a hearty meal of roast beef, mashed potatoes and gravy, string beans, and cole slaw, topped off with bread pudding, they retired to their room. Travel weary, they were eager to go to bed.

"Did you find Nate?" Peter asked as they undressed.

Matt shook his head, then told him about Nate's stallion.

"I hope he burns in hell," Peter said.

Two minutes later both men were asleep.

The next morning movement downstairs awakened Matt. He picked up his pocket watch from the small bedside table and peered at it. Six-thirty. "Wake up, Peter." He shook his bed partner's shoulder. "Let's eat breakfast and get our tobacco over to the auction shed. The bidding will start in an hour."

As they washed up and got dressed, both men were excited, but a little nervous. One never knew from one year to the next what the going price of tobacco would be. Sometimes the market was flooded and the farmer didn't see much profit from his summer's hard work. Other times when the growing season was extremely hot and they had to grow in drought conditions, prices soared.

Of course the quality of the plant had a lot to do with price. Matt wasn't concerned on that count. He raised the finest tobacco in all of Tennessee. His secret was that he grew a better, sweeter leaf than anyone else. The seed had been passed down from father to son since 1610, when John Rolfe had brought it to the states from Trinidad. Matt had shared his seedlings with Kaitlan, and if the price was decent, she stood to make a fair profit from her and Peter's hard work.

Half a dozen farmers were ahead of Matt and Peter, and a long line of wagons were headed toward the open-sided shed where buyers and the auctioneer stood around waiting for the bidding to begin.

The bids on the first three wagons from the other side of the Gap were mediocre. The following three wagons from downriver fared much better. Then it was Matt's turn to drive his wagon under the shed's roof, and interest picked up among the buyers. Matt's reputation for growing the finest tobacco was well known in the tobacco industry. When the auctioneer held up several stalks of hardy, well-shaped leaves, the bidding began with a fervor that ultimately brought him the best price he'd ever earned.

While Matt waited for his tobacco to be weighed and to receive a check from the man who had won the bidding, Peter drove his much lighter load into the shed. Ears pricked up when the buyers were shown plants equal in quality to Matt's. He thought the black man's smile would split his face, it was so wide. When he led his team outside, Matt slapped him on the back and asked, "Well, do you think all that hard work was worth it?"

"You damn betcha. I'm gonna put in twice the amount of tobacco next season."

Matt grinned in approval. "Let's go to the bank and cash our checks, then do a little shopping before we head home. I'm sure our womenfolk will be expecting presents."

"You know, this will be the first time I'll be able to buy Hattie a gift in all our years together."

"All that is gonna change now, Peter," Matt said, climbing into the wagon. "You're gonna be able to buy her a lot of things from now on. Let's get the teams back to the livery and then we'll go to the bank."

An hour later, money in their pockets, they walked into the largest mercantile in Nashville. "See that red dress over there?" Peter pointed to a rack holding women's garments. "That's what I'm buying for Hattie. That will please my color-hungry woman mightily. She's had to wear drab-colored clothing all her life."

Matt shopped first for Sammy, choosing a

soft rubber ball that would fit his small hands, then a set of tin toy soldiers. His next purchase was a blue velvet bonnet for Polly, and then there was Kaitlan, the hardest of all to buy for. What could he give her that wasn't too personal?

A rack of nightgowns caught his eye, and he wandered over to them. They were mostly flannels, high necked and long sleeved. But mixed in with them were some fancy ones, cut more daringly at the neckline. There was one in particular that he'd give half his crop money to see Kaitlan wearing. It was pink in color and of a sheer muslin that would reveal the body beneath it.

Knowing, however, that he'd never see Kaitlan in such a garment, he bought her a box of chocolates. For Hattie he chose a pair of red stockings to go with her dress.

Kaitlan sat on a willow tree trunk that hung out over the river. She stared unseeingly at six geese paddling along in the water.

She could no longer ignore the fact that she was expecting. She, like Claire and the other two girls in the Gap, had been used by Nate and then abandoned. She, too, would have to bear the shame of having a child out of wedlock.

Kaitlan heaved a sigh of resignation. She would manage somehow, but not in the way the first two girls had handled their misfortune.

She would not throw herself into the river, nor would she give up her baby. She would keep her child, and with the help of Hattie and Peter, she would raise it.

Her eyes glittered with unshed tears. Those two dear people would be devastated when they learned of her pregnancy. They had always held her in such high regard. Would that be shattered now? If only it hadn't been Nate who had fathered the child on her. Hattie had repeatedly warned her about him, that he couldn't be trusted.

One tear trickled down her cheek. What if her unborn child grew up to be like him? She would try hard not to let that happen, but who was to say she would be successful? Look at herself. She hadn't listened to Hattie and Peter.

She squeezed her eyes closed. When should she tell them? Right away, or should she let them live in ignorance until she began to show? She had gotten pregnant sometime in August, so the baby would be born in May. She had another month or so before she began showing.

Kaitlan dropped her head on her bent knees and let the tears flow.

It took Matt and Peter an extra half day to arrive at the Gap, due to the slow pace they had to keep for the recovering stallion. He had a name now. Matt called him Grit because of his determination to cling to life. It was high noon when their wagons rolled along the river road, and home was just a short distance away. Both men were eager to get back to the everyday routine of farm work.

As his team clomped around a bend in the road, Matt exclaimed with a wide smile, "There's Kaitlan sitting on that big willow trunk that the kids use for diving into the river. She must be fishing." He cupped his hands around his mouth and called out, "Hey, Kaitlan, you catching anything?"

Kaitlan's head jerked up. She stared a moment, then scrambled off the tree. But instead of coming to meet them as Matt expected, she struck out running toward the cabin.

"What's wrong with her?" Matt looked back at Peter. "I know she recognized us."

"You got me, Matt."

"Should I ride on up to the cabin with you? Maybe she's mad at me about something. I'd like to know if she is so we can get it straightened out."

"I doubt if you have anything to do with her actions, Matt. She thinks highly of you. Why don't you come over after supper, bring her that big box of candy you bought? Chances are she'll be in a better mood by then. That's the way she's been acting lately. One minute she's smiling and talking; then her face is full of gloom and she takes off for her room."

"If you think that's better, I'll see you later, then," Matt said and guided the team onto the fork that led to his farm.

# Chapter Twenty-two

Matt sat on the bottom porch step, oiling a pile of traps. Although he didn't trap for a living, as some of his neighbors did, during the cold season he laid out a short line mainly to have something to do during the cold and gloomy days of winter. It wasn't his nature to sit idle in front of his fire waiting for the hours to pass.

The Gap was enjoying a mild spell at the present, but that could change overnight. The nights were cold now, the fence rails silver with frost.

A burst of childish laughter drew Matt's attention to Sammy, who was throwing and chasing after his new ball. Matt's face softened as he remembered how the little fellow's blue eyes had sparkled when he was handed the gift from Nashville. He had insisted on taking it and the toy soldiers to bed with him.

As he laid a finished trap aside and picked up another, he wondered if Kaitlan's strange behavior toward him had anything to do with Sammy coming to live with him. Did she still care for Nate? Did the boy remind her of his father?

He had gone to the Barrett farm last night to give her the box of chocolates. And though it was early, only a little past seven, Hattie had explained without looking at him that Kaitlan had retired early with a headache. He knew the black woman was lying to save his feelings and he was more convinced than ever that Kaitlan was deliberately avoiding him.

She couldn't hide from him forever, he thought, picking up another trap. He'd catch her alone someday and insist on her telling him what he had done to make her act so strangely toward him.

"Kaitlan, isn't that Maybelle Scott riding this way?" Hattie called from the kitchen.

Kaitlan hurried from her room to stand behind Hattie and look over her shoulder. "I wonder what she wants. She's never come visiting before."

They watched their sharp-tongued neighbor awkwardly dismount and tie her mare to the hitching post. When she opened the gate and started walking toward the cabin, Kaitlan sighed and stepped out onto the porch.

"Good morning, Maybelle," she called, wondering at the woman's glowing face. "How nice of you to come calling. Hattie has just finished brewing a pot of her herb tea. We'll have a cup, along with gingersnap cookies."

"Thank you, Kaitlan, that sounds right good." Maybelle preceded Kaitlan into the kitchen and nodded pleasantly to Hattie as she removed her bonnet and dabbed at her moist forehead with a white, lace-edged handkerchief. "I didn't realize it was so warm today." She sat down in the chair Kaitlan pulled from the table.

"That's a real pretty handkerchief you have there," Kaitlan said as she sat down across from her guest.

"Yes, it is," Maybelle agreed with a simpering smile. "Mr. Stokes gave it to me. It came all the way from New York," she added importantly.

"Well, now, is there a new romance brewing in the Gap?" Hattie teased.

Maybelle's face pinkened. "Yes, there is," she answered, then blurted out, "Hiram has asked me to marry him."

Kaitlan and Hattie were so stunned at the old maid's news that they hardly heard her add, "I'd like for you to stand up with me, Kaitlan."

Kaitlan gaped at her another second and then hurried to say, "Of course, Maybelle. I'd be delighted to."

"When is the happy occasion taking place?" Hattie asked, still a little wide-eyed with surprise.

"Next Saturday, four days from now. At the church, with Reverend Turner officiating," Maybelle answered, hardly able to contain her happiness.

My goodness, Kaitlan thought, I hope I can find something dressy at Stokes's store. Hattie, of course, had her new red dress. And though the bright red was hardly the proper color to wear to the ceremony, nothing but death would keep her friend from wearing it.

Maybelle finished her tea, refused another cup, and after asking Hattie if she would have Peter ride around to their neighbors and spread the word about her coming marriage, she said good-bye to her still-stunned hosts and took her leave.

Kaitlan and Hattie waited until Maybelle had ridden out of hearing distance, and then broke into loud laughter. "I can't imagine any man having the courage to ask that one to marry him," Kaitlan said.

Hattie nodded. "I'd bet my red dress that she did the asking. In a roundabout way, of course."

At least she'll have a husband, Kaitlan thought, sobering suddenly. "I'm going out to take a walk," she said quietly, leaving Hattie shaking her head behind her.

It was an hour before lunch, and Matt had finished with his traps and was waiting for Polly to call him to the table. His attention was caught by the sound of hoofbeats. Looking in that direction, he saw Kaitlan astride her stallion riding toward the church and cemetery. He asked himself if she was going to visit her grandparents' graves, or going to his special waterfall, which she was in the habit of doing. After about ten minutes he decided to hike up to his special place. If Kaitlan was there, he would pry out of her why she had avoided him last night. If she had gone to the cemetery, he wouldn't disturb her.

Calling to Polly that he'd be back soon, Matt struck off through the woods.

Arriving at the waterfall Matt saw Kaitlan at once. She sat at her favorite spot, a flat rock where the fine smokelike mist of water barely missed her. Her knees were drawn up, and her head was resting on them. Was she crying, he wondered, or just daydreaming? She gave a startled jerk when he softly called, "Are you all right, Kaitlan?"

Drawing an arm across her eyes, she turned her head from him and answered weakly, "I'm fine."

"No, you're not." Matt climbed up and sat down beside her. "I think you've been crying."

"You're mistaken," she declared at the end of a hiccup.

Matt cupped her face with his hand and turned her head toward him. "You little liar. Your eyes are red and swollen and they're still wet. Now tell me why the tears."

"I can't, Matt. I'm too ashamed."

"Kaitlan, I can't imagine you doing anything that would be shameful." He put an arm around her shoulders and coaxed, "Come on now, tell me what's wrong."

The touch of his comforting arms, the softness of his voice opened a floodgate of more tears. Burrowing her head against his chest, gripping the material of his shirt in her hands,

286

Kaitlan sobbed out, "I'm going to have a baby."

Matt's body went rock-still and a sound like a groan issued from his throat. "Are you sure, Kaitlan?" he finally managed to ask.

"Yes," Kaitlan answered miserably. "Sometime in May Sammy will have a new little sister or brother."

As Matt held her close, unaware that her tears were soaking through his shirt, she wailed softly, "What am I going to do, Matt? How am I ever going to get up the nerve to tell Hattie and Peter? They will be so disappointed in me."

"Don't tell them anything yet." Matt continued to absentmindedly rub her back as he stared unseeingly at the rushing waterfall, swearing furiously to himself. "I'll think of something."

Kaitlan raised her head to look at him. "I won't get rid of it, if that's what you're thinking."

"Good Lord, no," Matt denied fervently, pushing her head back onto his shoulder. "I would never want you to do that."

When only an occasional sob escaped her, he took Kaitlan by the shoulders and held her away from him. "Bathe your face; then go home. I'll see you in a few days with some kind of solution."

"What would I do without you, Matt?" Kaitlan sighed as he helped her off her perch.

"I'm sure you'd do all right." Matt playfully

pinched the end of her nose. "Now go get some cold water on your face and eyes. You know eagle-eyed Hattie. Don't let her see that you've been crying."

Kaitlan gave him a weak smile, and when he left her she was kneeling at one side of the tumbling water, cupping it in her hands and carrying it to her face.

Kaitlan awakened from the best sleep she'd had in many nights. Since shifting her dilemma to Matt's shoulders, all her despair had dispersed like steam rising from a boiling pan. She felt carefree again. Matt would take care of everything. She never gave a thought to just how he'd do this, but she felt certain that he would come up with a solution.

When she walked into the kitchen, a bright smile on her face and a cheery "Good morning" on her lips, Hattie looked at her and wondered when her mood would change. But her high spirits lasted through breakfast and while she helped Hattie with the dishes. And later as she made up her bed and straightened up the cabin she sang little snatches of songs.

Kaitlan was peeling apples for a pie, wondering to Hattie if she would be able to find a nice dress at the Village to wear at Maybelle's wedding, when old Granny Higgins rode up on her mule. Hattie hurried outside to help the old lady to the ground and to assist her up the porch steps.

"Thank you, Hattie, my rheumatiz' is sorely actin' up this mornin'. It's bad every time the weather changes. I suffer somethin' turrible in the winter."

"You come close to the fire now and get warmed up." Hattie took the ragged shawl from her shoulders and bade her to sit in the rocker alongside the small cooking fireplace. "I'll get you a hot cup of coffee."

"That would hit the spot right well, Hattie. Put a hearty splash of moonshine in it, if you have some handy."

Kaitlan and Hattie exchanged amused looks; then Hattie asked, "What brings you out on this cool morning, Granny?"

"Two things, actually." Granny propped her feet on the hearth. "I wanted to tell you that the old Tyler place burned down last night."

"It did!" Kaitlan and Hattie exclaimed in unison. "How did it happen, does anybody know?" Hattie asked.

"Well, them who believes in haints and spirits are sayin' that the Tylers have come back from the dead and set fire to it. But more sensible people say that most likely some rowdy teenagers was in the old place drinkin' moonshine and got careless with matches. I'm inclined to think that too."

"I, for one, am glad it burned," Hattie said. "Maybe all those ghost stories will stop being told."

"They won't. There will be more wild stories

than ever goin' 'round."

"You said you came for two reasons, Granny," Kaitlan reminded her.

Granny nodded with a toothless grin. "What about skinny Maybelle marryin' fat ol' Hiram! Don't that take the whole biscuit? The women-folk don't know which to talk about first, the weddin' or the old cabin burnin'. It's like their tongues are tied in the middle and waggin' on both ends," she ended with a cackling laugh.

"We was talking about the wedding when you rode up," Hattie said. "Maybelle asked Kaitlan to stand up with her and Kaitlan was wondering if she could find a nice dress at Hiram's store."

"I doubt it. He mostly carries homespuns and calicos."

"Oh, dear, I was afraid of that." Kaitlan sighed. "Just when I can afford to buy a decent dress, there's none to be had."

"I know where you could buy a real purty one, but I don't know if you'd want to give the dressmaker your business," Granny said.

"I don't care who she is. I need a nice dress."

"It's that widder woman who lives at the edge of the Village. She sews dresses for Ruby and her girls. If you get down there today, she can most likely have a dress finished before the weddin'."

"What do you think, Hattie?" Kaitlan looked at her doubtfully.

"I don't know why not. Just because she sews

for whores doesn't mean that she's one."

"That's right," Granny said. "Bertha Hart is a real respectable, churchgoin' woman."

"Does she sew for the rest of the women who live in the Gap?" Kaitlan asked.

"My land, no. The womenfolk around here can't afford her price. The material she uses is silks, muslins, lawns, and velvets. You'd look real purty in a blue velvet, Kaitlan. It would match your eyes."

Kaitlan pushed aside the bowl of apples and stood up. "I'll go tidy my hair and ride down there right now."

Later that morning Kaitlan rode Snowy down the single dirt street of the Village. She asked the first person she saw, an old man shuffling along, where the widow Hart lived.

Raising his cane, he pointed to the end of the Village. "She lives back in the trees there." He spat a stream of tobacco juice on the ground, then leered at her. "Do you be a new girl of Ruby's?"

Kaitlan didn't bother to answer the old lecher, but rode on down the street.

She had no problem finding the dressmaker's cabin tucked in among some pines. After dismounting and looping the reins over a tree branch, she approached the small dwelling.

She raised her hand to knock on the door just as it opened and a big woman, the one she had seen Matt talking to, stood framed in the doorway. She received a pleasant smile and a cheery, "You must be Miss Kaitlan Barrett, Matt's friend."

"Yes, I am." Kaitlan smiled back, thinking that with the paint washed off her face Ruby Gentry would look like any other respectable woman in the Gap.

"How is little Sammy? Me and the girls miss the little fellow."

"He's fine. He wants to visit you. I think Matt intends to bring him for a visit soon, now that he's not so busy with his tobacco."

"Matt is a fine man and will make Sammy a good father." Without giving Kaitlan a chance to agree, Ruby said, "I must be getting along. My girls will be getting up soon and will want their lunch."

When Ruby moved her large bulk, Kaitlan was able to see the small woman who had stood behind her. She was greeted with a sweet smile and invited to step inside. "I assume you want me to make you a dress," the widow said, patting a chair and inviting Kaitlan to sit down.

Seating herself Kaitlan returned the smile and answered, "I'm standing up for Maybelle Scott's wedding and I'd like something nice to wear. The wedding is Saturday. Could you have something ready by then? I know it's short notice."

"Luckily I just finished making some dresses for Ruby's girls. I can finish one for you if I get started today. I'll show you some patterns and we'll look at the material I have on hand."

"Good!" Kaitlan heaved a sigh of relief, then said laughingly, "I was afraid I'd have to stand up in calico."

"And Miss Scott wouldn't like that." Amusement twinkled in the widow's eyes.

Kaitlan chose a pattern with a wide-cut neckline, long tight sleeves, a form-fitting bodice, and a draping skirt. She took Granny's advice and decided on a soft blue velvet.

"You've made a marvelous selection in both material and pattern." Mrs. Hart smiled her approval. "Let me take some measurements now and I'll get started right away."

Riding home later, Kaitlan fell into a fit of depression. Would she ever have the excitement of planning her own wedding?

# Chapter Twenty-three

A cold wind, unusual for mid-October, stirred the branches of the tall pines as Matt rode down the river road. The old-timers had been predicting an early winter, and maybe they were right, he thought. The mountain folklore they espoused often proved to be true.

They made their prophesies according to how thick and tough the cornhusks were, the way a squirrel grew a bushier tail and started gathering nuts early. Then there were those who swore by the fact that the beavers' lodges had more logs than usual, that the hair on their farm animals and dogs was thicker. Some claimed that a harsh winter was coming when more spiders were seen or when the butterflies left the mountain early. And Granny Higgins swore that if there was frost before mid-November it would be a bad winter.

The old folks' forecasting went on and on. Matt smiled his amusement, thinking how utterly ridiculous some of the signs were. But he had always heeded those that made sense. He had found that the hotter the summer, the colder the winter was. Also, if they didn't have too much rain in the summer, the lack of precipitation was made up by heavy snow in the winter.

As Satan loped along, Matt's thoughts turned to the wedding taking place tomorrow. That was the reason he was making the trip to the Village. He needed a new pair of boots to wear to it. He had tried to polish his old ones last night but they were too scratched and scuffed to take a shine. He wanted to look nice for Maybelle's big day, the biggest one the old maid would probably ever have. But not for her alone, he admitted to himself. He wanted to look his best in Kaitlan's eyes also.

For once, he wished he had his stepbrother's easy way with women, his endless fund of sweet talk. It would be so much easier to woo Kaitlan if he did. But maybe Kaitlan's pregnancy would simplify everything. If he were to ask her to marry him now, would she agree?

It was an outlandish scheme, but it just might work. Once they were married, he would have all the time he needed to win her heart. As his stallion neared the Village, Matt made up his mind. He would ask Kaitlan as soon as he got back home.

Hiram's good-natured face was all smiles when Matt entered his store, and he greeted his customer with a hearty "Good morning, Matt."

"The same to you, Hiram. I expect you're looking forward to your big day tomorrow."

"Yes, I am, but I'm getting a little nervous too. It's a big step for a man who has been a bachelor for fifty-four years. I've lived in two rooms over the store for fifteen years. I won't know how to act being married and living in a regular house. I'll have to watch my manners around Maybelle too, not belch or anything whenever I feel like it."

Matt grinned. "You'll sure have to watch that. Such things offend ladies' sensibilities. Maybelle will make you live in the barn if you're not housebroken."

"I reckon." Hiram's face lost the exuberance it had worn a few minutes before.

Matt felt sorry for the fat, easygoing man and spoke of the reason he was there. "I want to take a look at your dress boots, Hiram. I need a new pair to wear at your wedding. I've got to look my best or Maybelle won't let me in the church."

"Ain't that the truth." Hiram was beginning to sound henpecked already. "She's a very particular woman. Wants everything to be just perfect."

As Matt looked over the selection of boots, he hoped that he hadn't given the storekeeper cause to rethink getting married.

He pulled on three different pairs of boots, and found the last ones to his liking. He took them to Hiram and laid his money on the counter. The groom-to-be said as he wrapped them up, "I got a letter for you. It's from some lawyer firm in Nashville."

Matt walked over to a corner of the store where a portion of it had been walled in with a sign over the door that stated UNITED STATES

POST OFFICE. Why, he wondered, as he waited for Hiram to join him, would he get a letter from a lawyer?

Hiram finally lumbered across the room, handed him his package, and then walked into the small room where the mail was delivered.

When Matt was handed a long white envelope he looked at the left-hand corner and read, *Brock and Crawford, Attorneys at Law.* He became a little nervous as he tore it open, wondering if it had something to do with Nate.

Matt read the short message, then read it again.

Dear Matthew Ingram. On September twenty third, I drew up a will for your stepbrother, Nate Streeter. As the guardian of his son, Samuel Streeter, he asks that you handle his son's inheritance until he is of age. There is a house and furniture, and a sizable savings account. He also asks that at his passing you see to his funeral and burial.

I was informed this morning that he is on his deathbed. It is imperative that you come to Nashville as quickly as possible and see me in my office. Sincerely, Enos Crawford.

Matt folded the single sheet of paper and slipped it back in the envelope. He felt Hiram's questioning eyes on him and said briefly, "It's to inform me that Nate is dying." He quickly left the store before he could be questioned further. Climbing into the saddle, he set Satan down the street at a hard gallop.

What had sparked a sense of decency in Nate at this late date? he wondered as the stallion thundered along. Was it because he knew he was dying and was afraid of what the unknown would bring him? Did he hope that the gesture of providing for his son might atone for the evil life he had led on earth?

He urged the stallion to run faster. He must get to Nashville as soon as possible, to talk to Nate before he died.

When he arrived at home, Matt handed the lawyer's letter to Polly on his way to his room. There he threw clean underwear and a white shirt into a satchel, changed into his suit, and pulled on his new boots. When Aunt Polly wanted to discuss the surprising news from Nashville, he told her he had to get on the road, and that he would tell her everything when he returned.

"When will that be?" she asked, following him to the door.

"At least a week, maybe longer."

It was around noon when a tired Satan carried Matt into Nashville. Matt guided him down the street of the business district and had no trouble finding the building that housed the law firm he sought. After tying the stallion to a brass hitching rail alongside the wooden sidewalk, he brushed as much dust as he could from his clothes, then wiped off his boots with a handkerchief he took from a back pocket. After drawing a long, deep breath he hopped up on the boards and entered the brown-painted building.

Inside, he walked down a long hall until he came to a door that had the title in large letters, BROCK AND CRAWFORD. ATTORNEYS AT LAW. In answer to his rap a male voice invited, "Come in."

As he walked across a shiny hardwood floor, a tall man in his early fifties, dressed in a brown suit with a stiff white collar, stood up from behind a large desk. Smiling, he asked, "What can I do for you, sir?"

"I'm Matt Ingram. If you're Mr. Crawford I'm here in response to your letter."

"Yes, Mr. Ingram. I'm Crawford," the lawyer answered, solemnly offering his hand.

When his work-callused palm met the other man's soft one, Matt thought to himself that this one was a city fellow through and through. "Have a seat," Crawford invited, sitting back down.

"How is my stepbrother?" Matt asked, resting an ankle on his knee.

"I'm sorry to tell you that Mr. Streeter passed away about three hours ago. A young . . . woman came in to tell me." When Matt showed no sorrow, no emotion at his announcement, the lawyer added, "I have ordered that the body be taken to the Alder Funeral

Home, a block over. You can make all arrangements with them." He opened a desk drawer and brought out a ring of keys. "These are the keys to Mr. Streeter's house." When Matt had taken them, Crawford pulled a sheet of paper to him and spent a moment writing on it. He folded it in half and handed it to Matt, saying, "I've written down the address of the residence and the bank where Mr. Streeter did his business. They will be expecting you.

"If I can help you in any way, just let me know."

"There is one thing," Matt began hesitantly, "but I don't know if it can be done." When the lawyer sat quietly, waiting for him to continue, Matt said, "On my way here I thought a lot about Nate's son's mother. She was seventeen years old when Nate got her with child, and her parents threw her out when he refused to marry her. She's living somewhere here in Nashville. I'd like to find her, let her take over the raising of her son, live with him in his father's house. I'd like to let her have access to the money in the bank to help her do this. I feel that is no more than fair. Can papers be drawn up to transfer everything to her?"

When Crawford made no instant reply to his request, only stared down at his desk, toying with a pencil, Matt sat forward, anxiety on his face. He had given up hope that his idea would be practicable when Crawford looked up at him and spoke.

"It would require a lot of paperwork, and then we'd have to present your request to a judge to decide on. It is in your favor that the court most always thinks that it's to the child's benefit to be raised by its mother.

"While you take care of Mr. Streeter's burial and find the child's mother, I'll start drawing up the papers."

Both men stood up and shook hands again. "Thank you, sir," Matt said sincerely. "I expect I'll be staying in Nate's house while I'm here. You can reach me there, keep me informed of your progress."

After asking directions from a couple of people about how to find Nate's house, Matt finally stood in front of a two-story redbrick building. Well, Nate, he thought, staring at the attractive house on the respectable street, you've done quite well since leaving the Gap.

He lifted the brass knocker on the front door and let it drop. Seconds later he heard the sharp tapping of a woman's shoes from inside. The door was flung open and hard, cold eyes stared up at him from a heavily painted face. Her hands on her hips, the young woman snapped, "I'm in mourning for my man, so I won't be doin' any business today."

Matt ran an insulting look over her dress, the short hemline, the neckline so low it showed a good portion of her breasts. Had this one taken Claire's place? he wondered.

The woman grew angry at his scornful scrutiny and declared in a heated voice, "I told you I was grievin' for my man. Now go away."

"Like hell you are. Nobody grieves for Nate Streeter," Matt said coldly, and, brushing her aside, he walked into a wide, carpeted hallway. The woman ran after him, screeching, "What do you think you're doin'?"

Matt wheeled on her. "I know what *I'm* doing. Now I'm going to tell you what you're going to do in the next ten minutes. You're going to get your clothes together and get the hell out of here. And," he added, "I'll check you and your luggage to make sure you're not taking anything that doesn't belong to you."

The woman gave him a sullen look. "You must be the great Matt Ingram, Nate's stepbrother. He hated and envied you, you know. That's why he left all his money to his boy. He never wanted his son to be dependent on you the way he was."

Matt digested the news silently. "I think you'd better start packing. I'll just sit down here and make sure you don't steal anything on your way out."

A stream of foul language trailed behind the woman as she flew up the stairs to the rooms above.

When the whore, whose name he didn't know and hadn't asked for, came back downstairs with a minute to spare, Matt stood up. "Open up your satchel," he ordered, standing over her.

Giving him a hard look, she undid the straps of the valise and spread it open.

Matt went through its few contents: a couple of dresses of a flimsy material and a pair of hose. He said to himself with a wry grin, "Evidently she doesn't wear any underclothes." Beneath the clothing he found a bottle of cheap perfume and some gaudy colored-bead necklaces and matching earbobs. He motioned her to close the satchel, which she hurried to do.

But, still watching her, Matt saw her lips twist in a smirk as she started walking toward the door. He followed her and, taking her by the arm, stopped her and said roughly, "I haven't searched you yet."

"What do you mean, search me?" she screeched. "I ain't gonna have you pawin' my body."

It only took an instant to discover that she had nothing concealed in her scanty clothing. Still he wasn't satisfied. That grin he had seen on her face meant she felt that she was getting away with something.

"Take off your shoes," he ordered.

"I'll do no such thing." An uneasy look came into her eyes.

Matt didn't quibble with her, but reached down and grabbed her ankle. He jerked the low-cut pump off her foot. Sticking his fingers inside it, he pulled out several banknotes of large denominations. When he gave her a hard look, she wilted and made no fuss when he took off the other shoe. He found what he expected: another sheaf of banknotes.

As he shoved the money into his pocket the irate whore slipped on her shoes and stormed toward the door again. Before she slammed it behind her, she fired another barrage of oaths at him, some he had never heard before.

Matt had no problem finding the funeral home. When he stepped inside, the hushed atmosphere sent shivers up his spine. He gave a start when a voice spoke behind him.

"May I help you, sir?" The question was asked in low tones.

"I'm Matt Ingram. I've come to pay whatever is involved in Nate Streeter's burial."

Taken aback by Matt's curt announcement, the man hesitated a minute and then said, "Well, there is the fee for laying out the body and the cost of the casket. As for the burial, do you want the body sent home to be buried among friends and relatives?"

Matt was quick to shake his head. He didn't say so, but he knew that everyone in the Gap would object to Nate being laid to rest among their relatives. "You can bury him in a cemetery here in Nashville," he said out loud.

"I see. Will you want him to have a headstone?"

Matt shook his head again. "Just give me the bill for your services."

Matt heaved a long sigh of relief when he

stepped outside into the warm sunshine. Now, he thought, how in the world am I to find Judy Perkins? He didn't know the girl well, only that her folks lived farther up the mountain in a remote area, and that they tended to stay to themselves. He couldn't recall ever seeing the mother.

Matt spent three days and part of the evenings in the lower section of town, asking everyone he could think of if they knew Judy's whereabouts. To his dismay, no one had heard of her. Surely she couldn't have disappeared without a trace?

On his fourth day in Nashville, Matt sat on a bench in the small park across the street from Nate's house. Was Judy dead? he wondered. Should he give up his search and go home? He longed to be back in the mountains, to breathe fresh air again. And to see Kaitlan's lovely face. She was probably anxious for his return, waiting to see if he had come up with a solution to her serious problem.

But the lawyer had all the papers drawn up, and he felt that he should spend one more day looking for Sammy's mother.

A sheet of newspaper blew across the street and wrapped around his leg. As he removed it a thought came to him: Why not put an advertisement in the daily newspaper? If Judy was still alive, maybe she would read it and get in touch with him. He knew the building where the paper was printed. He had walked past it a dozen times since coming to Nashville.

Fifteen minutes later Matt left the residential neighborhood and entered the business district, where he made his way to the newspaper office. There, with a pen poised over a pad of paper, he thought for a minute, then began to write:

I am looking for a young woman named Judy Perkins. I have some important news for her. Judy, if you read this, contact Brock and Crawford, Attorneys at Law.

He signed his name, paid a young man the price of the ad, and walked out on the street. As he strolled toward Nate's house he hoped that Judy was in the habit of reading the newspaper.

Three days passed without Matt hearing from Judy. He had just about made up his mind it was useless to hang around Nashville any longer. For all he knew, Judy couldn't even read. Tomorrow morning I'm heading for home, he decided.

Matt was packing his saddlebag when the knocker sounded on the front door. When he answered its summons, he recognized a young teenager he had seen in Crawford's office. The boy took off his cap and said, "Mr. Ingram, Mr. Crawford would like you to return with me to his office."

Matt took his jacket off the coatrack in the

hall and said as he shrugged into it, "Let's go."

At first he didn't recognize the young woman sitting in the lawyer's office. With the exception of the rather gaudy dress she wore, she looked like a respectable young lady, not the poor mountain girl he'd known.

Then he looked into her large brown eyes and exclaimed, "Judy! You did read my ad."

Crawford rose from behind his desk. "I'll leave you two to talk. I'll be out in the hall. Call me when you've finished."

"I can't get over how you've changed, Judy," Matt said, sitting down beside her. "How have you managed since coming to Nashville?"

"It was hard at first," Judy answered with a shrug of her shoulders and a tight little smile. "No one would hire me. . . . I never had enough to eat. Then, I found someone to care for me . . . an older man. I'm his mistress now. I have been for two years. He supplies me with an apartment and money for food and clothing. I never know when I'll hear his key in the door, and although he treats me very nice, I'm really just a whore."

"All that is going to change, Judy," Matt said sympathetically. "From now on you're going to pose as a young widow who is raising her son alone."

"Have you taken leave of your senses, Matt?" Judy looked at him as though she believed he had.

"No." Matt grinned at her. "I'm quite sane.

Now, I'm going to tell you a story that will be harder yet to believe." For the next half hour he filled Judy in on the last three years, bringing her up to the present.

Nothing Matt told Judy seemed to surprise her until she learned of her son's inheritance. Thankful tears filled her eyes then.

"Oh, Matt," she cried, "my little boy is going to have a fine future. Are you sure of everything you said?"

Matt nodded with a wide smile. "The papers are all ready to be signed." He ran a glance over her attire. "Do you have a dress that is more . . ."

"Plainer?" Judy laughed. "Something a respectable young widow would wear?"

"Yes." Matt nodded, a sparkle in his eyes. "We have to see a judge and get his stamp of approval on the papers. He might frown on that red, ruffly one."

"I'll meet you in his office in half an hour, and I promise I won't embarrass you."

And she didn't. Judy had pulled her hair back into a sleek chignon that lay low on the back of her neck, then perched a small, narrow-brimmed hat on top of her head. Her dress was a dove-gray poplin, long sleeved and buttoned up to her chin. No young woman had ever looked more respectable.

When some twenty minutes later they were out on the street, Judy let loose a laugh that wasn't at all ladylike. Matt laughed and told her to calm down, then took her to Nate's bank. "You won't need to draw out any money yet," he told her and handed her the money Nate's whore had concealed in her shoes, "but I think you should introduce yourself to the bank's president."

Judy could only stare at the money she held clutched in her hand. It was more than she had ever dreamed of having in a lifetime.

She was equally stunned by her new home and the housekeeper that went with it.

When she had gone over every room, exclaiming her delight, she and Matt sat in the magnificent parlor, sipping coffee from dainty cups and nibbling on wafer-thin cookies. Every five minutes or so they had to hold back their laughter as they made plans for Judy to come to the Gap. They had decided it would be best to let Sammy get used to her before she took him away to live in Nashville.

When it came time for Matt to say good-bye, huge tears washed down Judy's cheeks. "How can I ever thank you enough, Matt? You have changed my whole life around for me."

"It's time you had something good happen to you for a change," he said, giving her a hug. "I'm glad that I could do it for you. Now dry your eyes and go gloat over your new home for a couple hours."

Judy chuckled and blew her nose. "That's exactly what I'm going to do."

"I'll see you in a week or so, then."

# Chapter Twenty-four

The log on the fire flamed, making Kaitlan jump as it burst into a shower of sparks. Her nerves were stretched to the breaking point.

When was Matt coming home? she asked herself as she had many times this past week. This was the second week he'd been gone. Surely it hadn't taken him this long to settle Nate's affairs and see to his burial . . . unless he hadn't died yet. Aunt Polly had told them that the lawyer's letter said he was at death's door.

What if something had happened to Matt? Her heart beat wildly at the thought. Maybe he had never arrived in Nashville. Maybe he had arrived and some cutthroat had dragged him into an alley and killed him.

But that wasn't likely. Matt was a big, strong man. He could fight off half a dozen men who might attack him.

Another fear entered Kaitlan's mind. What if he had been on his way home and a panther had leaped upon him? The big cats moved so silently, he'd never hear one over the plodding of the horse's hooves on the rocky trail. She'd never forget that day at the church social when Matt had shot and killed the panther.

She made herself stop worrying about Matt and switched her thoughts to Maybelle's wedding. Everything had gone just as the bride had wanted it to. Hiram's suit had been pressed with a crease so sharp it looked lethal. His shirt was snow white and his hair was slicked back.

As for Maybelle, she looked almost pretty. Her face glowed and her look of satisfaction put a glitter in her small eyes. When they had said their vows and everyone had gathered in the churchyard, Hattie poked Kaitlan in the ribs with her elbow. "She's started bossing Hiram already," she whispered. "I'll bet he's wondering what he's got himself into right about now." Flustered by all the orders shot at him by his new wife, the shopkeeper was sweating profusely as he hurried about doing Maybelle's bidding.

However, Kaitlan remembered that when Maybelle waited on her at the store last week there was a serene glow in her eyes. Kaitlan knew that look. She herself had worn it also after Nate's night visits. She cringed, remembering how that evil man was able to make her lose control and do things that made her blush now.

Kaitlan refused to let her mind dwell on those nights of passion, one of which had left her pregnant. Could she love a child of Nate's? she asked herself, then felt ashamed that she had let such a question enter her mind. Of course she would love the innocent little piece of humanity. *Only, please, God, don't let it look like Nate.*

Suddenly the cabin seemed to be closing in on her. She felt she had to get outside, had to clear the disturbing thoughts from her mind.

"I'm going for a walk," she said to the Smiths as she took her jacket off a peg beside the door.

Hattie and Peter looked at each other as the door closed behind her. Hattie sighed. "She's back in the glooms again. I'd like to know what's bothering that girl."

An icy November wind lashed Kaitlan in the face as she walked along, scuffing the fallen leaves on the forest floor. She didn't feel its pinch, for a familiar worry, one that never left her mind for long, returned to niggle at her brain. Had Matt thought of a solution to her predicament? He'd said that he had come up with one idea, but that he didn't think she would go along with it. At this late date, she felt that she would agree to anything he suggested, no matter how outlandish it might be.

The sun was going down. Kaitlan turned around and started homeward. She didn't want to get caught outside alone after dark. She still got the cold shivers every time she remembered the panther at the waterfall that day. She stopped in midstride and peered down the shadowed trail when she heard the clomping of hooves. She smiled and her eyes sparkled when she made out Matt's stallion jogging toward her.

"Oh, Matt!" she cried. "You're home." When Matt pulled Satan in and dismounted, she

312

threw herself at him. "I thought you were never coming home."

Matt put his arms around her, and every nerve ending in her body was aware of him. Without thinking she pressed her softness against his hard body. Becoming aware then of what she was doing, she blushed and pulled away, wondering what Matt must think of her, clinging that way to him.

"Well, I reckon you're glad to see me." Matt grinned down at her.

Kaitlan gave a nervous little laugh. "I was beginning to think that something had happened to you."

"It took longer to settle Nate's affairs than I thought it would. I'd like to tell you all about it tonight after supper. Right now I want to get home and soak in a tub of hot water. I sure am saddle-weary."

"Did you give any more thought to my problem?"

"I've thought on it, but haven't come up with anything except a plan I don't think you'll agree to."

"Well, you can tell me what it is tonight. Maybe I'll surprise you and like it."

"We'll see," Matt said doubtfully. He climbed back in the saddle. "I'll see you later, then."

When Kaitlan walked into the cabin, all smiles, Hattie and Peter stared at her. What could have changed her mood so quickly? When Kaitlan said on her way to her room,

"Matt is home," they looked at each other with raised eyebrows.

"Do you think it's possible she cares for Matt?" Hattie said hopefully.

Peter nodded. "It sure looks that way. Maybe she finally realizes that he's worth a thousand Nate Streeters."

"I certainly hope so. She was always such a levelheaded girl until she met that piece of sweet-talking scum."

Kaitlan kept up such a stream of chatter all through supper, Hattie rolled her eyes at the ceiling. When it came time to wash the dishes, Hattie said, "You go change your dress. I'll straighten up the kitchen. That gabbing of yours is giving me a headache."

Matt arrived about ten minutes after Kaitlan had changed her dress and brushed her hair. When she answered his knock, she thought how handsome and dear he looked, his collar turned up to his windblown hair, a few loose curls hanging on his forehead.

"Man, that wind is fierce," he laughingly said as it came swirling in behind him, causing the flames to leap in the fireplace.

"Go on in by the fire and warm up." Kaitlan smiled up at him as she hurried to close the door.

When everyone was settled in front of the fire, a glass of whiskey at Matt's elbow, Peter asked, "Well, Matt, what kept you so long in Nashville?"

Matt's lips twisted wryly. "Things that you will find hard to believe. First off, Nate passed away three hours before I arrived at his lawyer's office. The house he left Sammy is in a respectable neighborhood and very well built. And the money in his savings account is more than you and I can make in a lifetime raising tobacco."

Matt took a sip of his drink, then continued his tale. "I got to thinking about the boy's mother, the hard life she has led since his birth. It seemed to me that the decent thing was to try and find her and unite them, let her take over the rearing of him.

"It took me nearly a week to find her. When I told her why I was searching for her, she shed almost as many tears as she did on the day she handed her baby over to me."

"Well, I'll be jiggered," Peter exclaimed when Matt finished his story. "I guess you'll be losing the little fellow, then. It's gonna be hard on you, ain't it?"

"Yes, it will. I love him dearly, but he belongs with his mother. Aunt Polly is going to miss him a lot, too."

"Are you taking Sammy to his mother, or will she come get him?" Kaitlan asked.

"Judy is coming for him. We decided that she should spend a few days at the farm, letting Sammy get used to her before taking him away."

"That's a good idea," Hattie said. "The poor little fellow has already had two changes made

315

in his life. It's good that he'll spend the rest of it in Nashville, away from the Gap. He won't be looked down on there; people won't speak of him as Judy Perkins's little bastard."

Kaitlan flinched. Would that happen to her child? Would neighbors whisper to each other about Kaitlan Barrett's little bastard?

"Oh, Lord, I couldn't bear it," she wailed inwardly, knowing in that moment that she loved her unborn baby dearly. She could almost understand why that young girl had thrown herself into the river. She could feel her pain, her hopelessness.

Immersed in her gloomy thoughts, Kaitlan was startled to realize that Hattie and Peter were saying good night, preparing to go home to their little house. She withheld a relieved sigh. At last she could ask Matt what he had in mind for her.

As soon as the Smiths closed the door behind them, she slid her chair closer to him and said eagerly, "Now tell me what you think I won't like to do."

Matt finished the last of his drink, set the glass down slowly, cleared his throat a couple of times, and then blurted out, "Marry me."

Kaitlan blinked, thinking that surely she had misunderstood him. "Marry you?" she squawked.

"Why not?" he asked, almost defensively. "Your baby would have a name. I can give you a nice home, provide you with most anything you would want."

Kaitlan looked away from him and stared un-happily into the fire. Matt had given her the perfect answer to her plight, and she would like nothing better in the world than to marry him. Even now, she was so aware of his presence, her stomach was full of butterflies. How wonderful it would be if he had first said that he loved her.

She turned her head to look at him. "Do you think we would have a good marriage without love in it?"

Matt didn't answer right away, and in the gloom pierced only by the low flames in the fireplace, Kaitlan didn't see the pain in his eyes that her words had caused. After a moment or so, he said, "A lot of good marriages have lasted because the couple liked and respected each other. I think we have that between us."

"That's true," Kaitlan agreed weakly.

"Besides, it will be a marriage in name only. Our lives won't change all that much."

In name only. Kaitlan couldn't get past those three words. There would be no lovemaking be-tween them, she thought in frustration. But that was one way Matt might grow to love her. Could she live the rest of her life with every fiber in her being crying out to have his arms around her, his hard body moving on hers? And what about when his body cried out for the release that only a woman could give him? He was a young, healthy male who would want a woman often.

Her hands clasped tightly in her lap, Kaitlan

asked, "What about . . . you know . . . your needs? I don't think I'd like seeing you go to other women for that."

"Don't worry about that. I'd never embarrass you in that manner. Neither you, nor anyone else, will ever know when that happens."

Kaitlan felt crushed. Matt had admitted that he would find his pleasure in another woman's arms. Could she bear it, loving him the way she did, wondering what woman he was with every time he was gone for a few hours? Would she know when it happened? Would he come home with a contented glow on his face?

What should she do? she wailed inwardly. For her unborn child's sake, should she accept his proposal, such as it was, knowing that his heart wasn't truly in it?

"Well," Matt said after her long silence, "should we have the preacher announce it in church Sunday? We could get married the following Saturday."

Kaitlan hesitated briefly, then answered, "Yes, if you're sure you want to marry me."

"I'm sure." Matt picked up his jacket, which he had laid on the floor next to his chair.

Kaitlan followed him to the door. He smiled down at her, gave her a brotherly peck on the cheek, and stepped outside.

Kaitlan leaned her head against the door, listening to the stallion's hoofbeats fade away. A sob choked her; then hot tears washed down her cheeks. She would be getting her man, but she wouldn't be getting his love.

As Matt rode down the well-trodden trail, whose muddy ruts were frozen ridges now, his head was bowed in defeat. He had thought, had hoped, that Kaitlan's recent actions toward him meant she felt toward him the way he felt for her. He'd had his answer tonight. She was fond of him, but she didn't love him. She had admitted it when she answered his proposal with the question, "Do you think we would have a good marriage without love in it?" What cut him the deepest was that she expected him to go to other women for what she wouldn't give him. She only wanted him to be secretive about it so that she wouldn't lose face in front of their neighbors.

What would it do to him, he asked himself, living in the same house with her, knowing night after night that only a wall separated them? He had only to look at her and his body tightened. Would he, after a time, be forced to go to the Indian village to visit one of the pretty maids there? He hadn't been there for months.

And what about Kaitlan? She knew the pleasures of lovemaking. Hope flared inside him. Maybe she would turn to him to ease the ache in her body. He didn't like to think that was the only way he could possess her, but he knew he wouldn't hesitate a second to welcome her into his bed.

Aunt Polly was still up when Matt walked into the warmth of the cabin. He shed his jacket and hung it up and tried to put an elated look on his face. "Kaitlan has promised to marry me, Aunt Polly."

Polly's elation was real as she cried, "Oh, Matt, I'm so happy for you. I know you have loved her ever since she came to the Gap. When will your marriage take place?"

"A week from Saturday. After Reverend Turner announces it in church this Sunday."

"I must start getting my things together. I'll be going to live with my sister on the other side of the Gap. She's been wanting me to move in with her for a long time."

"You mustn't do that, Aunt Polly. There's room for you here. Besides, you don't get along with your sister."

Polly gave a little shrug of her shoulders. "I get along with her well enough until she starts trying to run my life. She's one of those people who thinks that her way is the right way, the only way. I'll just ignore her.

"Anyway, a newly married couple should be alone as they start their life together."

Matt had been thinking it would save him and Kaitlan a lot of embarrassment if Polly wasn't around to see their sleeping arrangement.

"I'll agree to it for a month; then I'll expect to see you back here," he said firmly.

"We'll see." Polly smiled at him and put her knitting away in its basket. "I'll say good night now," she said, and left Matt to stare gloomily into the fire.

# Chapter Twenty-five

The cold weather was definitely here to stay, Kaitlan thought as she pulled her knitted hood snug around her red, chilled cheeks. Every morning the valley was white with frost and the creek pools were gradually icing over.

Ordinarily she would be close to the fire on such a bitter, windy day, but she wanted to say good-bye to Sammy. His mother had arrived at the Ingram farm yesterday and she wanted to meet Judy Perkins.

Sunday, two days ago, everyone had been shocked when the Reverend Turner had announced that she and Matt would marry this coming Saturday. After the sermon everyone had gathered around her and Matt, offering them sincere congratulations, saying that the two of them were meant for each other, that they would have a good life together and have many children.

She had forced back a bitter laugh at their predictions. There would be only one child in the Ingram family, and that one wouldn't belong to the head of the house. Would Matt grow to hate her when the little one arrived, looking just like Nate? She vowed that if that were the case, she would take her babe and leave the Gap. Matt was too dear to her to have him embarrassed by cruel gossip.

As Kaitlan neared the Ingram farm, the first thing she saw was Matt, Sammy, and a young woman playing together in the yard. Sammy's boyish squeal and the adult laughter rang out as they grappled with each other in a pile of leaves.

They looked so good together, her heart contracted. Just like a mother and father playing with their child. She gasped her pain when the young woman straddled Matt's waist and, fighting off his hands, piled leaves in his face. When he flipped her on her back and did the same thing to her, Kaitlan could stand no more and she urged the stallion forward, pulling him up just in time to avoid trampling the laughing pair.

When Judy's eyes widened at the sight of the big horse and the girl staring down at them, Matt turned his head and looked up at her. His face flushed red, because he knew how he and Judy must look to Kaitlan.

After scrambling to his feet, he helped Judy up and stammered, "I . . . didn't . . . expect to . . . see you today, Kaitlan. This is Judy Perkins, Sammy's mother." The young woman stopped brushing leaves off her person and gave Kaitlan a friendly smile.

Kaitlan dismounted and, returning the smile, held out her hand. "I heard that you have come to take your son back to Nashville with you. I've come to say good-bye to him. He's a dear little boy."

She looked at Matt then and said coolly, "Your hair is full of leaves." With that she took Sammy by the hand and led him toward the cabin. "I have a going-away present for you," she said, smiling down at him.

Matt looked after her, dumbfounded. When she'd told him about his hair, her voice had dripped ice and her eyes had shards of it in them.

"Whew" — Judy laughed — "she is furious. You're going to have to do a lot of sweet-talking to get back in her good graces."

"If you mean she was jealous of our horsin' around, you're mistaken. She's probably upset about something else."

"You don't know much about women, do you, Matt?"

"I don't know a lot, but I do know that Kaitlan wasn't upset at seeing us together."

After they had brushed the leaves and twigs off their clothing, Matt and Judy found Kaitlan at the kitchen table with Sammy on her lap. The child was playing with a wooden pony Peter had carved for him. Polly had poured four cups of coffee and was cutting into a pumpkin pie. "I figured coffee and pie would be quite welcome after your being out in the cold." Her smile included them all.

"What a nice horsey Kaitlan has given you." Judy sat down next to Kaitlan's chair. "May Mama see it?"

Instead of handing it to his mother, he

scooted off Kaitlan's lap and crawled onto Judy's. As he jabbered away to her about his gift, Kaitlan could see the love Judy felt for her son as she cuddled him close to her and stroked his head.

She's very pretty, Kaitlan thought, and wondered if she and Matt had made love while he was in Nashville. The way they had been wrestling around in the leaves, it looked to her as if they were on intimate terms. Matt had never acted in that boyish way with her. Would he rather be marrying Judy? He wouldn't lose Sammy if they were to wed.

She refused a second cup of coffee. "I have to get home. Hattie wants to discuss with me when she and Peter can move into my place." She gave a little laugh. "You know Hattie, everything must be arranged to her satisfaction." Turning to Judy she said, "I am happy that you have your son back." She gave Sammy a smacking kiss that made him giggle, then pulled on her jacket.

"I wish you and Matt all the happiness in the world," Judy said, sincerity in her voice.

Kaitlan smiled her thanks, and Aunt Polly beamed at her and said, "I guess I'll see you Saturday then."

"You don't have to go with me," Kaitlan said to Matt when he put on his jacket to walk her to her horse.

"I know that." This time there was a coolness in his voice too. "Come along now."

When he had helped her to mount, Matt laid a hand on her knee. "You're acting so strange today. Have you changed your mind about getting married?"

"No, I haven't." Kaitlan gathered up the reins. "Have you?"

"Not in the least."

"Then I'll see you in church Saturday." Kaitlan reined the stallion around and without another word turned its head homeward.

Matt stared after her as the horse cantered away. He didn't care how much she might try to hide it; her stiffly held back told him that she was displeased about something.

At least she still wanted to marry him, he told himself, so he should be thankful for that. Maybe she just had prewedding jitters.

When he returned to the cabin, Polly and Judy noticed right away that some of his high spirits had waned. When he retired early, Judy looked at Polly and remarked, "As nice as Kaitlan seems, I wonder if she's the right wife for Matt. When she's around you can see he's crazy about her, but she doesn't even show any affection for him, let alone love. He's a fine man. I'd hate to see him trapped in a loveless marriage."

"You're mistaken about Kaitlan." Polly was quick to defend her young friend. "She cares deeply for Matt." She frowned and added, "She certainly wasn't herself today, though. Something is bothering her."

"Whatever it is, it's affecting Matt. He really looked down when he went to bed."

"I'm sure they'll work it out," Polly said with conviction. "They're the best of friends."

Kaitlan stood at the kitchen window, staring outside. A bright sun shone warmly, as though to make up for the past few days of gloom and misty rain.

*My wedding day.* Kaitlan leaned her head against the glass pane. *Happy is the bride the sun shines on.* What a mockery that old saying was. The brightest sun in the world wouldn't take the place of her intended saying that he loved her.

She laid a palm on her still-flat stomach, whispering, "Only for you, little one, will I go through with it. Only for you would I do this to Matt. He is marrying me out of the goodness of his heart."

She hadn't seen Matt since the day she had gone to tell Sammy good-bye. She imagined he'd been too busy with Judy. According to Peter, the young woman from Nashville had left the Gap yesterday, taking her son with her.

Was Matt feeling sad today? she wondered. He would miss Sammy, she knew, but what about the little boy's mother? Had Matt finally fallen in love, now that he was already promised to another?

"Well, that's done," Hattie said, breaking into Kaitlan's disturbing thoughts. "I've written down all my easiest recipes. With them and all that I've taught you the past two weeks, you should be able to make decent meals for Matt."

Kaitlan sat down at the table and scanned the six pages filled with Hattie's cramped handwriting. "Thank you, Hattie." She folded the pages together. "I'm afraid what I put on the table won't come close to what Aunt Polly has been serving him."

"Don't worry about that. Matt will like anything you cook for him. Now, have you packed everything you want to take to your new home?"

Kaitlan gave a light laugh. "Yes, it took me all of fifteen minutes to put my wordly goods into that battered old trunk of mine."

"You know, Kaitlan, sometimes I think I must be dreaming that a black couple who never had anything but their names are now part owners of a fine little farm and a nice sturdy cabin. And you, child, have found a good man to marry."

"It's been a long time coming, hasn't it, Hattie?" Kaitlan laid her hand on Hattie's and gently squeezed.

"Let's not think back, Kaitlan. We must let the past go and only think of the future. Now, I expect we should start getting ready to go to the church." She stood up and, pushing the chair back in place, said, "I've got Peter's clothes laid out, but if I'm not there to watch him, the fool will put on a pair of his homespuns."

Kaitlan smiled and shook her head as Hattie left. Peter would do no such thing and Hattie knew it. She just liked fussing over her man. He was her husband and child, all wrapped in one. The tough facade she showed the world hid a softness of heart that few people had. Kaitlan recalled the way Hattie had cried the day she asked her friend if she would stand up with her.

"It will be the proudest day of my life," Hattie had sobbed.

But Hattie couldn't be much prouder than Lish Jones. Matt had passed over his younger friends and had asked Lish to stand up with him. The old fellow would brag about that for the rest of his days.

As Kaitlan went to her bedroom to change into the dress that she had worn when she stood up for Maybelle, she thought dispiritedly that everyone but herself was looking forward to her wedding. Excepting Matt, she amended. He was probably feeling the same way she did, maybe worse.

"I mustn't think about it anymore," she said, feeling a tension headache coming on.

As Matt dressed for his big day, he was not only nervous, but also dead tired. For the past two weeks he and three friends had worked from first light until dark, building Kaitlan's surprise wedding gift. He had taken a few hours off to spend with Judy and Sammy, but the rest of the time had been used in building a snug cabin whose windows looked out on the special waterfall that Kaitlan loved so much. He had remembered her saying one day that it was a beautiful spot for a cabin, where one could see the falls through a window and could fall asleep at night listening to the muted splash of the water hitting the gravel bed below.

The cabin had been finished the day before yesterday, and yesterday the new furniture had been delivered. With Aunt Polly directing him and his friends, each piece had been put in place. All it needed now was Kaitlan's personal touch.

This morning he had gone to the new place and built a fire in the huge fieldstone fireplace in the sitting room and kindled a blaze in the cookstove in the kitchen. Elam Cook's eldest son, Paul, would keep the fires going until Matt arrived with his new wife.

His wife. Matt paused in pulling on his other boot. He still couldn't believe that Kaitlan had agreed to marry him. She hadn't had much choice, though. It was marry him or bear the shame of having a baby out of wedlock.

Considering her attitude toward him the last time he'd seen her, he wouldn't be too surprised if she didn't show up for her wedding a half an hour from now.

"My, but you do look handsome." Aunt Polly gave him a wide, approving smile when Matt walked into the kitchen. "Your new suit fits you perfectly. I was afraid it might be too tight across your broad shoulders."

"Will you help me with this tie?" Matt asked in frustration.

"Don't be so nervous, Matt," Polly scolded as she deftly tied a proper knot. "It's not like you're marrying a stranger. You and Kaitlan know each other well enough."

"I'm not sure that we do. The way she's been acting lately makes me wonder if I know her at all, and God knows there's plenty she doesn't know about me."

"Now what could you have ever done that would be too shameful for Kaitlan to know about?"

"There's only one thing I dread her finding out about."

"I'm sure she'll forgive you if she ever learns about it, whatever it is. I guess it's time we get goin' to church. I hope Lish will show up in time, and I pray he cleans himself up some."

"I don't know about that, but he'll be there. He's probably been there for the past hour," Matt said in amusement as he helped Polly with her cape and shrugged into his best jacket.

Polly gave a delighted cry when they stepped outside. Matt had hitched up his buggy for the special occasion. "I see we're going to ride in style today," she said as he helped her into the seldom-used conveyance.

"You're dressed too fancy to be riding in our old wagon today." He grinned down at her as he gathered up the reins and slapped them against the horse's rump. "It wouldn't do for my bride to ride in a wagon, either. Anyway, I've got the wagon loaded with everything I want to take to the new place."

"What about your livestock? Won't it be a nuisance for you to come back and forth every day to take care of them?"

"I'm starting on a barn tomorrow. Until I get it finished, Peter is going to take care of them."

"You'd better get your barn up fast. It's gonna snow any day now."

When they came within sight of the church, Polly gasped. "Good Lord, Matt, everybody from miles around must be here. I've never seen so many horses and wagons and buggies. Do you think we can find a spot to pull into?"

As if in answer to her question, one of Matt's drinking friends came loping up to them. "Howdy, Matt, Aunt Polly. We saved a spot for your buggy and the Smiths' wagon over there beside that big pine. Ol' Hiram is standin' guard over it. We knew that everybody and his brother would be comin' to see you get hitched. Nobody thought you'd ever let a woman put a ring in your nose."

A wide grin split Cal's face. "Don't fall down dead, but even Ruby Gentry and her girls are here. They're seated in the last row in church. You might not recognize them, though. They ain't got no paint on their faces and their breasts ain't fallin' out of the plain dresses they're wearin'. Ruby said there ain't no way she was going to cause you any embarrassment, but that she intended to see you get married."

"Ruby and her girls are as welcome as anyone else," Matt said, "She's . . ." He stopped short and stared. Peter had driven up and Matt couldn't take his eyes off Kaitlan. How lovely she looked. In just a short time all that beauty would be his. His to hold and keep, but never to make love to, he reminded himself.

Kaitlan wore the same dress she had worn to Maybelle's wedding. Matt hadn't attended that marriage, and he thought that Kaitlan looked like a queen as he stepped forward and lifted his arms to swing her to the ground.

"Thank you, Matt." She gave him a shy smile. "You certainly look grand."

"I don't have the words to describe how you look," he said as he placed her arm in the crook of his. "Shall we go in? I expect everybody is waiting for us."

All the hushed conversations ceased as they entered the church, and necks were craned to watch them walk down the narrow aisle to where Reverend Turner stood waiting at the pulpit.

Peter took a seat and Hattie continued on to stand beside Kaitlan. Lish had seated himself in the first row, and when he stood up Matt noticed from the corner of his eye that the old man was clean shaven, and the customary wad of "chaw" was missing from his cheek. He wore his usual clothes of homespun, but they were clean and neatly pressed.

The look of pride in the old fellow's face made Matt doubly glad that he had asked Lish to stand up with him. It was probably his one day of glory.

When the preacher opened his Bible and began, "Dearly beloved, we are met here today . . ." Matt reached for Kaitlan's hand. She grasped it instantly. Her fingers were ice cold and he knew that she was as nervous as he was.

Matt only caught an occasional word the reverend said. He was too aware of Kaitlan's hand gradually tightening around his and growing warmer. He thrilled to the fact that he had been able to give her the confidence she needed. If he could continue to do that, maybe before long she would be his wife in all ways.

When Matt received a sharp poke from Lish and saw the wedding ring he was pushing at him, he heard the reverend saying, "With this ring I now make you man and wife." His hand trembled slightly as he slid the gold band on Kaitlan's finger. He breathed a sigh of relief that it fit.

When he was smilingly told, "You may kiss your bride now, Matt," he looked at Kaitlan, wondering if he should claim her lips or kiss her cheek.

Kaitlan answered his question by lifting her lips to him. They were warm and clinging and he dared to deepen his kiss. They stood so long in each other's arms, the kiss going on and on, the congregation began to laugh, and Matt's rowdy friends started clapping their hands. Kaitlan pulled away then, her face crimson.

Not so with Matt, though. All he was aware of was the fact that Kaitlan had returned his kiss with a hunger that matched his own.

Outside in the churchyard they were nearly smothered by their friends and neighbors gathering close around them to shake Matt's hand or steal a kiss from Kaitlan. Matt came to her rescue by threatening good-naturedly that he would flatten the next man who tried to kiss his bride.

With an arm around her, Matt managed to push his way through the crowd of people. But even once they were free of the crowd, they were followed and showered with rice. Matt knew that the stinging blows on his head and rear were caused by small stones thrown by his drinking friends.

As he helped Kaitlan into the buggy he grinned to himself. With that bunch he was lucky they hadn't pelted him with rocks. There was nothing gentle about them.

Those same friends weren't finished with him yet, he discovered. When he started the horse down the rocky road, a clamorous sound of pans and cans followed them.

"You've got something caught in the wheels, Matt," Kaitlan exclaimed. When Matt laughingly told her what their neighbors had done, she laughed too. After they had left the yelling and carrying-on behind, Matt pulled the horse in and cut the rope that held the noisemakers to the back of the buggy.

"I've never seen this road before." Kaitlan frowned as Matt turned the buggy onto a narrow, recently cut road leading through the woods. "Where are we going?"

"I want to show you my wedding gift to you."

Several minutes later the horse pulled the buggy around a big pine, and Kaitlan gasped her pleasure. "Oh, Matt, you remembered what I said about a cabin being built here! When did you do it?"

"I started felling the trees the day after you said you'd marry me. Those rough friends of mine helped me build it."

Kaitlan understood now why she hadn't seen much of Matt during the last two weeks and felt ashamed of the suspicions she'd had about him and Judy.

She mustn't tell him of her thoughts, though. She mustn't let him know how jealous she had been of Sammy's mother. He would know then that she loved him, and it would make him feel uncomfortable.

The waterfall seemed to welcome her as Matt took her arm and led her up the two wide steps to the porch that ran along the entire front of the cabin. The sun's rays hit the waterfall, making it appear like millions of diamonds twinkling on their rush to the ground.

She clapped her hands in delight when Matt

pushed open the door and stepped aside to let her enter. A cozy fire burned in the huge fire-place, sending its warmth out as though it too welcomed her. Everything smelled of new wood and the beeswax Aunt Polly had rubbed into the furniture — furniture the likes of which Kaitlan had never expected to own in a life-time.

From the sitting room a short hall led to three bedrooms. All three were furnished, but to Matt's surprise and frustration, Polly had only made up one bed, the one in the larger, middle room.

He slid a glace at Kaitlan, to see her reaction. The only thing he saw on her face was her plea-sure at the sight of the panther skin on the floor beside the bed. "Is it the one you shot that day?" she asked.

"Yes. I thought it would keep your feet warm this winter," he explained.

Matt took her into the kitchen next, a large room adjoining the sitting room. She went into rhapsodies over the big black cookstove, the first one ever to be installed in the Gap.

"Do you know how to use it?"

"Yes, we had one in Philadelphia, but it wasn't so grand. Wait until Hattie sees it." She smiled up at Matt. "What do you want for supper?"

Matt turned her around and pushed her out of the kitchen. "I'll not have my new bride making our supper on our wedding night. Aunt

Polly packed us a basket. A real wedding feast, she said. It's in the buggy. I'll go unhitch the horse and bring it in."

When Matt was gone Kaitlan went through her new home again, taking time to examine all that was in it. When she stood in the bedroom, she gazed at the bed. The big four-poster was made up too neatly for Matt to have done it, so it had to be Aunt Polly's work. Did Matt tell Polly to put linens on only the one bed, or did she simply assume that there was no need to make up the other two?

Should she ask Matt, or should she wait and see if he brought up the subject?

She decided she would follow his lead.

When Kaitlan had finished her inspection of the cabin she walked out onto the porch and sat down in one of the chairs Matt had thoughtfully bought. She feasted her eyes on the waterfall. A few minutes later Matt joined her and they sat together in silence, each one aware of the other, each one wondering what the evening would bring.

Matt broke the silence. "I hope those dark clouds in the north mean rain, and I hope we have a real gully-washer."

"Why in the world do you wish that?" Kaitlan asked, laughing.

"No one will come out in the rain to shivaree us." When Kaitlan gave him a look that said she didn't understand his meaning, he explained, "Friends and neighbors watch for the lights to go out of the newlywed couple's bedroom; then after about half an hour they descend on the cabin, banging pots and pans, shooting guns in the air, making an earsplitting racket. I, for one, can do without that."

When the last rays of the sun dipped behind the mountaintop, Kaitlan said, "I'm hungry. What about you?"

"I haven't eaten much all day. Let's go see what Aunt Polly fixed for us."

Taking the cloth off the basket, Kaitlan found several slices of baked ham, half a fried chicken, herb-seasoned potatoes, string beans, yams, and a beautiful white wedding cake. Matt put out two plates of their new dinnerware, and after he added knives and forks, they sat down and began to eat their first meal as man and wife by the soft glow of the two candles in the center of the table.

They were in the middle of eating a slice of Aunt Polly's cake when rain began to slash across the window. Kaitlan and Matt looked at each other and said in unison, "I hope it pours."

While Kaitlan cleared the table, setting aside the plates and flatware because Matt had forgotten to bring in a pail of water to wash them in, he went into the family room to smoke his pipe. As he laid a log on the fire, he thought to himself that there was nothing more cheery than a blazing fire on a cold winter night. Unless, he thought wryly, it was making love to a woman you love.

Kaitlan joined him shortly and they sat in silence, tension growing between them. The fire hissed as the wind sporadically blew the rain down the chimney, but neither noticed. In each of their minds was the image of the bed in the room only a few feet away from them. Each was wondering if they would share it tonight.

Each wanted to.

Finally the strain became too much for Kaitlan. She gave a sham yawn and said, "I don't know about you, but I'm ready to go to bed."

"Me too. It's been a long day."

Kaitlan hesitated, uncertain what to say before leaving the room. If she said "Good night," it would sound like she wouldn't see him until tomorrow morning. If she asked, "Will you be retiring soon?" it might sound like an invitation.

In the end, she smiled at Matt and left him smoking his pipe and staring into the fire.

Kaitlan had changed into her nightclothes and snuggled into the covers when a light knock sounded on the door. Her heart pounding, she called, "Come in."

The door swung open and he stood there, looking like a little boy who was about to be rejected. He cleared his voice and said awkwardly, "I can't find the bed linens to make up one of the other beds."

Instinct being a million years older than

339

reason, Kaitlan turned back a corner of her covers and, with a twinkle in her eyes, asked, "Why prepare another bed? This one is plenty big for the two of us."

# Chapter Twenty-six

Matt caught his breath as Kaitlan sat up. The thin material of her gown hid nothing of the proud uplift of her breasts with their rosy-tipped nipples.

"Are you sure?" His voice was husky. "You know, don't you, that I will want more than just to sleep with you."

Kaitlan gave him a wicked smile, and lay back down. "I certainly hope so," she said softly.

"You do?" Matt asked eagerly.

"I do." Kaitlan sounded shy, but breathlessly sincere.

In the soft glow of the candlelight Kaitlan watched Matt practically tear the buttons off his shirt in his hurry to get out of it. She had seen him bare to the waist before, the times he had worked in his tobacco fields. Now, as she had done then, she let her eyes roam over his broad back and shoulders with pleasure and admiration as he sat down on the edge of the bed to remove his boots. Her eyes followed him as he stood up, faced her, and began unbuckling his belt.

She knew it wouldn't be ladylike to watch him take off the last piece of clothing. But there was no power on earth that could keep her from watching as he slid his trousers down over his lean waist, then down his narrow hips. He impatiently tugged them over his feet and left them crumpled on the floor.

Was there ever another man with a body more perfect than her husband's? Kaitlan wondered as wave after thrilling wave washed through her. Not only was his body large, but the manly part of him was in proportion to his size. She couldn't wait to feel its strength inside her.

And Matt was just as eager to give her its power, to slide deep inside her and stay there the rest of the night. He blew out the candle and climbed into bed. With only the faint light coming from the fireplace in the other room bathing their bodies, he took Kaitlan into his arms.

Kaitlan responded to him as though it was the most natural thing in the world to press against him, to throw a leg over his waist.

Catching his breath Matt grasped her shapely bottom and pulled it tight against him as his lips sought hers in a hot, clinging kiss.

Although Kaitlan could feel Matt bucking his hard maleness against her throbbing femininity, the thinness of her nightgown was a hindrance. She wanted to feel his naked flesh rubbing against her.

She slid her lips from his and whispered, "Let me get out of my gown."

She sat up and whipped the thin garment

over her head and tossed it on the floor. When she lay back down this time, Matt's long leg was thrown across her waist. All coherent thought deserted her as he lifted one of her breasts to his lips and drew on her nipple.

"Oh, Matt," she whispered, running her fingers through his hair, "I have dreamed of this so often."

His response was to hold her tighter, letting her know that it had been his dream also.

Kaitlan gave herself over to him, to let him do as he pleased with her.

Sensing her surrender, Matt moved his head to suckle her other breast, at the same time stroking the wet abandoned one. When both breasts were swollen with passion, he left them to run light kisses down her body.

Kaitlan expected him to stop when he came to her waist, but the kisses continued past there. Before she could guess his intent, he knelt between her legs and lifted them up to rest on his shoulders. She gasped a small protest as his head lowered and his mouth closed over the throbbing part of her. It was too reminiscent of what Nate used to do to her and she didn't want memories of him intruding into her wedding night.

But when Matt had found his way through the silky thatch of curls and his tongue was swirling around the little nub of her desire, she felt herself weakening. When he began nibbling with gentle teeth she forgot all else. Beyond her control she was reaching a climax.

Her body was still throbbing when Matt positioned himself and took his manhood in his hand to enter her. Kaitlan's body went stiff. Her mind couldn't accept it. Matt was following the same pattern Nate had. She pushed at his shoulders, crying, "I'm sorry, Matt, but I can't go on. Everything you do is the same as what Nate used to do to me. I had hoped it would be different with you."

She began to cry. "Do all men make love the same way?" she sobbed.

Matt rolled over on his back, all passion and desire leaving him. With an arm drawn across his eyes, he wondered with a ragged sigh what had made him think he could get away with it.

He sat up, pulled on his trousers, and lit the candle he had recently blown out. Sitting back down on the edge of the bed, he took Kaitlan's hand and with great reluctance said, "Nate never made love to you. It was always me."

Kaitlan could only stare at him, appalled. She had thought him the most honorable man in the world, and he had done this dastardly thing to her! He had sneaked into her bed, time after time, and vented his lust on her.

Blazing anger wiped out all other emotions. She sat up, and in her hurt and disappointment, rained blows on his back and shoulders, all the time yelling at him to get out of her room and never enter it again. "If it wasn't for my baby's sake" — she paused, her eyes

344

growing wide — "your baby's sake, I'd leave you tomorrow."

"But, Kaitlan, let me explain," Matt began, but the wild look in her eyes told him that this wasn't the time to try to talk to her. He gathered up his clothes and left the bedroom with Kaitlan's ragged sobbing beating against his ears.

Kaitlan made Matt's meals to the best to her ability and kept the cabin spotlessly clean. She also washed and ironed his clothes. She intended to be the perfect wife in all ways, except in the bedroom.

However, she grew thin and drawn in the process. Her heart still ached at Matt's duplicity. During those endless nights of lovemaking she had foolishly thought that he loved her as she did him. She hadn't denied him anything, and he had demanded much.

But why had he gotten her with child? Was it because he wanted to put something over on Nate? Didn't he take her into consideration at all? Hadn't he cared that her baby would probably look like him? Didn't he care that people would know that he had been sleeping with her when all the time she had promised herself in marriage to his stepbrother?

Each time her mind dwelled on what Matt had done to her, a voice inside her whispered, "Aren't you glad though that Nate didn't deflower you?" She had to admit she was thankful for that.

Matt went around like a whipped dog, staying out of Kaitlan's way as much as possible. He lost his appetite, but forced himself to eat the meals Kaitlan put on the table, so as not to hurt her feelings.

Finally, in desperation, he set out a short trapline, so he would have an excuse to stay out of the cabin. He and his friends had built his barn and driven up his livestock. But a man could only find so many things to do in a barn.

Kaitlan was on her way home from visiting Hattie and Peter. In the three weeks she and Matt had been married, they had come calling once, and this was the first time she had gone to see them. Hattie had questioned her about her weight loss and Kaitlan had laughingly said it was due to her cooking. But Hattie hadn't looked satisfied with her answer and Kaitlan had cut her visit short, for she knew that Hattie would continue to question her until she got the whole embarrassing story from her. Kaitlan had used the black clouds that threatened snow as an excuse to shorten her visit.

Her excuse became reality when she was barely out of sight of the farm. Great white flakes were suddenly falling on her head and shoulders. Kaitlan loved the first snowfall of the winter and had always looked forward to its arrival. As she had done when a child, she lifted her face skyward and stuck out her tongue to catch the cold flakes on it.

As Kaitlan rode on there was a stillness in the air. She wondered if Matt was enjoying the silent snowfall as she was.

When she arrived at the cabin, the stallion's fetlocks were deep in snow. She rode straight to the barn, unsaddled Snowy, and removed the bit from his mouth. After she had rubbed him down with a piece of an old blanket, she gave him a helping of oats.

Kaitlan opened the cabin door, but before stepping inside she removed her boots. Once in the kitchen she put a thick rug, woven from rags, in front of the door. She and Matt, and any company they might have, would wipe their feet on it before walking onto her clean floor.

The early darkness brought on by the clouded sky soon became dusk. Matt would be home soon, Kaitlan thought, and set about preparing supper. In the middle of frying pork chops and fries, she had to pause to light the two candles on the table. She stood thoughtfully a moment, then lit another to set on the kitchen windowsill. She told herself that Matt might need its light to guide him home.

Supper had been ready and pushed to the back of the stove to keep warm for close to an hour. Kaitlan had made numerous trips to the window, peering through the snow, hoping to see Matt riding in. When another half hour passed and there was no sign of him, she began to worry in earnest. Something had happened to him. He had never been late getting in be-fore.

The thought of him lying in some ravine, his body all broken, grabbed her by the throat. She grabbed up her jacket, tied a scarf on her head, shoved her feet into her boots, and lit a lantern she took from the storage room. She was going to go look for him.

As Matt lay helpless in the snow, his thoughts were on Kaitlan. Was she worried that he was late getting home? Had she even noticed? They never even spoke to each other unless it was ab-solutely necessary. Now, their estrangement might cost him his very life.

He had been removing a mink from a trap when he became vaguely aware that it was snowing. He was well aware of it by the time he had finished running his line and had started home.

"We'd better hurry along, Bucky," he had said to the sturdy little mountain horse he used to check his trapline. "We don't want to get caught up here after dark. Panthers can see at night, and there will be plenty of them roaming around looking for their supper."

The horse shook his head as if he was just as anxious as his owner to get home. He also knew the dangers of the big cats and wanted to be safely stabled in the barn, out of harm's way.

There was only the whisper of the pines as the snow fell silently, and Matt wasn't prepared for the chilling sound of the panther's scream. His stunned reaction was to swear under his breath when he spotted the panther, high in a tall pine, only feet away. It had gathered all four feet together, ready to spring on Bucky.

Matt dug his heels into the little horse, urging him to run. But the horse was terrified, and with a frantic squeal he rose up on his haunches instead of running. The panther chose that moment to spring at the little horse, landing on its rump, only inches from Matt's back. It sank its claws into Bucky's flesh and hung on as the horse reared again, screaming in pain.

This time Matt was unseated. He found himself lying on the ground, on his back. Luckily he'd managed to free his rifle. He raised it, took aim, and squeezed the trigger. The bullet hit the animal in the head. But even though the shot was a fatal one, the angry cat used its last strength to pull Bucky to the ground.

A thousand pounds landed on Matt's lower body. As the cat breathed its last Matt struggled to get out from under the weight pinning him down. It was a useless attempt. He was caught there until someone came along to help him.

The little horse was moaning his agony as his lifeblood spilled into the snow. With tears in his eyes, Matt knew what he must do. Once more his rifle spoke, and the sturdy little horse he had raised from a colt lay still, at last out of his unbearable pain.

The horse's deadweight, however, pushed Matt deeper into the snow. As he lay there, helpless, his lower body going numb, he asked himself if it was from pressure, or frostbite. It was freezing cold.

Now, in the dead calm of the snow-covered land, he strained his ears for the sound of another panther slipping up on him. He had only two empty shells in his rifle, and he couldn't get to the three full ones in his pants pocket. If he should be attacked, he would only have his hands to fight the beast off.

The snow was becoming heavier by the minute, and an inch of the white stuff covered the horse and panther. He often had to brush the large flakes off his face. He must keep his eyes clear so that he could peer through the darkness.

Matt's upper body was beginning to be chilled now, and he was struck with the realization that he could lie there and freeze to death before anyone found him.

He closed his eyes in denial. It was unbearable to think that he would never see Kaitlan again, never see his son or daughter.

Kaitlan hurriedly saddled the stallion and, keeping him at a slow pace, began making her way down the mountain. She could only see a few feet ahead of her.

She urged Snowy to a faster pace when they entered the foothills where the light was better

350

and there were fewer rocks for him to stumble on.

Her worry for Matt was growing by the minute. She wouldn't let herself think that something fatal had happened to him. She couldn't bear that, for she knew now that she loved him with her whole heart.

Kaitlan at last arrived at the Village and, covered with snow, she burst into the tavern. The men at the bar turned around and stared at her. Then Matt's friend Cal exclaimed, "It's Matt's wife." He strode swiftly to her, asking anxiously, "Has something happened to Matt, Kaitlan?"

"I don't know," she almost wailed in a breathless voice. "He's hours late getting home from running his traps."

She didn't see his friends exchanging worried looks. They knew that something had happened to their friend. The big man, Cal, who had come forward, said soothingly, "We'll head right out and look for him. We'll have him home in no time. Can you find your way home?"

"I'm not going home." Kaitlan's eyes sparked. "I'm going with you."

"Now, Kaitlan, you can't do that. It's dangerous terrain up there. Not fittin' for a woman to ride at night, and in a snowstorm at that."

"I'm going," Kaitlan declared, her chin set stubbornly. "He's my husband."

Cal had never before argued with a determined wife, let alone one so beautiful. He reluctantly gave in. "But you can't ride your stallion. For sure he would step in a hole and break a leg. I'll saddle one of my little mountain horses for you. Go stand before the fire and warm up while we get ready to ride."

"Don't you dare go off and leave me. If I have to, I'll go alone."

"I give you my word we won't do that."

After Matt's four close friends left the tavern to prepare to ride, Kaitlan paced back and forth in front of the fire, fretting at the delay in hunting for Matt. Didn't they realize that every minute counted?

It was less than five minutes later when Cal stuck his head in the door and said, "We're ready to ride, Kaitlan."

The horse he helped her to mount was very small in comparison to her stallion, which someone had taken to the livery. But she could feel his wiry strength as she settled into the saddle.

"I'm going to put you between me and Harry. When we leave the foothills and begin to climb, you take hold of my horse's tail and don't let go. That way we won't lose you," Cal said as he mounted his own horse.

When they left the protection of the foothills and began to climb, Kaitlan gladly grasped the rough tail of the horse ahead of her, for she could barely see a foot in front of her.

"Give him his head, Kaitlan. Let him pick his

own way," Cal called back to her.

Kaitlan let the reins rest on the little animal's neck as the group inched their way up the rock- and boulder-strewn mountain. Cal knew where Matt had laid his line and headed in that direction.

They had climbed about half an hour when the men began to loudly shout Matt's name. Kaitlan joined in, her voice ringing out as loudly as the others'.

She lifted her head heavenward in thanks when they heard Matt's answering call on the still night air.

In the blinding snow Cal's horse almost stepped on the dead horse and panther. They saw Matt then, and Cal exclaimed, "He's pinned under his horse. And dammit, he's fallen asleep now. We've got to work fast, men. Sleeping is a bad sign.

"Kaitlan," he said, as she scrambled off her horse, "see if you can wake him up while we try to free him."

Kaitlan ran to kneel beside Matt's head. She wiped the snow off his face and shook his shoulders. When he didn't respond, she began to slap his cheeks, crying raggedly, "Wake up, darling, you mustn't sleep now."

Matt's eyes fluttered open. "Is that you, Kaitlan?"

"Yes, Matt, it's me." She smiled tenderly at him. "I'm going to leave you a minute so I won't be in the way while your friends lift

Bucky off your body."

She stepped aside and Cal took her place. As the other three men positioned themselves along the dead horse, Cal took hold of Matt's shoulders. Grunting and straining, they finally managed to lift the crushing weight off Matt far enough for Cal to pull him free.

"How do you feel?" Cal asked anxiously.

"I don't feel anything." Matt lifted worried eyes to his friend.

Cal hid his own worry. Had Matt broken his back in his fall? "You're probably just cold and numb from the weight on your body." He made himself speak calmly. "I'm going to check your legs for broken bones now."

Kaitlan knelt down beside Matt again and moved his head into her lap. She held her breath as she watched Cal carefully check Matt's legs and then his hips.

Her breath came out with a whoosh when Cal announced with a wide smile, "You don't have any broken bones. You just need some circulation in your legs."

He gave Matt a teasing grin. "Ain't none of us boys gonna carry you home. You're gonna mount up on Kaitlan's horse and ride home."

He looked up at Matt's grinning friends. "Come on, you yahoos, start rubbing them trunk-sized legs."

The men rubbed and kneaded Matt's flesh for a good five minutes before he began to moan with the pain of the feeling returning to

354

his legs. They helped him to stand on his feet then and walked him around for another five minutes.

Finally he was allowed to climb stiffly onto the little mountain horse Kaitlan had ridden. Cal lifted Kaitlan up and set her in front of Matt. With his arms around her, Matt gathered up the reins and they all started to make their careful way home.

The snowfall had abated enough that the four friends could make out the fork that would take them back to the Village. With a wave of Cal's hand they left Matt and Kaitlan.

Matt wished that he and Kaitlan had another ten miles to ride, she felt so good in his arms. It might be the only time he would get this chance.

But in only another half mile they would be home.

The candle still burned in the window. It made a cheery sight, Matt thought as he swung stiffly to the ground and then helped Kaitlan to dismount. When she said that she would take care of the horse, he didn't argue. His legs were still a little weak, and his feet hurt.

He didn't object either when Kaitlan put her arm around his waist to help him climb the steps to the porch. He didn't need her help, but he needed the closeness of her body.

"Now," Kaitlan said as soon as they had shed their jackets and hung them up, "the first thing I want you to do is sit down and eat your supper. You must be starved. I'm going to put some water on the stove to heat while I go take care of the horse. When you have finished eating, you're going to sit in a tub of hot water awhile; then you're going to sit in front of the fire until you're thoroughly thawed out."

"You're awfully bossy all of a sudden." Matt grinned in amusement. "Are you going to change into a Hattie Smith?"

"Would that be so bad?" Kaitlan asked, only half joking.

"Well," Matt said after swallowing a mouthful of meat and potatoes, "I guess I could stand it."

"You know it's not my nature to boss people around," Kaitlan scolded, "unless, of course, they need it." Her eyes smiled at him. "Now finish your supper."

By the time Kaitlan got back from drying the little mountain horse and giving him some grain to eat, she found that Matt had finished his supper and had filled a wooden tub with the heated water. She didn't stay in the kitchen to watch him disrobe and climb into the tub. She didn't dare look at his body bared in all its splendor. She might just throw herself at him and beg him to make love to her. She knew he wouldn't hesitate to do so. She'd had plenty of proof of that. When it came to her body, he never seemed to get enough of it.

She stared into the flames. Why couldn't Matt love her? What was it about her he didn't

356

like? She stopped thinking about it when Matt came from the kitchen with nothing but a quilt wrapped around himself. When he sat down in the chair next to her, she jumped up and brought him a footstool to rest his feet on. When she started to sit back down he grabbed her wrist.

"Sit here." He urged her down on the stool. "I want to talk to you."

"Of course, Matt. What do you want to talk about?" Kaitlan felt tension growing inside her. Was he going to say that their marriage was a mistake and that she should return to her own farm? She waited, her fingers tightly gripped together.

"First off, I feel fine. The hot bath was all I needed to bring me back to my old self.

"But that isn't what I want to talk about. I want to explain why I took advantage of you last summer."

When he paused as if thinking just how to put his next words, Kaitlan watched him, eager to hear those words, whatever they were. She needed to know the truth, even though it might break her heart.

"That first night," he began again, "when I took your innocence, I knew that Nate planned to do it. I knew he wouldn't take you with care or gentleness. I knew that he would hurt you terribly, even scar your mind.

"After spending that night with you, I knew that I would go to any lengths to keep Nate

357

away from you, so I threatened to beat him within an inch of his life if he made love to you before he married you. My hope was that you'd discover how evil he was before you became his wife.

"Every time he came home from that supposed job of his and stayed for a while, I'd go to you. By then, making love to you had become as necessary to me as breathing.

"I never meant for you to get with child, though, but one night I lost control and spilled my seed inside you. When I learned that you carried my babe, it was the happiest and saddest day of my life. The woman I loved with all my being was having my baby and I couldn't shout it to the world."

Kaitlan stared at Matt, astounded. Had she really heard the words that she had lost hope of ever hearing? Her eyes shimmering with the happiness engulfing her, she asked breathlessly, "You love me, Matt? You never said that you did."

"I never said that I loved you?" Matt looked at her as if he couldn't believe what she had said. "You must have known. Everybody in the Gap knew I was wild about you.

"Kaitlan." He took her hands and, gazing deep into her eyes, said, "I thought I might scare you away if I said the word *love* to you. I didn't want to chance losing your friendship. I couldn't believe my luck when you agreed to marry me, even though it was for the baby's sake."

"Oh, Matt, how foolish we've been. All the time you were loving me, I was beginning to love you." She threw herself at him, dislodging the quilt he had been holding around himself. As Matt folded her into his arms, she drew back, and with a happy little laugh exclaimed, "Matt Ingram, I do declare that you are naked."

"I do declare you're right." Matt's voice was low and husky. "And every piece of my nakedness is hungry for you."

Before he claimed her mouth with a devouring kiss, she said in throaty tones, "I'll decide if that's true," and slid a hand down his body.

Matt spread his legs, giving her full access to what she sought. Her fingers closed around him, and when he groaned at the feel of her, she softly laughed in delight. He was hard and waiting for her.

"Oh Lord, Kaitlan," Matt whispered hoarsely after she had fondled him a minute or so. She sank down onto her knees and replaced her hand with her mouth.

Matt's body trembled and he continued to moan his pleasure as her soft lips moved on him. But finally he could bear no more. He gently, but urgently, pulled her up into his arms and whispered, "It's time to go to bed."

With her still in his arms, he stood up and carried her into their bedroom. He stood her on the floor beside the bed and with shaking

359

fingers helped her out of her clothes. They fell onto the bed then, their eager hands on each other's body.

Their lips seared together as Matt kneaded her breasts and Kaitlan stroked his hardness. When her breasts longed for the feel of his lips on them, Kaitlan broke off the kiss, and, scooting up in the bed, she leaned over him and lifted one of her full, heavy breasts to his mouth. He quickly clamped his lips on the pink, pouting nipple and she moaned her pleasure as he suckled her hungrily.

When he had attended to both breasts, Matt whispered huskily, "I'd like to feel your lips again."

Kaitlan teased him a minute by nibbling on the throbbing head of his desire. When he whispered, "Please, Kaitlan, don't torment me any more," she opened her mouth and slid it over his large, hard length. Matt leaned up on his elbows and watched her lips move on him. Within seconds he was clenching his fists, trying to hold back the release his loins were demanding. He lifted her from him, and, turning her on her back, he crawled between her legs. She reached down and, taking his wet hardness in her hand, guided it inside her. With one smooth push of his hips Matt buried his full length as far as it could go. He slid his hands under her smooth cheeks and lifted them slightly off the bed. Holding them steady to receive his thrusts, he stretched out on top of her and began to stroke in and out of her. Kaitlan gave a soft cry of delight and brought her arms up around his shoulders.

After only a few thrusts of his hips they were both crying out their release, a release so intense, so satisfying, it left them weak. But after they had caught their breath, Matt gathered Kaitlan tightly in his arms, and with a full erection his hard buttocks rose and fell again, pumping rhythmically into her.

This time, long, exquisite minutes passed before, together, they joyfully cried out their release of passion.

After they had napped for a while, renewing their energy, they were hungry for each other again. This last time was a slow, almost lazy coupling as Matt moved his strength in and out of Kaitlan, her femininity sucking at him with each drive of his hips. This time lasted longer than the others, and when they found their satisfaction, they only sighed in complete contentment.

At last, lying side by side, loosely clasped in each other's arms, Kaitlan felt the coldness of the room. With a smile, she moved closer to Matt's warm body. She need never feel cold again.

# Epilogue

Kaitlan and Matt stood on the porch, watching their twins tumble around in the grass. They were a year old and just beginning to take uncertain steps.

The little girl, Sarah, so much like her father in coloring and easy nature, let her brother, Caleb, the spitting image of his mother, direct where they would go.

Matt chuckled. "I pity the woman who ever marries Caleb. He'll give her a merry chase."

"But it will be a lucky man who gets Sarah," Kaitlan said, watching her dainty little daughter follow her brother.

"Yes, but not half so lucky as I was when I married you." He pulled Kaitlan into his arms and, giving her a wicked look, said huskily, "Isn't it time those two took their nap?"

Kaitlan ran a hand down the front of his trousers and, giving him a saucy look, said, "I see it's time I took you to bed for . . . a nap."

# Norah Hess

Always a daydreamer, and often scolded for it by the grandmother who raised her, Norah Hess always wanted to be a writer. At eighteen, she was sent to Chicago to live with an aunt after her grandmother's death. It was there that she met her husband. After raising three children, Norah decided to write her first novel, and since then has had over fifteen published romances. After her husband passed away, she and her two cats moved to Palm Springs, where the desert and mountains inspire her to write her Western romances.